A WINTER IN ZÜRAU

Fiction and non-fiction are two sides of the same coin. Or are they? Franz Kafka is in flight. After spitting blood and being diagnosed with tuberculosis in the summer of 1917, his thirty-fourth year, he escapes from Prague to join his sister Ottla in her smallholding in Upper Bohemia. He leaves behind, he hopes, a dreaded office job, a dominating father, an importunate fiancée and the hothouse literary culture of his native city. Free of all this, he believes, he will at last be able to make sense of his existence and of his strange compulsion to write stories and novels which, he knows, will bring him neither fame nor financial reward.

But this is not fiction. It is an exploration of eight crucial months in the life of one of the greatest writers of the twentieth century, months of anguish and reflection preserved for us in his letters and journals of the time, and which resulted not just in the production of the famous Aphorisms but, as Josipovici shows in this compelling study, of some of his most resonant parables and story-fragments.

A WINTER IN ZÜRAU

GABRIEL JOSIPOVICI

CARCANET

First published in Great Britain in 2024 by
Carcanet
Alliance House, 30 Cross Street
Manchester, M2 7AQ
www.carcanet.co.uk

A CIP catalogue record for this book is
available from the British Library.

ISBN 978 1 80017 431 3

Book design by Andrew Latimer, Carcanet
Typesetting by LiteBook Prepress Services
Printed in Great Britain by SRP Ltd, Exeter, Devon

The publisher acknowledges financial
assistance from Arts Council England.

In memory of my dear friends and teachers

Del Kolve, George Craig, Jonathan Harvey

PARTITA

GABRIEL JOSIPOVICI

CARCANET

First published in Great Britain in 2024 by
Carcanet
Alliance House, 30 Cross Street
Manchester, M2 7AQ
www.carcanet.co.uk

A CIP catalogue record for this book is available from the British Library.

ISBN 978 1 80017 431 3

Book design by Andrew Latimer, Carcanet
Typesetting by LiteBook Prepress Services
Printed in Great Britain by SRP Ltd, Exeter, Devon

The publisher acknowledges financial assistance from Arts Council England.

PARTITA

Fiction and non-fiction are two sides of the same coin. Or are they? Michael Penderecki is in flight. Someone has threatened to kill him. But who is the woman dead in the bathtub? And why does the voice of Yves Montand singing 'Les Feuilles Mortes' surge from the horn of an antiquated phonograph in an otherwise silent villa in Sils Maria?

This is the most enigmatic – and melodramatic – of Gabriel Josipovici's novels to date. It is as though one of Magritte's paintings had come to life to the rhythms of a Bach Partita.

For Rosalind

It turns out that black holes are in fact good children, holding on to the memory of the stars that gave birth to them.

Newspaper report

CONTENTS

I PRAEAMBULUM

1

He is dozing when the telephone rings. He puts it to his ear.

A voice says:

– Karim.

– I'm sorry?

– I am speaking to Michael? the voice says.

– Yes. Mike Penderecki here.

– This is Karim, the voice says.

– Do I know you? Mike says.

– I am the husband of Angela, the voice says.

– And who is Angela?

– The lady you are sleeping with, the voice says.

– I see, Mike says.

– I am here, the voice says. Outside your house. You will speak with me?

– Of course, Mike says.

– Then I will ring the bell.

2

– Please, Mike says, motioning to a chair on the other side of the coffee table.

The man sits and Mike sits in his turn.

– You see this? the man says, taking a small object from the pocket of his windcheater and putting it on the table between them.

– Yes, Mike says.

– It is a knife, the man says.

– Yes, Mike says.

– You know how to use it? the man says.

– Use it? Mike says.

The man presses the handle and the blade flicks out. He runs his finger along the sharp edge, then closes it gently and lays it back on the table.

– Look, Mike says. This is quite unnecessary. Angela and I have already agreed to part.

The man looks at him, smiling.

– It wasn't going anywhere, Mike says. We both realise that. It's over. Finished.

– You know from where I come? the man says.

– Angela told me, Mike says.

– From Homs, the man says.

– I know, Mike says.

– You do not know, the man says. I have business in Homs. It is destroy. I have house in Homs. It is destroy. I have wife and children in Homs. They are kill. You do not know.

– I'm sorry, Mike says.

– I come to England, the man says. I have cousin here. He give me work in his business. I meet Angela. We have children. You understand?

– Angela told me. I'm very sorry.

– Then you come, the man says.

– I told you, Mike says. It's all over between Angela and me. Finished. This is an irrelevant conversation.

– Now I will explain, the man says. If I come tomorrow and you are here I will kill you.

– Hold on, Mike says. You haven't been listening to me. It's all over between us. This is an irrelevant conversation.

The man stands up.

– Look, Mike says, standing up in turn. This is where I live. Where do you expect me to go?

– I go now, the man says.

He moves towards the door, opens it.

– Where the hell do you expect me to go? Mike calls out after him.

He runs to the door but the man is already on the next landing.

– Where the hell do you expect me to go? he shouts again. But the man does not look round.

3

He makes a call.

– Giles here, a voice says.

– Giles, this is Mike.

– Mike?

– Mike Pen.

– Mike! Giles says. Good to hear you! How are tricks?

– Listen, Giles, Mike says. There's a madman here who wants to kill me. I've got to get out of the house.

– A madman? He's in there with you?

– Not right now, Mike says. He's gone. Listen, Giles, I've got to get out of the house. Can I come over?

– Come over?

– You don't understand, Mike says. I need to get out of the house. He wants to kill me. He told me if he finds me here tomorrow he'll kill me.

– Kill you? Why?

– It's a long story.

– Why don't you call the police?

– This isn't a police matter, Giles. Can I come over?

– Now you mean?

– Yes. Right away.

There is a silence.

– Giles, Mike says, you've got to help me.

– All right, Giles says. But it's awkward.

– My life's in danger, Giles, Mike says.

– Are you sure?

– Of course I'm sure. Do you think I'd have called if I wasn't sure?

– All right, Giles says. Come on over.

4

Giles opens the door.

– What's that? he says, pointing.

– My suitcase, Mike says.

– You're not thinking of staying, are you? Giles asks as he rolls it in.

– Listen, Mike says.

– It's out of the question, Giles says, shutting the door. I'm expecting Annabel for supper.

He gestures towards the kitchen, visible through the open door, as he leads him into the living room.

– I should be getting on with the risotto, he says.

– The man's trying to kill me, Mike says. Don't talk to me about risotto.

– There's no need to get excited, Giles says.

– Of course there's a need to get excited, Mike says. I keep telling you. The man's trying to kill me.

– Go on then, Giles says, motioning towards an armchair as he sits down on the sofa.

– Tell me.

– It's like this, Mike says, sitting down. I've been seeing this woman. Angela. Her husband's abusive to her and the kids. He's from Syria and half-crazed with what he's been through.

– I can't do anything about this, Giles interrupts. You need to go to the police.

– I thought you were a friend, Mike says.

– I am, Mike, I am, Giles says. But it sounds as if this is beyond both of us. You've got to get protection.

– You're not listening to me, Mike says. If he finds me in the flat tomorrow he's going to kill me. He's got a knife. He showed it to me. An ugly flick-knife affair. The man's crazy. He'll think nothing of using it.

– Can't you settle this thing amicably? Giles says. Maybe it's money he's after.

– The ridiculous thing, Mike says, is that we'd already parted, me and Angela. She decided he'd never let the children go.

– Then it's clearly money he wants, Giles says.

– Giles, Mike says. I need to get out now.

– You need to go to the police, Giles says.

– You don't understand, Mike says. My life's in danger. Even if the police give me protection twenty-four seven he'll find a way. The man's mad. I could see it in his eyes.

– I'll tell you what, Giles says. Why don't I call Gerry?

5

– Have another, Gerry says.

– No thanks, Mike says.

– You don't like it? Gerry says.

– I do, I do, Mike says. But, really, no.

– It's the best single malt in this benighted country of ours, Gerry says. Believe me.

– I'm sure it is, Mike says. But, really, no.

– You don't mind if I do?

– Please! It's just that I've had quite a day and –

– Relax, Mike, Gerry says, going over to the drinks table. Breathe in, breathe out. Look at the view. There isn't a better one the length of the South Coast.

He refills his glass.

– On a good day, he says, lifting up the glass and looking through it, you can see all the way to Dieppe.

– Dieppe? Mike says.

– Cross my heart, Gerry says, returning to his deep leather armchair. Feast your eyes, he says, gesturing towards the window.

– Listen, Gerry, Mike says. It's really good of you to take me in like this but –

The other raises a hand to silence him.

– Think nothing of it, he says. Any friend of Giles' is a friend of mine. We're like brothers.

– Then if you don't mind, Mike says, I think I'll turn in.

– You can't do that, Mike, Gerry says. Sue hasn't got back yet. You've got to meet Sue.

– It's been a long day, Mike says. I think Giles explained that –

– He gave me the gist of it, Gerry says. But you know what I always say? It's all in the mind. If you think you're tired, you're tired. If you think you're raring to go, you're raring to go. Know what I mean?

– There's only one place I'm raring to go, Mike says. And that's to bed.

– Ah, bed, Gerry says. He gets up again and pours himself another drink. What a word, bed. The images it conjures up. The dreamless sleep of childhood. The fervent nights of love. What do you think of my phonograph?

– I've been admiring it since I came in, Mike says.

– Picked it up a couple of months ago, Gerry says. Been looking for that model for donkey's years. Peter Ustinov had the exact same one. Put your ear to the horn you can hear the sound of the sea. Like a shell. Same principle. They talk about the shell of the ear. Same principle. I must play you my favourite song of all time.

– Tomorrow, Gerry, Mike says. OK? I'm bushed. I just want to get to bed.

– One short song, Gerry says, moving to the table. Send you to bed a happy man.

He finds the disc, sets it in place, winds up the mechanism. One short song, he says. Yves Montand. The king of them all, in my humble opinion. *Les Feuilles mortes. Autumn Leaves.*

A quiet voice of great beauty begins to tell a story. It tells of memory and of those happy days when the sun always shone, days when we were friends; it tells of the dead leaves of autumn swept up into piles, like our memories and regrets; it tells of the song you used to sing to me, and as it does so, without effort it swells in volume and turns into song, singing now in that lovely voice, breaking at times with emotion yet always beautifully controlled, of how life parts those who love and on the sands of time even the footprints of those who once loved are effaced by the tide; it sings of ways not taken and memories buried but brought to life again. Brought to life by the song that fills the room.

When it is over they sit in silence. The disc on the turntable makes a slow whirring sound.

Finally Gerry says: – Ivo Livi. The son of a broom salesman from the north of Italy. I ask you! A broom salesman! Did you even know there was such a thing? Crossed over to France when Mussolini putsched. The boy was two. Grew up in Marseilles. Worked in his sister's beauty salon before he was discovered. I ask you!

He sips his drink.

– He's the one, he says. Piaf has the voice but she's basically singing the same song all her life; Aznavour has the skills but he's always retelling you he doesn't belong; Brel has the voice but little else; Brassens has the Gallic wit but after a while it wears thin. Only Montand can do it all. Only Montand can inhabit us all, can give it everything and yet – and that is his secret – hold something back. Hold something back.

He is silent. Then he says:

– I wonder what happened to Sue?

Mike stands up.

– If you'll show me my room, he says.

– The night's young, Gerry says. Have another.

– No, Mike says, making for the door. I need to lie down.

Gerry heaves himself out of his armchair.

– You'll like it here, he says, leading the way down the corridor. Stay as long as you like. Sue'll look after you. But don't fool with her, if you know what I mean.

He throws open a door and stands back.

– The bathroom's en suite, he says. Have a good night.

6

A bright morning.

In the kitchen Mike locates the kettle, the tea, the mugs and the milk.

The tea made, he takes his mug to the table and sits down facing the big window with its wide sea view.

The door opens and a beautiful young woman with long auburn hair enters.

– I'm Sue, she says.

– So you got back.

– Back?

– Gerry seemed concerned about you last night.

– Gerry's sweet, she says.

She switches on the kettle, goes to the window, looks out.

– I don't actually know him, Mike says. He's a friend of a friend of mine. He very kindly agreed to put me up when I was in a bit of a hole. Perhaps he told you?

– Gerry's sweet, she says again.

She sits down opposite him and stares at him, her green eyes open wide.

– He's your father? Mike asks.

– My father? she says. That's rich.

– I'm sorry, Mike says.

– Look, darling, she says. If there's one thing I can't stand it's men who say sorry the whole time.

– Sorry, Mike says. Oops!

– Have an egg, she says. Have two. Have three. There's bacon in the fridge. And tomatoes. And mushrooms.

– No thanks, Mike says. I don't eat much breakfast.

– Personally, she says, getting up and opening the fridge door, I like a good fry-up in the morning. Mind you, it's not much good for my figure or my gut, but, hey! you're only young once if you know what I mean.

She's at the stove, sets the bacon sizzling, breaks a couple of eggs.

– Do you mind if I open the window? Mike asks.

– Do what you like, darling, she says.

She brings her plate to the table, sits down opposite him again and starts to eat.

– I like the look of you, she says, looking up and wiping her mouth slowly with her napkin. Do you have a name?

– Michael, he says.

– My angel! she says.

– Hardly, he says.

– Don't be so modest, she says. The rule of the house is we say what we mean and we mean what we say. It saves time.

– Sorry, he says. Oops!

– Look, Michael, she says. I'm going to tuck into this and then I'm going back to bed. It would be a pleasure if you would join me.

– I'm not sure I –

She stops him with a finger to her lips.

– You don't have to decide now, darling. Have another cup and think it over.

She bends over her plate again.

He looks at her glossy head.

– I expect Gerry'll be down any minute, he says.

– Gerry? she says. Oh no. He's out for the day. Gerry works. He commutes. Up and down on the train every day bar the weekends.

– I see, Mike says.

– So there you are, my angel, she says, wiping her plate clean with the last of her bread. I may see you in a little while or I may not. Suit yourself. Second door on the left if you're so inclined. Or if you want to have a wander on the beach there's a spare key hanging by the front door. Make sure you take it.

– You've got egg on your nose, he says.

– My angel! she says, rubbing her nose with the back of her hand as she stands up.

She takes her plate and mug over to the sink and disappears, leaving the door wide open.

7

In bed she breathes 'my angel!' into his ear, then hoists herself on top of him and puts her tongue into his mouth.

The doorbell rings.

– Fuck! she says, rolling off him, the boys have forgotten their keys. Lie there quietly, my angel, and I'll be back.

– All change, she says when she returns. They saw your coat in the hall and naturally they're curious.

– What do I do? he asks.

– Sit up, she says.

– In bed?

– Relax, my angel, she says. They won't eat you.

Three young men in black jeans and white shirts file into the room, mugs in hand.

She introduces them:

– Edward. Edmund. Edgar. And this is Michael.

– Hullo Michael, says the one called Edward.

– Hi, Mike says.

They stand at the door.

– Come inside, boys, Sue says. Don't stand on ceremony with Michael, he's a gentle soul.

– Are you? asks the one called Edmund.

– I don't know, Mike says. If she says so.

– We're gentle souls too, Edward says.

There is a silence.

– Doesn't it get confusing when people call you Ed? Mike asks.

– Nobody calls us Ed, Edward says.

– I see.

– And you?

– Me?

– They call you Mike?

– Yes.

Another silence.

– Staying long? Edmund asks.

– No no, Mike says. Gerry very kindly –

– OK, boys, Sue says. Now we've got to know each other, out please. We've got to get dressed.

They file out again.

– Right, Sue says when the door has closed behind them. We've got to get you out of here. Have you got your passport?

– Yes but –

– No buts, my angel, she says, putting a finger to his lips. The boys saw you in bed with me. They don't like it. I suggest you take the next train to Ashford and jump on the first Eurostar to Paris.

– Paris? Mike says.

– You can get a ticket at Ashford, she says.

– But where am I supposed to go?

– You don't have friends in Paris?

– Not to stay with.

– Brussels?

– No.

– And you wouldn't consider a hotel?

– For how long? he says. I can't afford to stay in a Paris hotel for months on end.

– Hold on, my angel, she says. I'll make a call. Get yourself sorted. The bathroom's in there.

When he comes out she says:

– Right, my angel. Xavier will put you up. Here's the address and phone number. Don't lose them.

– But when am I going to see you again?

– Who knows? she says. Life's short, but not that short. Our paths may cross again one day.

– Give me your number at least, he says.

– I don't think that would be wise, she says. Now the boys have seen you in my bed.

Standing on tiptoe she kisses him lightly on the lips.

– Goodbye, my angel, she says. Then she pushes him down the corridor and out of the front door and closes it quietly behind him.

8

Xavier Roche, in white linen suit and lavender shirt, greets him with open arms:

– Welcome, my English friend! You arrive just in time. Tonight we are going to a party.

He embraces him.

The young woman standing beside him says:

– Do you want a drink, Michael?

– Yvonne, Xavier says, gesturing. If we decide to have a child, he says, we will call her Zazie.

– A charming name, Mike says.

– XYZ, Xavier says.

– I see, Mike says.

– I asked Michael if he would like a drink, Yvonne says.

– No time, Xavier says.

– There's plenty of time, Yvonne says. Besides, I would like one myself. Will you join me, Michael?

– Thank you, Mike says.

– I said there's no time, Xavier says.

– Here in France, Yvonne says, thank you means no thank you.

– I forgot, Mike says.

– Don't forget, Yvonne says. You might miss out.

9

At the party there are so many people there is hardly room to move. Yvonne introduces him to Mia, who is small, with a tight cap of bleached hair.

– Come out of the crush, she says, taking his hand and pulling him after her through the crowd.

Outside, on the landing, she says:

– Ouff! One can't breathe in there with all that smoke.

People keep coming up the stairs, pushing past them into the room.

– Come! Mia says. I will show you something.

He follows her up the stairs to the next landing. She pushes open a door and stands back to let him pass.

A bathroom. Steam.

– Go on, Mia says, pushing him towards an old-fashioned claw-foot bathtub. A woman is lying in the tub, her naked body submerged with only the head and feet protruding.

They stand side by side, looking down at her.

– She's dead! Mike says suddenly.

Mia begins to laugh. He turns and stares at her.

– She's dead! he says again.

– Touch her, Mia says.

– Touch her?

– Go on, she says.

– Are you mad? he says. What's going on?

– Don't be afraid, she says. It's only art.

– Art?

– Body art, she says.

He looks down at the body again.

– Go on, Mia says again. Touch her.

– I can't, he says.

– What do you think of the face? she asks.

– What do you mean what do I think of the face? he says. It's horrible.

– Rachel would be pleased, she says. The face gave her the most trouble, you know.

– Who's Rachel?

– The artist. That's her in the bath. It's body art. That's her thing.

There is the shrill sound of a police whistle.

– Shit, Mia says. They're busting us.

10

– Tell us, the first policeman says.

– I've told you, Mike says.

– Tell us again.

– I was taken to this party by a friend, Xavier Roche. And when we got there I was introduced to a woman called Mia. She took me upstairs to a bathroom where there was a woman lying in the bath. I thought she was dead but it turns out it was body art and then you arrived and everyone had gone.

– Body art? the man says. What's that?

– I've no idea, Mike says.

– But you said body art.

– That's what this woman Mia told me.

– And you believed her?

– I don't know, Mike says.

– You don't seem to know much, the man says.

– Who is Mia? the second one asks.

– I told you, Mike says. A woman I was introduced to at this party.

– What is her full name?

– I don't know. I was introduced to her as Mia. She took me up the stairs and –

– Yes, the man says, you told us.

– And you believed her when she told you it was body art? the first one asks.

– I told you, Mike says. I didn't know what to believe.

The two confer.

They turn back to Mike.

– Tell us again, the first says.

– Tell you what?

– The whole thing.

He tells them again.

– Does that sound convincing to you? the first says.

– What?

– What you've just told us.

– It's the truth, Mike says.

The man consults his notebook.

– You have not explained this body art, he says.

– I told you, Mike says. I don't know. It turns out it was her in the bath. Not dead at all.

– Mia?

– No no. Rachel. The artist.

– The artist? In the bath? Why did you not tell us this before?

– You didn't ask.

– We asked you to tell us everything.

– What is everything? Mike asks.

The men wait. Finally the second one asks:

– This Rachel. Who is she?

– The artist, Mike says. I told you.

– In the bath?

– That's what Mia said.

– And you believed her?

– I had no reason to doubt her.

– The house, the first one says. Who does it belong to?

– I told you, Mike says. I've just arrived in Paris. Surely you must know who the house belongs to.

– We are asking the questions, the second one says.

– You say you had just arrived to stay with a friend, the first one says. You had arrived from London?

– No. From Brighton.

– You live in Brighton?

– No. I was staying with friends.

– You have many friends, the man says.

– Not really, Mike says.

– Why did you come to Paris? the second asks.

– I wanted to visit Paris.

– Why?

– I hadn't been for a while. It's a city I'm very fond of.

– Everybody is fond of Paris, the other man says.

Mike waits.

– And you stayed with Xavier Roche? the second asks, consulting his notebook.

– Yes.

– He's a good friend?

– A friend of a friend. He offered to put me up.

– The dead woman you saw in the bath, the first says. When you saw her did you not think of alerting the police?

– It was not a dead woman. It was art.

– You said you thought she was dead.

– I did at first, yes. Then Mia explained to me that it was art.

– And you believed her?

– It all went by very fast, Mike says.

– Did she move?

– No.

– Then why did you think she was not dead?

– I did at first. But then Mia explained to me.

– And if we explained to you that it was a dead woman, what would you say?

– I wouldn't know what to say.

– You don't think it strange when the police find you alone in a house that stinks of drugs standing in a bathroom looking at a dead woman lying in a bath?

– So she was dead? Mike says.

– We ask the questions, the second one says.

– You do not think it suspicious? the first one says.

– Of course, Mike says. Who wouldn't? But I swear I am innocent.

– We do not think you are guilty, Mr Penderecky, the man says, looking at the passport.

– Penderetzky, Mike says.

– It says here Penderecky, the man says, pointing.

– It's pronounced Penderetzky, Mike says.

– Polish? the man asks.

– Yes, Mike says.

– This is a British passport, the man says.

– Polish name, British passport, Mike says.

– You are British?

– Yes.

The two men get up, move to the side of the windowless room, confer.

They return, sit again.

– We do not think you are guilty, Mr Penderetzky, the first one says, but we do not think you are telling us the whole truth.

– You don't?

– No.

– You can check what I've told you, Mike says. You can ask Xavier, Mia…

– We will ask them, the man says.

– Mr Penderetzky, the second one says. How do you think a judge would view the evidence presented to him in this case?

– I don't know, Mike says.

– He would convict you of murder, the man says.

– But I don't know the victim, Mike says. I have no motive.

– You are an art lover?

– I wouldn't say that. I am interested in art.

– In modern art?

– All art.

– Is that why you went to the house?

– No. I told you. My friends took me to a party there.

– And when you saw this… body in the bath, you thought it was art?

– I told you. I had no doubt it was a dead body. And then Mia explained to me.

– You have already told us.

He waits.

– And if we told you it was indeed an artefact, the first one says. What would you say?

– I would heave a sigh of relief.

There is a silence. Then the first one says:

– Mr Penderetzky, we are going to let you go.

– Let me go?

– You can pick up your belongings on the way out.

– You mean I'm free?

– You're free.

He makes a dismissive gesture. Mike gets up.

At the door he turns and looks back. The two of them are sitting there in their stiff uniforms, their faces turned towards him.

– Go on, the first one says. Fuck the hell off.

11

The phone in his pocket rings and he brings it to his ear.

– Giles? he says.

– Mike! Why the hell has your phone been off all this time?

– The police confiscated it.

– The police? What happened?

– It's a long story.

– I'm sorry it didn't work out with Gerry, Giles says. He told me you scuppered off to Paris with the spoons.

– What spoons?

– His little joke. I gather you're staying with Xavier.

– Who is Xavier?

– What do you mean who is he? You're staying with him.

– I mean how do you know him.

– He's a friend of Vicky's. Is it good there?

– No, Mike says. It's not good. I'm getting out. I haven't even unpacked my bag.

– What happened?

– It's a long story.

– You're in trouble with the French police?

– It's a long story, Giles. Another time.

– Listen, Giles says. This may work out very well. I have a proposition for you. Nancy's flat in Nice has just become vacant and she's looking for someone.

– Who the hell's Nancy?

– Sylvia's friend. Her tenant's let her down and she's not planning on getting down there herself till June and she doesn't want to leave it empty.

– I couldn't afford the rent, Mike says.

– No rent, Giles says. You'd be flat-sitting. Doing her a favour. It's right in the heart of the Old Town. You'd love it.

– How do I get in?

– Just ring her friend Raoul. I'll text you the number. You'll love it.

– This Xavier, Mike says. What do you know about him?

– Great guy, Giles says. Sorry, can't really talk now. Shall I tell Nancy it's sorted?

– Yes but –

– Raoul will explain everything. Ring him as soon as possible.

– Giles, listen.

– Sorry Mike, Giles says. Got to dash. You'll love it down there. I know you will.

II ALLEMANDE

1

Walking past the *Pépito* at three in the morning, the heaving night life of Nice Old Town having once again driven him, sleepless and exhausted, from Nancy's third-floor, oak-beamed flatlet, he is surprised to find the door, usually so firmly shut, standing wide open, and even more surprised to hear, coming from within, a light female voice intoning a familiar song.

As he enters the applause is dying away. A large, low-ceilinged room, barely half-full, with a bar to the left and a small stage at the far end on which a woman with a bob of blonde hair is absent-mindedly sipping a drink while, to the right, the members of a small ensemble in white shirts and dark trousers chat idly among themselves. As he advances the musicians begin to return to their places and start tuning their instruments, while the woman walks across the stage and deposits her glass on the upright piano, then moves back and, as the lights dim and the spotlight is turned on, cradles the microphone and whispers her way into a new number.

There is a curious echo where he is standing but he is able to make out what she is saying. 'Deshabillez-moi', she sings, undress me – but not straight away, and not too quickly. Desire me, she sings, take me captive, undress me, but don't be like the others, don't rush me, don't rush it. Choose your words with care, she sings, touch me, but move your hands over me. Not too slow, not too quick. And there, she sings, I am trembling now beneath your hands, undress me, quickly now, undress me – and you – now get your clothes off quick.

Scattered applause. Graciously, she indicates the musicians and they stand and take their bows.

He makes his way to the bar and orders. As the man places the drink in front of him he asks:

– C'est qui, celle-là?

– Au micro?

– Uhuh.

– Charlie.

– Charlie?

– Charlie.

She is standing beside him. The barman places a glass on the counter before her and pours from a bottle.

– I liked that, Mike says.

She turns and looks at him.

– I really did, he says.

– You've got to be joking, she says, her voice surprisingly deep.

– Not at all, he says. Lovely words, lovely song.

– You're easily satisfied.

– I don't think so, he says.

She is sipping her drink.

– The other one, he says. *Autumn Leaves.* I heard it only the other day.

– Oh yes? she says.

– In another town, he says. Another country.

She has returned to her drink.

– On an old phonograph, he says. Yves Montand.

– Really? she says.

She puts down her empty glass and makes her way back to the platform. There are barely two dozen people left in the room.

Once more she cradles the microphone. 'Speak Low', she announces in English.

'Speak low when you speak love', says the song, and it goes on to tell of how our summer days have fluttered away too soon, too soon. It tells of ships adrift and the end of love.

'We're late, darling', she sings and goes on to sing of how the curtain descends and everything ends, while the room empties, leaving the air heavy with the smell of sweat and cigarettes.

Mike asks the barman for a refill.

And once again she is standing beside him.

– For you? he asks, pointing to her glass.

– Marcel knows, she says.

– I liked that, he says.

– Is that all you know how to say?

– No, Mike says. But I did.

– I told you, she says. You're easy to please.

– On the contrary, he says. My friends think I'm very discerning.

– Do you always speak like that? she asks.

– Only when I'm nervous.

– And you're nervous now?

– Yes.

– Why?

– Because I'm talking to you.

– Look, she says abruptly. I don't feel so good. Will you take me home?

– With pleasure, he says.

– Wait while I get my things.

The big room is now empty. Marcel lights a cigarette and wipes down the zinc.

– Does no one sleep in this town? Mike asks.

– We sleep in the mornings, Marcel says.

– I wish I could, Mike says. But however late I go to bed I always wake up at the same time. Then I feel wretched for the rest of the day.

– It's to do with the biological clock, Marcel says.

And she's there again, in a long white coat.

– Come, she says, putting her arm through his. Let's go.

2

Outside, in the now silent street, he says:

– Are we walking?

– I told you, she says. I don't feel well.

– Where do we get a taxi?

– You're new here?

– Newish.

– Follow me.

Wrapped in her long white coat she leads him through the silent streets.

On the promenade he flags down a taxi. He holds the door open for her and she gets in and immediately curls up in a corner.

– Where are we going? the driver asks.

He nudges her:

– Where do we go?

She mumbles an address. He repeats it for the driver.

She dozes, curled up in her corner. He looks out of the window, watching the hotels and restaurants of the town centre give way to villas and gardens as the road starts to climb. Then they are in tree-lined residential streets, silent and empty.

The driver brings the car to a stop.

– Eh voilà! he says.

– Pay him please, she says, opening the door on her side.

He follows her up the steps of a three-storey balconied building. She activates the code and holds the door open for him.

– Quiet, she says.

Inside she fumbles in her bag, finds the keys, opens the door and goes in. She puts on a light as he follows her inside and closes the door behind him.

She is leaning against the open door of the bedroom.

– Are you all right? he asks.

– There's the kitchen, she says, pointing. Make me some hot chocolate please. You'll find everything.

When he returns with the mug of hot chocolate she is sitting on the bed, still in her white coat.

– Are you all right? he asks. You don't look good.

– Put it there, she says, indicating the bedside table. Then go.

– Do you want me to call a doctor?

– No. Just go.

When he is at the door she says:

– Thank you for seeing me home.

He goes out into the night.

3

He arrives at the *Pépito* soon after the advertised opening time to find the door shut.

He rings the bell.

A window in the door opens and a man's voice says:

– Yes?

– I want to come in.

– Member?

– No.

– Members only.

– I was in here yesterday. Nobody said anything about membership.

The door opens and he steps inside. The man, who is sitting on a high stool with a newspaper open on his knees, shuts the door behind him.

– How do I become a member? Mike asks.

The man points with his chin towards the bar and returns to his paper.

Marcel is still polishing the zinc.

– I want to join, Mike says.

– Join?

– Yes.

– Weren't you in here yesterday?

– Yes.

– What will you have?

– Same as yesterday.

– You expect me to remember?

Mike tells him.

When the man puts it down in front of him he says:

– Now tell me how I join.

– Search me, Marcel says.

– The guy at the door told me I had to join.

– No idea, Marcel says.

– Where's Charlie?

– She's not in today.

– Why not?

– How should I know? Marcel says.

– Is she ill?

– How should I know? Marcel repeats. Mireille's in tonight, he adds.

– Is that Mireille over there?

– Uhuh.

Mike swallows his drink and pays. At the door the man is still reading his paper.

– I want to leave, Mike says.

The man looks up from his paper.

– You just came in, he says.

– That's right, Mike says. I want to leave.

With a sigh the man opens the door.

4

He rings the buzzer and waits.

Silence.

He rings again.

– Who is it?

– Me. Mike.

– What do you want?

– I want to see you.

The door clicks open and he steps into the hall.

She is standing in her dressing-gown by the half-open door of the flat, bleary-eyed.

– You're ill, he says.

– Come in.

He follows her into the bedroom. She lies down, pulling the covers over her.

– Are you ill? he asks.

She motions him to the chair by the bed.

He sits.

– Why did you come? she asks.

– I was worried about you.

– You sound like my mother.

– I am your mother, he says.

– Thank God not.

She has her eyes shut.

– Have you got a temperature? he asks.

– You really are like my mother.

– You haven't answered my question.

– What was your question?

– I asked if you had a temperature.

– I don't have a thermometer.

– You don't believe in them?

– Please, she says, opening her eyes and looking at him.

– I'm sorry, he says.
– Can you straighten the blankets please.
When he has done so he asks:
– Can I draw the curtains? Open the window? It's fuggy in here.
– Fuggy? she says.
– It smells of illness.
– You want to leave?
– I want to open the window.
– Open then.
He draws the curtains, opens the window. A neat garden, several tall trees.
He sits down by the bed again.
– How come? she says.
– How come what?
– That you're here.
– I went to the club. They said you were ill.
Her eyes are closed. She says:
– You are kind.
He waits.
Finally he says:
– You want me to go?
– No. Stay.
After a while he says:
– Are you often ill?
– More questions! she says.
– I'm sorry.
She is silent, seems to have gone to sleep.
He waits.
Suddenly she says:
– You can go, you know.
– Why are you here? he asks.
– Here?
– In Nice.

She is silent.

– You're not French, he says.

– No.

– What then?

– Allemande.

– Allemande?

– Allemande.

– Why Nice?

– Why not?

– A man?

– Maybe.

– Still with him?

– Enough questions, she says. Make me a cup of tea. Verveine.

He pulls up the blinds in the kitchen, finds the packet, makes the tea, brings it in and sets it on the table by her bed.

– Now go please, she says.

– I don't want to leave you like this.

– Please, she says. You tire me with your questions.

– When he is at the door she says:

– Will you come tomorrow? Bring me some food?

– I'll get it now.

– I don't need it now, she says. Bring it tomorrow.

– You need to eat.

– You'll make me angry, she says.

– I'm concerned.

– There's stuff in the fridge.

– What do you want me to bring you then?

– Anything, she says.

– But – ?

– Use your common sense, she says.

– But is there anything you can't eat? Don't like?

– Please, she says. Just go.

5

Again she is waiting at the open door of the flat.

– I'm glad to see you, she says.

– Are you starving?

– It's you I'm glad to see.

She takes his hand and draws him in.

– Come, she says. I'll make coffee.

– You're feeling better?

She puts a finger to her lips:

– No questions.

At the kitchen table, with the coffee between them, he asks:

– How long can you take off from the club?

– I told you, she says. No questions.

– I'm sorry.

She pushes the cup across to him.

He says:

– Perhaps you're right. I only know how to ask questions.

– You English are so complicated, she says.

– I'm not English.

– No?

– Polish.

– Polish?

– My father.

She is silent.

– Do you want to know any more? he asks.

– No.

She gets up, holds out her hand.

– Come, she says. She draws him after her to the bedroom.

– See? she says, pointing. I opened the windows.

She takes off her dressing-gown and then her nightdress and gets into bed.

– Come, she says.

– Into the bed?

– Take off your clothes first.

At the climax she says: Ha ha. Ha ha. Then falls asleep.

6

He dozes, wakes up when she nudges him.

– I made coffee, she says.

– I went to sleep.

– I know, she says.

She sits on the bed.

– You're lovely, he says.

– Why? she says.

– You just are.

He sits up as she hands him the mug and the abrupt movement knocks it out of her hand.

– Shit! he says, jumping up. I'm sorry.

She sits on the sodden bed and starts to cry.

– It's all right, he says. It's all right, Charlie.

– It's not all right, she says, between sobs. It's all wrong.

He goes into the kitchen finds a cloth, comes back into the bedroom. She is still sitting on the bed, her head in her hands, her body heaving.

– Get up, Charlie, he says. Let's change the sheets.

She doesn't move.

– Charlie, he says. Don't worry. It'll come off in the wash.

– You must go away, she says, her head in her hands.

– Go away?

– You bring me bad luck.

– Charlie, he says.

– Please, she says. Go away.

– I can't go away, he says. I'm going to help you get this mess cleaned up. You'll see, we'll do it in a second.

– No, she says, looking at him, the tears still streaming down her cheeks. You don't understand. I want you to go away.

– But –

– Go, she says. Go away.

– When shall I come back?

– Don't come back, she says. You bring bad luck.

– What are you talking about? he says.

– Go, she says. Please go.

– I'm just clumsy, he says. I always have been. I don't bring bad luck.

– I don't want you here, she says, wiping her face with the back of her arm. Go. Don't come back.

– What does that mean? he says. You don't want to see me again?

– I made a mistake.

– A mistake?

– Go, she says, pointing. Now. Please.

– Charlie, he says.

She sits on the bed, her head in her hands.

7

He pays a visit to Mme Esther. Her flyers, plastered over the walls and billboards of the Old Town, read: 'Mme Esther, Déformations du temps'. Her waiting room resembles that of a doctor or dentist of the old school, upright wooden chairs with worn leather seats line the walls and ancient copies of *Elle* and *National Geographic* sit forlornly on a low table in the centre.

The only occupant is a stern-looking young woman at the reception desk who silently motions him to one of the chairs.

He sits.

After a while the woman says:

– You may go in now.

In Mme Esther's consulting room there are no crystal balls or packs of cards, only the furnishings of a bourgeois living room. Mme Esther herself, tiny and elegant in dark slacks and white silk shirt, is of indeterminate age. Her handshake is surprisingly firm and cool.

– What can I do for you today? she asks, smiling, showing perfect white teeth.

– I thought you foretold the future, Mike says.

– There is no future, Mme Esther says. And no past. There is only our perception of the present, variously deformed.

– Deformed?

She waves this away and motions him to sit down in a deep armchair while she herself perches on the edge of the sofa, legs elegantly crossed.

– Tell me about my present then, Mike says.

– But that you already know, she says, smiling.

– Then what are you offering?

– Give me your left hand, she says.

She leans forward as he holds it out and takes it in her right, looking all the while into his eyes.

– I see a dead woman, she says. Lying on a daybed.

– In a bath, Mike says. Only she wasn't dead. It was body art.

– A bed, a bath, she says, releasing his hand but maintaining eye contact. It makes no difference.

– But it does, he says. You see, she wasn't dead.

– Mr....? she says.

– Penderecky.

– Penderecky.

She leans back on the sofa, closing her eyes.

He waits.

Finally she says:

– I see an ear on a table.

– A phonograph, Mike says.

– Please do not interrupt, Mr…, she says, opening her eyes and looking straight into his own.

– I'm sorry, he says, but you see, Mme Esther, that is all in the past. I want the future. Otherwise why would I consult you?

– Mr…, she says reproachfully.

– Penderecky.

– Please do not interrupt, Mr Penderecky, she says.

– I'm sorry, he says. Go on. I just meant I know all that. I want to know what I don't know.

– We always know everything, she says, smiling, showing her beautiful teeth. But we don't always know we know, you understand? Or we are not always prepared to acknowledge what we know.

– And so? he says.

– I help you to know what you know, she says. To acknowledge it.

– You sound like a psychoanalyst, he says.

– Sir, she says, you must understand. I sound like no one but me. Mme Esther.

He stands up.

– You are leaving us? she asks, still deep in the sofa.

– How much do I owe you? he asks, taking out his wallet.

– My secretary will tell you, she says, motioning towards the door.

– Thank you, he says, holding out his hand.

She does not take it.

The waiting room is still empty but for the young woman at the reception desk.

– It's not cheap Mike says, examining the bill she hands him.

– You pay for what you get, she says.

– In that case, he says, it is extremely expensive.

– Mme Esther is never wrong, she says, putting the money carefully away in a metal box in a drawer of the desk. – Would you like a receipt?

8

Now he has taken to sitting on the beach at night as he waits for the Old Town to go quiet.

He listens to the sounds of the waves lapping the beach.

Sometimes footsteps crunch on the beach behind him and a dog out on its late-night walk sniffs around him till called away by its owner.

Sometimes lovers stroll down arm in arm and stand at the edge of the beach, looking out over the water.

Sometimes he falls asleep there. One night he only wakes as dawn is breaking. He had been elsewhere.

Once a philosopher seeks to engage him in conversation and he has to get up to escape.

The weather grows warmer, the town more crowded.

And one night she is there, seating herself down beside him on the sand.

They sit.

Finally she says:

– You disappeared.

– What did you expect?

– Expect?

– You threw me out, he says. You said you never wanted to see me again.

The lights from the Promenade dance on the little waves.

She sighs.

– I looked for you, she says. You hadn't given me an address. Nothing.

He sits.

She says: – You should never pay attention to anything I say.
– That's helpful, he says.
They sit.
The dancing lights. The sound of the little waves lapping the shore.
– You're not working today? he asks.
– I finished early. Everyone had left.
She puts a hand over his on the sand.
– I'm sorry, she says.
– What's the use, Charlie? he says.
A dog sniffs around them, goes away.
– I thought you had gone, she says.
– Gone?
– Left town.
– No, he says.
– Please forgive me, she says.
– What's the use? he says again.
They sit.
He gets up.
– Where are you going? she says.
– What's the use? he says again.
– Don't leave me, she says.
He stands beside her.
– Please, she says. I beg you.
He sits again.
– Please, Mike, she says.
He sighs.
– Say yes, she says.
The town has grown quiet behind them.
– Please, she says. Say yes. Say you forgive me. Now I've found you.
– Yes, he says.
She sighs.
– I'm glad, she says.

9

What he likes most, in the days that follow are the desultory conversations after sex.

– What gets me about that Juliette Gréco song of yours, he says, is the *vous*.

– *Vous*?

– In English it can only be direct, brutal: 'Undress me.' But in French you have that decorous plural, just peeping out in '*Sachez me convoiter*', then a little more prominent in '*Ne soyez pas comme tous les hommes*' and '*de vôtre main experte, allez-y*', before bursting out with magical effect in the last stanza: '*Et vous, déshabillez-vous*.' Doesn't that make it ever so much sexier? *Déshabillez-vous*?

– I don't know what you are talking about, she says.

– Language, he says. And sex.

He falls asleep again.

When he wakes up it is day and she is in the kitchen, making coffee.

She comes back with two mugs.

– No, he says as she hands one to him. I'll join you in the kitchen.

– Are you afraid I will throw you out again?

– Yes.

As they sit at the kitchen table she says:

– Will you come with me or stay here?

– Come with you where?

– To the club.

– Sure I'll come. You know I'm your greatest fan.

– I don't know if you are laughing at me or not, she says. But I like having you there when I sing.

– Are we walking?

– Of course, she says.

10

Marcel, the barman, seems to have time on his hands.

– There was another shooting last night, he says.

– Here?

– No. At Jo-Jo's.

– You don't say.

– Two dead, Marcel says.

– Why don't the police do something about it?

– They know to keep out of it, Marcel says.

He rubs his cloth meditatively over the gleaming chrome.

– These things go in cycles, he says. When honour's satisfied on both sides, it stops.

– It sounds like the Middle Ages to me, Mike says.

– Here it's still the Middle Ages, Marcel says. The Middle Ages with offshore banking.

11

Sometimes he does not even go in with her but spends the day in the flat and its surroundings. He likes to roam through the quiet residential streets, so different from the incessant bustle and noise of the downtown area. He discovers a garden café close to the archaeological museum and sits reading a book. There are few clients and the waiters leave him alone.

Once a week the cleaner comes. She's from Alsace. Meussieu Pendère, she calls him. I was once in your country, she says. What country was that? Mike says. I can't remember, she says. You know I come from England, Mike says. England? she says each time they have this conversation. I thought you came from… over there. From Poland? That's right. Poland. No, Mike says. I come from England. I was once in England, Mme Stranitz says. Oxford Street. Piccadilly Circus. Very nice, Mike says. Very nice, says Mme Stranitz.

When Charlie lets herself in he often does not wake up. She undresses in the bathroom and slips into bed beside him.

12

He wakes up in the dark to sense her moving about.

– What are you doing?

– Go back to sleep.

– But what are you doing?

– Dressing.

– Dressing? What time is it?

– Five.

– Five? What are you dressing for?

– I've got to go.

– Go where?

– I've got to catch a train.

– A train? What for?

– I'm going to Zürich.

– Zürich? What for?

– I'm going to see my boyfriend.

He sits up in bed and puts on the light.

– Boyfriend? he says. What are you talking about?

– Don't make a fuss, she says. I'll be back the day after tomorrow.

– Boyfriend? he says again. But I'm your boyfriend.

She comes to the bed, lays a finger on his mouth.

– Please, she says. It's not important.

– Not important? he says. Are you crazy? Why didn't you say?

– I've got to go, she says. Just go back to sleep.

– Charlie, he says. What is this?

– I don't want to talk about it, she says. It's not important. I'll come back soon.

– Charlie, he says. You can't go. What's this about a boyfriend?

– You've got the key, she says. I'll be back soon.

– Charlie, he says. We've got to talk.

– No, she says. And when I come back, please, no questions. Understood.

– Charlie! he says.

But she is gone.

13

She puts his mug of coffee down on the bedside table, then sits on the bed, cradling her own mug in both hands.

– You know what I would like to do?

– What?

– I would like to go bicycling with you.

– I don't have a bicycle.

– We could rent one.

– Where would we go?

– Just around. I want to freewheel down a hill with you in front of me.

– Why not behind?

– That's just how I see it, you in front and me behind.

– To go down a hill, he says, you first have to get up it.

– Why do you always look on the dark side of things?

– No, seriously, he says. It's pretty hilly round here.

– Bicycles have gears, you know.

– But still. I'm unfit. Look at me.

– We can go along the coast road to Monaco, she says.

– Monaco? Isn't that miles away?

– It's not that far.

– Won't the road be full of cars?

– There you go again, she says.

– I'm sorry.

– I'll plan it, she says. You'll see. We'll have a good time.

14

She is waiting for him at a bend in the road.

He dismounts, panting.

– Where are you taking me?

– I want you to meet some friends of mine.

– You said it would be flat all the way.

– It is flat, she says.

– Funny sort of flat, he says.

– It's only a kilometre or two into the hills, she says. Think of it as flat and it'll be easier.

– It's just that I haven't cycled for ages.

– It's a beautiful day. And you made it, anyway.

They are on the outskirts of a village just off the coast road.

– You'll like my friends, she says. They'll give us lunch. And it's not much further.

She is on her bike again.

– Hold on, he says. I need to get my breath back. Who are these friends of yours?

– You'll see, she says. You'll like them.

After a few minutes he gives up the struggle, gets off his bike.

– You go on, he says. I'll walk.

– It's just up there, she says, pointing.

– Up there? It's practically vertical.

– You'll see. The road's quite gentle. We'll be there in no time.

They push their bikes up the hill. A scooter zooms noisily past them, trailing a cloud of petrol fumes.

15

– My children: Armand, Antoine, Annette, Alphonse and Alma, says Rose, their mother, pointing to each in turn seated at a long table on the shaded terrace. You will eat with us? she asks them.

– With pleasure, Charlie says.

– You cycled all the way from Nice?

– All the way, Charlie says.

– Mamma mia, the mother says.

Chairs are brought out and space is made for them at the table.

– Why all the ayes? Mike asks Annette, who is seated on his right.

– The ayes?

– Your names.

– They are always aye in my father's family, Annette says. It is a tradition.

– He's not here?

– He?

– Your father.

– He passed away, she says, holding out the salad bowl for him to help himself.

– I'm sorry.

– So are we.

– You're still singing at the *Pépito*? Rose asks Charlie, seated on her left.

– Sure.

– Mémé still there?

– Still there.

– And Pépé?

– He left.

– Well, Rose says, I'm glad to see you.

– I'm glad to be here.

– And what do you do? Mike asks Antoine, seated on his other side.

– Nightguard, Antoine says, wiping his plate with a piece of bread.

– That's interesting, Mike says.

– It's a job.

– Think of it, Mike says. You guard the night.

– It's offices we guard. Down in Nice.

– I see.

– There's lots of crime in Nice.

– Is that so?

– Mike, you're not eating, Rose calls down the table.

– I am, I am, Mike says. It's delicious.

– Wait till you taste my mother's tart, Armand says, leaning across his sister.

– I can imagine, Mike says.

– The reality is better than anything you can imagine.

– I'm sure, Mike says.

– People identify Nice with terrorist crimes, Antoine says. But it's the local crimes we think about the whole time. It's getting as bad as Naples, believe me. On top of the Corsican mafia we've always had we now have the Chechen mafia, the Iranian mafia, even the Indonesian mafia.

– Really? Mike says.

– You've no idea, Antoine says. It's a sinkhole. Nothing but a sinkhole.

– What do you think of it? Annette asks, pointing to his plate with her fork.

– Delicious, Mike says.

– No one cooks meat better than my mother, Annette says. Every kind of meat. Pork. Beef. Lamb. She's the best.

– The Chechen gangs work with the Corsicans to wipe out the others, Antoine says. But they don't succeed. Or they do for a bit but then the others regroup and come back at them.

– Is that so? Mike says.

– That's the truth of it, Antoine says.

– How long have you and Charlie been together? Annette asks.

– I'm not sure we are together.

– If she brought you here to see Mama, believe me, Annette says, you are together. We're family to her. Try that cheese. It's local.

– I'm not sure I can have anything more, Mike says.

– It helps the digestion, Annette says.

– That's what they always say, Mike says. I don't believe a word of it.

– It's true, Annette says. These old sayings always have some truth in them.

– Come, Mike! Charlie calls out to him across the table. We must be on our way.

– I'm not sure I can even get up, Mike says. Let alone get on a bike.

Charlie has stood up and is kissing Rose.

– Now you are being taken from us, Annette says.

– I'm afraid so, he says, pushing back his chair.

– Goodbye, Rose says, waving to them from the terrace. Come back soon!

16

– We're going home, Charlie says as they retrieve their bikes. OK?

– I was going to suggest it myself.

– I'll take you back a different way.

– Not too steep?

– Not really.

When they arrive she asks: – How was that?

– My legs are like jelly.

– You'll feel it tomorrow.
– I feel it now.
– It'll be worse tomorrow.
– Thanks, he says.

They sit at her kitchen table with the coffee between them.

– What happened to the father? he asks.
– The father?
– Your friends.
– Oh, him. He was killed.
– Killed? How?
– They think he was mistaken for someone else.
– Murdered, you mean?
– Killed.
– They found the killer?
– No.

After a while she says:

– It happens all the time.
– You have nice friends.
– Are you being ironic?
– No. I really liked them.

He sips his coffee.

– You know what I want? she says.
– What?
– I want you.
– Jelly legs and all?
– Jelly legs and all.

17

He presses the buzzer.

Nothing.

He presses again.

Again nothing.

He activates the code, enters the building, crosses the vestibule, knocks on her door.

Silence.

He tries the door and finds it unlocked.

Darkness.

He calls out:

– Hello! It's me!

Silence.

Again he calls out:

– Hello! Anyone there?

He feels his way to the living room.

Darkness. Silence.

Then he sees her in the faint light of the shuttered window. She is sitting upright in the armchair by the wall.

Gradually, as his eyes adjust, he sees that her eyes are wide open.

– What are you doing? he says.

– Sitting, she says.

– Why in the dark?

Silence.

– Why didn't you answer when I called?

Silence.

– Can I put on the light? he asks.

– No, she says.

– Open the curtains?

– No.

He makes his way into the room, sits down on the sofa.

– What are you doing? he asks again.

– Sitting.

– Why in the dark?

– I like it like that.

– Charlie, he says.

Silence.

– Talk to me, he says.

– Go away.
– I'm not going away, he says. I want to know what's going on.
Silence.
– Charlie, he says at last. We've got to talk.
– Why?
– I can't go on like this.
Silence.
– I can't, he says again.
Silence.
– Charlie, he says. Talk to me. What is it?
– Nothing.
– Then what's all this about?
– I don't want to talk about it, she says.
– But don't you see you need to?
– I told you, she says. Go away.
– For good?
She is silent.
– Is that what you want?
Silence.
– Is it?
– Come tomorrow if you like, she says.
– But what do *you* like?
– I like for you to come tomorrow.
At the door he looks round. She hasn't moved. Her eyes are still open, her arms on the arms of the chair.
He goes.

18

Now he has taken to arriving at the *Pépito* near to closing time and standing at the bar while she performs.

She sings: 'Our summer day flutters away too soon, too soon.'

A hand on his arm. He turns.

– Alphonse! he says.

And there they all are.

– What will you have? Armand says.

Mike gestures towards his full glass.

– When you're done, Armand says.

– You've come down for the evening? Mike asks.

– You know how it is, Antoine says.

She sings: 'Like ships adrift we're swept apart too soon, too soon.'

– You know what I said to Annette after seeing you both the other day? Alphonse says.

– What?

– I said you did her good.

– Well, that's nice, Mike says.

– And you know what she said?

– No.

She said she agreed with me.

– She always agrees with you?

– Not always, Alphonse says. Sometimes.

She sings: 'The curtain descends, everything ends, too soon, too soon.'

– Look, Armand says. About that drink. Let's take a rain-check on it. OK? We've got to be going.

– Already?

– A bientôt, Antoine says, waving.

– Ciao, Mike says.

The place is almost empty. The band strikes up with a show of energy that does not last.

She sings: 'Sachez me convoiter me desirer, me captiver. Déshabillez-moi.'

19

– Did you see your friends? he asks when, in her long white coat, she rejoins him.

– What friends?

– The three ayes.

– Three ayes?

– Rose's sons.

– Oh, them.

– Did you see them?

– Were they in tonight?

– Just for a moment. Checking up on you.

– On me?

– Uhuh.

– They don't check up on me.

– I don't know why else they should drop in like that.

– Come on, she says. Let's go.

As they walk up the hill in the moonlight he says:

– I hadn't seen them in before.

She takes his hand:

– I don't want to talk about them, she says.

20

In bed she says:

– I like having you here.

And, later:

– Black moods come over me like a sack over my head. You must bear with me.

– It's always been like that?

– As long as I can remember.

– Do you know why?

– I don't want to talk about it. I just want you to say you will always forgive me.

– I will always forgive you, he says.

– Now make love with me.

At the climax she says: Ha ha. Ha ha. Then immediately falls asleep.

21

She brings him coffee in bed. Sits on the bed while he drinks.

– You know what I'd like to do one day? she says.

– Get rid of me.

– I would like to take you to my favourite restaurant.

– I didn't know you had a favourite restaurant.

– Have you been to Saint Paul?

– I thought it was a tourist trap.

– What is that?

– A place that attracts many tourists and then makes them spend their money on rubbish.

– I will take you to *A l'Ombre des Vieux Tilleuls*, she says, and then you can tell me if it is rubbish.

– How do we get there?

– Bus.

– I was afraid you were going to suggest cycling, he says. My bum's still sore from that last outing.

– A nice comfortable bus, she says. Except you have to hold on tight when the driver goes round the bends.

– Thanks for telling me, he says.

22

Now they are sitting on the terrace of the restaurant with the valley spread out below them. He reaches for her hand.

The waiter arrives.

– You deal with it, he says.

– When the man has gone he says: – I'm happy.

– And me, she says.

– To us, he says, lifting his glass.

– To us, she says.

He sips.

– Very nice, he says.

– I said you would like it here, she says.

– You are always right, he says. We are even sitting in the shade of the old lime tree.

The *hors d'oeuvres* arrive.

– Perhaps Nice is where I was always meant to end up, he says.

– And me.

They eat.

– When I was small, she says, I thought of the day as a refuge from the terrors of the night.

– Why terrors?

– When I was put to bed and the light was turned off it was as if a cloth had been pulled over my head. Like a parrot. And then I was afraid I was no longer there. I was conscious but my body had disappeared. Gone forever. It was terrible. And during the day the thought of what would happen when the night came would paralyse me and I could do nothing at all. My mother would beg me to go into the garden and lie down on the grass and look up at the sky. She said if I looked my fears would go away, but instead they got worse. There was no end to the sky. At first it was very far away. And then it would come closer and closer and I felt that if it came any closer it would suffocate me and I would scream. So they took me indoors and I would sit in a corner of the room and wait for the night to come.

– And didn't they try to do anything about it?

– They pleaded with me. My mother was very kind.

– Why didn't they just leave a light on during the night?

– They tried that, she says. But it only made it worse. I felt the light was burning my eyes and hid myself under the blankets.

– They didn't take you to see someone?

– What do you mean?

– To help you.

– I didn't need help, she says. I needed to be somebody else.

The main course arrives.

– Everything fine? the waiter asks.

– Super, she says.

The man goes.

– And then? he asks.

– Then?

– When did it pass?

– What do you want me to say?

– I'm sorry, he says.

– It doesn't matter.

They eat.

– What matters is us, here, she says.

Afterwards they walk round the ramparts.

– I was in Siena once, he says. I stayed in a hotel on the edge of town. There was a garden. Tall trees. There are very few trees in Siena. It's a stone city. It's hard to escape the sun. But in that garden you could walk under the shade of the tall trees. The guests wandered through those trees, talking in low voices. You could hear the murmur from the bedrooms. Many voices. Many languages. But indistinct. And at the end of the garden the ground fell away abruptly, just like this, and you could see the vineyards, the fields, and on the other side of the valley, more hills, rolling away to the horizon.

– Here you can look right down to the sea at the bottom of the valley, she says, pointing. But it's too hot today. There is a haze.

They are back at the entrance to the restaurant.

– Saint Paul is much smaller than Siena, she says. But of course Siena sits on the top of the hill. Here we are only half-way up.

Then they take the bus back to Nice.

23

Now he divides his time between the studio flat in the Old Town and her apartment in Cimiez, not far from the archaeological museum. Sometimes, on his way up to the flat, he goes in to explore Nice's ancient past. Around 350 B.C., he learns, Greeks from Marseille founded a permanent settlement and called it Nikaia, after Nike, the goddess of victory. Through the ages the town has changed hands many times. From 1388 it was under the dominion of Savoy. Between 1792 and 1815 it became part of the French First Republic, after which it was returned to the Kingdom of Piedmont, before its final re-annexation by France in 1860.

The dry facts fail to grip him, yet there is something soothing about the museum, nearly always empty, and its old stones.

She has given him a key and there are days when he lets himself in so as to have an early night, for his weeks of living in the Old Town, trying to sleep in the face of the pounding music all around him, his weeks of only going to bed when she has finished her stint at the *Pépito*, have failed to alter in any significant way the workings of his biological clock.

– If you only knew what it takes for a lark like me to take up with an owl like you, he says as he walks up the hill with her.

– I don't know what you are talking about, she says.

– Larks sing early in the morning, he says, and owls are night birds.

– You want me to be grateful? she says.

– I want you to understand me.

They climb the hill.

– I like Cimiez at night, she says. I like the quiet.

They reach the house. She puts a finger to her lips:

– Sshhhh. My neighbours also want their sleep.

She activates the code and they enter the building.

– They disapprove of you? he asks in a whisper.

– Why should they disapprove of me? Sometimes I invite them to the club to hear me sing. The old ones especially like it.

– Everybody loves you, he says, as she switches on the lights in the flat and takes off her coat.

– You too?

– Me too.

– Now I have a shower, she says.

He sits on the bed and takes off his shoes. Then he lies back and stares up at the blue ceiling.

24

He has lost track of time and only arrives at the *Pépito* at half past two. But the place is packed and he remembers that it is a Saturday night.

He stands at the bar waiting for Marcel to serve him.

A young man in a tuxedo with a handsome, ravaged face, steps onto the platform and, as the band strikes up, cradles the microphone and begins to sing. He sings 'Our summer day flutters away'.

Marcel has finally come over to his end of the bar.

– Where's Charlie? Mike asks.

Perhaps because it is so noisy the man does not appear to have heard.

– Where's Charlie? he asks again.

– Charlie?

He has to shout to make himself heard.

– Where is she?

– Gone.

– Gone where?

– Gone. She's left.

The young man on the stage has a pleasant light baritone. He sings: 'I wait darling, I wait'. He sings: 'Will you speak low to me, speak love to me?'

Mike has to raise his voice to make himself heard.

– What do you mean gone?

– Gone, Marcel shouts. *Finito.*

– *Finito?*

– *Finito.*

– She can't be gone, Mike shouts. She works here.

But Marcel is serving another customer.

– Gone where? Mike shouts, when the man returns to his end of the bar.

The answer is drowned in the applause. The ravaged young man on the platform launches into another song. This time he sings how thousands of years would not suffice to express the second of eternity when you kissed me.

– Where? Mike shouts again.

– Genoa, Marcel shouts back.

– Genoa? Why Genoa?

– Her brother.

– She's gone to her brother? In Genoa?

– Uhuh.

– Give me an address, Mike shouts.

The young man sings 'Où to m'as embrassé, où je t'ai embrassé, un matin dans la lumière d'hiver, au Parc Montsouris'.

– An address! Mike shouts.

Marcel points with his chin: – The patron.

– He'll tell me?

The young man sings: 'À Paris, sur la Seine'.

Mike pushes his way through the crowd till he reaches the table where the patron is sitting talking to a bald man in a white suit.

He taps him on the shoulder.

The man looks up.

– Where's Charlie?

– She no longer works here.

– Where is she?

The man has returned to his conversation.

Mike leans down and shouts:

– I want to know where she is!

The man looks up again.

– Go away, he says. Do you understand me? Then he returns to his conversation.

Mike walks to the door.

The doorman smiles at him over his paper. Mike takes out his wallet.

– Do you know where Charlie has gone, Philippe?

– Charlie? the man says. Genoa.

– Do you happen to know why? Mike asks, extracting a note from his wallet.

– Who knows?

– But you can guess.

– With women how can one guess?

– Give me an address, Mike says, holding out the note.

– Thank you, M. Penderecki, the man says taking it and slipping it into his pocket.

He produces a pencil stub and a piece of grubby paper. He writes, tongue between his teeth. He hands it to Mike.

– Via Santa Maria di Castello 22, Mike says, reading.

– Goodnight, sir, the man says as he opens the door.

– You're sure this is the right address?

– Sure.

– The brother?

– Goodnight, the man says again.

Mike goes out into the night.

III CORRENTE

1

The train journey from Nice to Genoa, according to the timetable, is 4h 55m. But not if there is a hold-up in Ventimiglia.

Two uniformed officers are systematically going through the train, checking passports. One of them slowly turns the pages of the document while the other waits, staring into space. The first closes the passport and hands it to his comrade, who goes through the same routine while his partner assumes the passive pose. When they have both thoroughly examined it they confer in hushed tones, in Italian. Finally the first turns to the passenger and, tapping the passport, says:

– M. Penderecki?

– Penderetzky.

– It says here Penderecki.

– Pronounced Penderetzky.

– Polish?

– Polish name.

– But you have a British passport.

– That's right.

The man looks up at the rack and gestures with his chin.

– Yours? he asks.

– Yes.

– Open, the man says.

– Open? Mike says. Why?

– Open.

The other occupants of the carriage draw as far as they can from the offender as is possible without giving the impression of so doing.

– Why? Mike asks again.

– Don't ask, the man says. Open.

Mike gets up, takes his suitcase from the rack and places it on the seat he has just vacated, opens it and steps back.

– Sorry! he says, turning as he steps on a foot.

With just one hand the second officer turns over the contents of the suitcase.

Then he steps back and invites his companion to do likewise.

When they have finished the first says:

– Close.

– Satisfied? Mike asks.

He closes the suitcase and heaves it back onto the rack, then sits down.

The first officer says:

– Where are you going?

– Genoa.

– Why?

– Private business.

– What business?

– Private.

– What business?

– I'm going to see my girlfriend.

– What is the name?

– Is this necessary? Mike asks.

The men wait.

– Charlotte, Mike says.

– Surname?

– Deutsch.

– German?

– Bravo.

– Answer please.

– Yes.

– Address?

He takes out his wallet, produces the slip of paper, reads:

– Via Santa Maria di Castello 22.

– Her house?

– Her brother's.

The men confer. The first gets out his phone and has a long conversion, slipping out into the corridor as he does so and shutting the compartment door behind him.

He is visible in the corridor walking up and down, talking on the phone.

He re-enters the carriage and pushes the passport into Mike's hand.

The two men leave the compartment, once more closing the door behind them.

The other passengers avoid Mike's eye.

With a creak and a groan the train starts to move again.

2

Via Santa Maria di Castello 22 stands between a hotel housed in a medieval palazzo and the church of Santa Maria di Castello, its Romanesque façade of white polished stone typical of the city of Genoa.

Mike rings the doorbell and waits.

An elderly woman wrapped in black opens the door.

– I'm looking for Charlotte Deutsch, Mike says.

– On the part of whom?

– Michael Penderecky.

– A moment.

She closes the door.

A time.

The door opens again and this time it is a man, youngish.

– Yes? he says.

Mike repeats his request.

– She's not here, the man says.

– Am I speaking to her brother?

– She's not here.

– Where can I find her?

– Why do you want to see her?

– I'm a friend from Nice. She left abruptly. I need to talk to her.

– What's your name?

– I told the lady. Michael Penderecky.

– Polish?

– English.

– She's not here.

– You're her brother? Mike asks again.

The man stands at the door, looking at him.

– I was told she had come to stay with her brother, Mike says.

– Who told you?

– At her workplace.

– She's not here, the man says again.

– Where can I find her?

– What do you want with her?

– I told you, Mike says. I'm a friend. She didn't mention me?

– She has many friends.

– Please. I need to see her.

– A moment.

The door closes again.

A time.

The street, at mid-day, Italian, empty.

The door opens again. Another man appears, older, balding, blowing his nose in a large polka-dotted handkerchief.

– Yes? he says.

– I'm looking for Charlie.

– Why?

– I need to see her.

– She's gone.

– Gone where?

– Milan.

– Milan?

– Yes.

– Why?

– To see friends.

– Do you have an address for her? I need to see her. It's urgent.

– Ring her up.

– Her phone appears to be disconnected.

The man is busy blowing his nose.

– I need to see her, Mike says. Do you have a new number for her? An address?

– A moment.

This time the large door is left ajar. A dark hall. Somewhere in the recesses of the house someone sneezes.

The man returns with a piece of paper in his hand. He thrusts it at Mike as he brings his handkerchief to his mouth again and stifles another sneeze.

– Splendore, Mike reads. Via Pietro Orsolo 48, Milan. What's Splendore?

– The name.

– What name?

– The name of her friend.

He sneezes again.

– Excuse me, he says. I have a cold.

Mike puts the piece of paper away in his wallet.

– Thank you, he says.

– That girl, the man says. Always running.

He steps back inside and shuts the door. Inside, he goes on sneezing.

Mike walks down the hill.

3

Via Pietro Orsolo 48, Milan. Mike bends at the car window as he pays the taxi.

A freshly-painted lime-green door.

He rings the bell, waits.

A young-looking middle-aged woman opens the door.

– Hi, I'm Mike. I'm looking for Charlie.

– Mike! Welcome! The woman says. She talked so much about you!

– She's here?

– Come in, come in. You will eat lunch with us?

– She's here? he asks again as he follows her inside.

– Come, come.

She pushes him before her and into a large light room where a great many people are sitting round a food-laden table.

– Sit! Sit!

He looks round.

– Where is she?

– Carlotta?

– Her brother told me she was here.

– You have seen her brother?

– He told me she was here.

– She was here but she was in a hurry. Always running.

– Running where?

– When she gets something into her head, that one… Come, I will introduce you. This is Mike, Carlotta's friend. I am Lucia. These are my children: Fabia, Federica, Antonio, Anna-Maria and Michaela. And my husband, Roberto, and his brother, Ronaldo, and the wife of Ronaldo, Margareta, and their daughter Albertina and their son Alberto.

– She's gone where?

– Sit, sit, Lucia says. Antonio, put a chair for Carlotta's friend. I will tell you everything. You will have some pasta?

– Thank you, Mike says as she pushes him into a chair between herself and Ronaldo.

A plate laden with different-coloured pasta is put in front of him.

– Eat! Eat! Ronaldo says.

– I need to find her, Mike says to Lucia.

– Eat, eat, Ronaldo insists. Do not insult the cook.

Mike takes up a mouthful, eats.

– How do you find it? Lucia asks him.

– Delicious.

– You like it?

– How could I not like it?

– Eat, Lucia says. When you have eaten I will explain.

– Eat, Ronaldo says.

He eats.

– This morning she was here, Lucia says. It is a pity you could not come earlier.

– But where did she go? Why is she running?

– You ask these questions of Carlotta? Lucia says. You do not know her. She runs. She always runs. Like there is a demon pursuing her.

– But where has she run to?

– I think Sils Maria, Lucia says.

– Sils Maria?

– She said Sils Maria. Villa Serafina.

– What's that?

– You know Carlotta. Very melodramatic. She said to me: Lucia, I have an appointment with death at the Villa Serafina, Sils Maria.

– An appointment with death?

– You know Carlotta. Always with her melodrama. Opera.

– You don't believe her?

Lucia shrugs.

– You know Carlotta, she says. Now eat. You have not finished the pasta and now comes the meat.

– How long does it take to get to Sils Maria?

– You have a car?

– No.

– Pity.

– By train. How long by train?

– No train.

– No train? What do I do?

– You want to catch her?

– Yes. That's why I'm here.

– You must take the train to Domaso and then the bus to Sils.

– How long does that take?

– Roberto, how long does it take to Sils Maria by train and bus?

– Why Sils Maria?

– Mike wants to go there. He wants to find Carlotta.

– Carlotta is not in Sils Maria. She is in Zürich.

– No, she said Sils.

– She said Sils?

– Yes. That is where she was going.

– She said to me Zürich.

– How long? Mike asks. How long?

– To Sils?

– Yes.

– Three hours train, two hours bus.

Mike pushes back his chair and stands up.

– Sit, Ronaldo says, pulling him down.

– No. I'm sorry. I have to go.

– Mike! Lucia says. The meat!

– You must taste her meat, Ronaldo says. No one cooks meat like Lucia.

– I'm sorry, Mike says, pushing away his hand. I need to go. Please, Lucia, call me a cab. I must run.

– Everybody is running, Lucia says sadly as she accompanies him to the door.

4

The bus station in Domaso is across the square from the railway station.

– Single one-way to Sils Maria, Mike says to the young lady behind the grille.

– No bus today to Sils Maria, the lady says.

– No bus?

– Not today.

– Why?

– Avalanche.

– Avalanche?

– Road blocked.

– What shall I do? Mike asks. I need to get to Sils Maria as soon as possible.

– Take the train to Zürich, she says, and then the train to St. Moritz. Then the bus to Sils.

– How long does that take?

She consults her screen.

– Four-five hours, she says.

– That long?

– Yes.

– And what time is the next train to Zürich?

She studies her screen again.

– You missed the last train she says.

– What?

– It just left.

– It can't be the last train, Mike says.

– Last train, she repeats.

– What shall I do?

– Stay in Domaso till tomorrow, she says. Maybe then the road will be unblocked.

– And if it isn't?

– Take the train to Zürich and then –

– Shit, Mike says.

She waits, impassive.

– Does this often happen? Mike asks.

– Avalanche?

– Yes.

– It is the mountains, she says.

– Shit, Mike says again.

She waits.

– You're sure there's no other way?

– No other way.

– And what time is the first bus to Sils?

– Seven o'clock.

– And the second?

– Ten o'clock.

– And it takes two hours?

– If the road is open.

– Shit, Mike says for the third time.

– Domaso is a very nice town, the woman says.

5

Domaso is a very nice town. It sits at the northernmost tip of Lake Como, and the little harbour is lined with pleasure-boats while the hotels and guest houses all advertise wind-surfing facilities and ferry trips across the lake. Noisy families roam the streets in the evenings and eat out in the many lakeside restaurants after a long day on the water.

– One night, Mike says to the sour man at the reception desk of the Villa Angelina.

– Special price for three nights, the man says. Including lessons in wind-surfing.

– No thanks, Mike says. Just the one night.

– No wind-surfing?

– No wind-surfing.

– With dinner?

– No. Just the room. With breakfast.

– Passport please.

The man puts it away in a drawer and hands him a key without meeting his eyes.

– Second floor, he says. On the right. Lift in the corner.

Domaso is a very nice town, but not if you are in a hurry. The restaurants are crowded, the lakeside throbs with music, the side-streets are dreary. After a dull meal he goes back to his hotel room, shuts the shutters, shuts the window, draws the curtains and gets into bed wondering if he will be able to sleep.

6

He is at the bus-station at nine-thirty the next morning. The same young woman behind the grille.

– Are the buses to Sils Maria running?

– How many?

– They're running?

– Yes.

– The road's been cleared?

– All clear.

– Thank God for that, Mike says.

– How many? the woman asks again.

– Just the one. Single.

– To Sils?

– To Sils.

– Is the bus here? he asks as he slips the ticket into his wallet.

– Over there.

– It leaves at ten?

– At ten.

– Thank you.

– You enjoyed our town? she asks.

– Very much.

– It's a very nice town, she says.

IV SARABANDE

1

The small Alpine resort of Sils Maria consists of a broad main street lined with the usual cafés, sports shops and hotels, against a background of three snow-capped mountains under a slate-grey sky. There is a stone fountain, rippling gently, in the middle of the street, opposite the Tourist Office. Minor roads, some no more than dirt tracks, sparsely dotted with Alpine villas, snake out towards the green fields and then the mountains, beyond.

A loud bell is activated by opening the glass door of the Tourist Office. Inside, a carefully made up young woman is looking at her phone. She glances up as he enters.

– Good morning, Mike says. I'd like a map of the town please.

She reaches out to the pile beside her and pushes a mimeographed sheet across the counter.

– Do you know how I get to the Villa Serafina?

– Villa Serafina?

– Yes.

– It's a hotel?

– I don't know.

She purses her lips:

– One moment.

She disappears through a door at the back and returns with a colleague who resembles her in every way. Together they bend over the map, leaving him to gaze at their glossy heads.

Eventually the first one says:

– Here.

She makes a cross in pencil on the map and pushes it across to him.

– And we are…?

She circles their location on the map.

– Is it a hotel?

– You are looking for a hotel?

– No. I want the Villa Serafina. But I want to know if it is a hotel or a private residence.

– It is a private residence.

– How long does it take to get there?

– Ten minutes.

– Thank you.

– This evening, she says, at the dance hall, *Sarabande*, there is a dance.

– Thank you.

Holding the map in one hand and his briefcase and the handle of his wheeled suitcase in the other he manoeuvres his way through the glass door. The bell rings shrilly, then ceases abruptly as the door closes behind him.

The sky is still grey. The fountain still ripples. He crosses the road and sits down on the stone rim.

He sits there for a while, dipping his hand into the water and passing it over his face. It leaves a faint metallic taste in his mouth.

2

Following the map, always open in his hand, stopping every now and again to flatten it out, he turns off the main street onto a smaller, tarmacked road. Large villas set in gardens enclosed by high hedges. He turns off this again onto a still smaller, winding road. Soon he is walking between small fields, the mountains with their white caps always there ahead of him.

Villa Serafina stands alone facing the fields in a large bare neglected garden. A rusty swing. Three open deck-chairs.

He leaves the suitcase on the little path leading to the front door and climbs the five marble steps to an imposing shiny black door. He rings the bell and hears it echo through the house, but there are no answering footsteps within.

He rings again.

Silence.

Slowly he descends and, leaving the suitcase where it is, starts to walk round the house along a narrow gravel path.

On the ground floor, raised high above the garden, the tall windows are all shuttered, but on the floor above the shutters are open and pinned back against the white-washed walls.

The back door.

No bell. He knocks.

Silence.

He tries the handle. Locked.

He continues on his slow circuit of the house until he is back once more at the steps and the front door.

He climbs the steps again, rings again, hears again the bell echoing through the house, then silence.

He tries the door. Locked.

He stands for a while on the top step, surveying the surrounding fields, the leaden sky, the mountains.

He descends, turns back down the path to the gate, trailing his suitcase in his wake.

He starts back to the town along the way he has just come.

3

In the main street he turns right instead of left.

A sign, 'Nietzsche-Haus', and an arrow. He follows the arrow.

The Nietzsche-Haus is another large Alpine villa, similar in style to the Villa Serafina. It is where Nietzsche stayed when, in the last years of his lucidity, he spent his summers in the Alpine resort. Today it consists of a hall and ticket office, cloakroom and lockers on the ground floor and, on the first floor, three rooms of exhibits, a library and a conference room. It also doubles as a guest house, catering mainly for admirers and disciples of the philosopher, with rooms on the top floor.

He buys a ticket, consigns his suitcase to a locker and, keeping his briefcase in his hand, climbs the broad spiral staircase and enters the first of the museum's rooms. He is the only visitor.

In vitrines, first editions of the Master's many works. He bends over and tries to decipher the gothic lettering. Tiring of this he moves to the far wall, where a framed letter is hung. An English translation, clumsily typed on a yellowing card, is tacked to the wall beside it. It reads: 'Well, my dear friend, I am once more in the Upper Engadine. This is my third visit to the place and once again I feel that my proper refuge and home is here and nowhere else.' The letter is addressed to Carl von Gersdorff and is dated June 1883.

He moves to the second room. More vitrines and another framed letter on the wall, this time addressed to Jacob Burckhardt: 'Dear Herr Professor, when it comes to it I would very much prefer a professorial chair in Basle to being God; but I dare not go so far in my private egotism as to refrain for its sake from the creation of the world.'

Three men in dark suits, speaking German, have entered the room. They bend over one of the vitrines, tapping the glass, commenting loudly on what they have found.

He crosses the room to the door, hurriedly descends the stairs and leaves the building. Taking long strides he returns the way he has come to the Villa Serafina.

4

Everything is as he left it: the three open garden chairs, the swing, the shuttered ground-floor windows, the silence.

His briefcase in his left hand and his raincoat over his right arm, he climbs the steps to the front door and rings the bell.

Silence.

He rings again, putting his ear to the shiny black door. As before, he hears it ring within but there are no answering footsteps approaching.

He tries the door and this time it opens.

He steps inside and with a gentle whoosh it closes behind him.

A large entrance hall, filled with shadows. An imposing staircase leading upwards in a wide spiral.

Against the walls, a few heavy dark wood chairs.

He starts to walk slowly round the hall, keeping close to the walls.

A door. He turns the handle and it opens.

Darkness.

He closes the door and moves on round.

Another door. Same story.

He returns to the foot of the stairs and gazes upwards.

Light floods down from above.

Keeping close to the wall he starts to climb.

Half-way up he turns to look down at the dark hall below.

Silence.

And then, very faintly, music.

He listens: a familiar tune.

He proceeds with his slow, silent ascent.

The landing.

He stops again.

The music can be heard more clearly now. It comes from behind the door facing the stairs.

Yes, he knows the melody. Was perhaps, even, secretly expecting it.

He crosses the landing and tries the door.

It opens.

Here on the first floor the shutters are open, though the windows are firmly shut.

In the window, facing him, the isosceles triangle of the central mountain, its summit gleaming white and, on either side, the lower slopes of the other two.

Just above the sill, framed by the mountains, three bare-headed silent watchers.

In the centre of the room, on a table covered with a red cloth, an old-fashioned phonograph, its enormous horn turned to the window. It is from this that the music is emerging. Of course, Yves Montand singing 'Les Feuilles Mortes'.

Next to the table, an upright chair. Between table and window a chaise-longue on which, quite naked, her hands resting on her small breasts, his lover Charlotte Deutsch is reclining, her eyes closed.

He stands and surveys the room.

He looks at Charlie. At the window. At Charlie again.

He stands.

After a while he moves towards her, stops.

He stands, looking down at her.

He looks up. The three watchers at the window have not moved.

Abruptly he turns and walks towards the door, opens it.

On the landing, on either side of the door, immobile, two men in dark suits and bowler hats. The one on the right holds in his right hand a large wooden cudgel, like a rough police truncheon. His fellow on the left holds a sort of fishing net which trails on the floor in front of him.

They stand, looking out over the landing and the staircase.

He turns back into the room, closing the door behind him.

Swiftly, he walks to the chair, puts his briefcase and raincoat down on it and turns back to the phonograph.

Leaning on the table with his left arm, his head bent a little to the left, he gazes into the horn's cavernous mouth.

Yves Montand intones confidentially:

> Tu vois, je n'ai pas oublié
> La chanson que tu me chantais.

He turns quickly, moves to the chaise-longue, kneels by the reclining woman and looks into her face.

Her eyes are now open.

– Charlie, he says.

Silence.

– What are you doing here? he says.

Silence.

Yves Montand sings:

> Et la vie sépare ceux qui s'aiment
> Tout doucement, sans faire de bruit.

At the window, the three watchers. Behind them, the mountains.

He stands up, returns to the table, gazes once more into the mouth of the horn.

Yves Montand sings:

> Et la mer efface sur le sable
> Les pas des amants désunis.

He turns back to the window. The three watchers.

He walks to the door, opens it.

The two guards.

From the room behind him, a scream, piercing, prolonged.

He closes the door, returns to the chaise-longue. He crouches once more at her side.

Her eyes are closed again. He reaches out to touch her face, stops, lets his hand drop.

– Charlie, he says.

He waits. She doesn't move.

He stands up.

Abruptly, he turns, picks up his coat and briefcase and walks to the door, opens it and looks out.

The two guards.

He steps out, shuts the door behind him and faces them.

The one on the right, with the cudgel, points to the briefcase.

He holds it out. The man turns and pulls a small table from the shadows behind him, lays his cudgel down on it, takes the briefcase, opens it, holds it upside down.

A large kitchen knife and a coil of green rope fall onto the table. The man shakes the briefcase just to make sure, turns it right side up, closes it and hands it back.

He makes a gesture of dismissal.

Mike takes the briefcase, moves towards the grand staircase.

He starts to descend, keeping close to the wall.

Behind him the voice of Yves Montand and its musical accompaniment gradually fade:

> Et la mer efface sur le sable
> Les pas

At the bottom of the stairs, the hall full of shadows.

He crosses the hall, takes one last look round and up, then steps out into the sunlight.

V TEMPO DI MINUETTO

1

With a light step he walks down the path, past the swing and the garden chairs, through the gate and back towards the town.

The fields. The villas.

The main street is still empty, the water still patters into the fountain.

A taxi is parked in front of the tourist office, the driver's window down. Mike leans in and asks the young woman at the wheel: – How long to St. Moritz?

– Fifteen.

– Minutes?

– Minutes.

– And by bus?

– Forty-five.

– Take me to St. Moritz then. The railway station.

He throws his briefcase and raincoat into the back seat and climbs in after them.

2

At the railway station the ticket office is empty except for a tired-looking man behind the grille.

– Zürich please, Mike says.

– Return?

– No. Single.

As the man deals with his request he asks: – When does the next train go?

The man studies his screen.

– Forty minutes, he says. Platform One. Via Chur.

– Is there a café?

– Platform One.

The café is called the Minuet Bar. It is empty save for a tall blond young man behind the counter.

– Coffee, Mike says. With milk. And a cheese sandwich.

– You like our town? the man asks as he takes the sandwich out of the perspex stand and puts it, still in its plastic wrapper, on a plate.

– Very much, Mike says.

– You have come for the Fiesta? the man asks as he puts a saucer and spoon down next to the plate.

– No. I've been to Sils.

– Ah, Sils, the man says. There is the Fiesta there too.

He fusses with the coffee machine and asks, his back to the customer:

– Holiday?

– No, Mike says. I was just there for the day, he adds.

The man turns back to him with the steaming cup.

– To visit the Nietzsche-Haus? he asks as he carefully sets the cup on its saucer.

– That's right, Mike says.

– American? the man asks.

– No. English.

– English?

– Does that surprise you?

– Here in St. Moritz, the man says, we have every nationality. Russian. Chinese. Many Japanese. Many Americans. In winter many Germans and Austrians. Much skiing. The Winter Olympics was here in St. Moritz two times, 1928, 1948.

– How much? Mike asks, taking out his wallet.

He takes his coffee and sandwich over to a table in the corner, overlooking the platform. A few people stand waiting, their suitcases beside them.

The two guards from the Villa Serafina enter, the one with his cudgel and the other with his net. They talk in German with the barman.

Mike slits open a packet of sugar, pours the contents into his coffee, stirs.

The one with the net shows it to the barman, who examines it, says something, and all three laugh.

Mike unwraps the sandwich, looking out of the window.

The men laugh again, absorbed in the objects before them.

Mike finishes his coffee and sandwich, looking out of the window.

He glances at his watch, gets up.

The train is waiting further up the platform. He finds an empty carriage and sits down by the window, facing the engine.

A time.

The train starts to move. Soon the Swiss landscape is rushing past: mountains with their snowy tops, pine trees, meadows, streams, brown and white cattle.

Smiling as he catches a glimpse of his ghostly self hovering over the landscape – the mountains, meadows and the rest – he briefly wonders why it is he feels so light-hearted.

VI PASSEPIED

1

He dozes. He dreams.

The compartment door opens and three men in dark suits and soft hats enter, close the door behind them take off their hats and take their seats facing him with their hats on their laps.

Occasionally, he notes through half-closed eyes, they glance at their watches.

The train slows. He sits up and looks out of the window. To judge by the growing number of houses they are approaching a town. He looks out for a sign and is soon rewarded: *Thusis.*

A station. The train comes to a gentle stop.

No one on the platform and no one apparently getting off.

The three men stare impassively ahead.

With hardly a sound the train starts to move again.

The compartment door opens and two uniformed men appear:

– Passports please.

He fumbles in his pocket. The three men opposite do not appear to have heard.

He hands over his passport. The first official takes it and begins to examine it. When he is done he passes it to his colleague, who examines it in turn.

– Michael Penderecki? he asks, looking up.

– Penderetzky.

– It says here Penderecky.

– It's pronounced Penderetzky.

The two bend over the document again.

– Why are you in Switzerland? the first asks.

– Tourism.

– You have been in St. Moritz?

– Sils Maria.

– Hotel?

– No hotel.

– No hotel?

– I didn't stay the night, Mike says.

– You did not stay?

– Flying visit, Mike says.

– There is no airport in Sils, the man says.

– I mean I just came for the day.

– For one day?

– I visited the Nietzsche-Haus.

They resume their perusal of the passport.

– I came from Milan, Mike says. I'm going to Zürich.

– Case, the man says, pointing up at the rack.

Mike stands up, takes his briefcase off the rack and hands it to him.

He looks inside.

– Empty, he says, handing it back.

– I left my suitcase behind, Mike says. In the Nietzsche-Haus.

– Why?

– I forgot it.

– Sit, the man says.

The two officers sit down on either side of him.

In the seats opposite the three men sit, impassive.

The officer on his right speaks into his phone.

– What's this about? Mike asks the one on his left.

The man does not answer.

– Are you arresting me? Mike asks.

The one on the phone gets up, still talking, leaves the compartment closing the door behind him.

He walks up and down the corridor, talking on his phone.

– I want to see a lawyer, Mike says.

The officer in the corridor puts his head into the compartment, motions to his companion, who gets up and follows him out again, closing the door behind him.

The two men can be seen talking animatedly in the corridor.

The three men opposite stare straight ahead, their hats on their laps. Their suits, Mike notes, are not as clean as they might be.

He catches the eye of one of them and turns quickly to the window.

The Swiss landscape flows past, picturesque, unchanging.

The second officer returns, hands Mike back his passport and rejoins his fellow in the corridor.

The train starts to slow. They are approaching another small town. *Chur*, says the sign on the platform.

There are plenty of travellers on the platform, waiting for the train to stop.

It does so, with a gentle sigh.

The two officers reappear on the platform, heading for the exit.

Someone opens the compartment door, looks in, closes it again.

With another sigh the train starts to move again.

2

He goes in search of a coffee.

A queue. Most take their purchases back to their compartments but a few sit down at tables next to the bar.

He waits.

When his turn comes he asks for a coffee, with milk, and a sandwich.

The woman behind the bar points to a menu on the counter. He glances at it and says:

– Cheese.

– No more, the woman says.

– It's on the menu.

– No more.

– Then just the coffee. With milk.

– Ham? the woman says. Ham and cheese?

– No. Just the coffee please.

He takes his cup and moves along the carriage, finds a table with two empty seats and settles into the one by the window facing the engine.

The landscape flows on past: the fields, the cows, the mountains and the rest.

Someone sits down in the vacant seat opposite.

He looks up. He stares.

Finally he says:

– You?

– Me? the woman opposite says.

– I can't believe it, he says.

– Can't believe what? she asks.

– What are you doing here?

– I'm having coffee she says, pointing.

– Charlie, he says.

The woman stares at him.

– Charlie, he says again.

– No, the woman says. I'm Johanna.

– I'm sorry, he says. I took you for someone else.

He examines her.

– Well? she says.

– Charlie, he says. What is this?

– Don't keep saying Charlie, she says. I'm Johanna.

– But why did you sit down here?

– I'm sorry? she says.

He looks round.
– There are all those empty seats, he says, gesturing.
– You want me to move?
– Of course not, but –
– Then tell me about this Charlie, she says.
– I can't believe it, he says, looking hard at her.
– What? she says.
– You don't live in Nice? he says.
– Nice?
– You weren't in the Villa Serafina?
She sips her coffee, looking at him.
– Charlie, he says.
– Why don't you tell me all about it? she says.
– You weren't at the Villa Serafina? he says again.
– You need to start at the beginning, she says.
– The beginning?
– Yes.
– Charlie, he says. Don't do this to me.
– Tell me your name, she says.
– Me?
– Who else.
He tells her.
– Pleased to meet you, Mike, she says.
– And you're Johanna?
– I told you.
– Where are you going?
– Zürich.
– Why?
– You're inquisitive, she says.
– Why?
– If you want to know, she says, it's to see my boyfriend.
– You've got a boyfriend in Zürich?
– Why not? she says.
He looks out of the window.

– And you? she asks.

He turns back to her, examines her face again.

– Do I look like her? she asks.

– And where have you come from? he asks.

– Chur, she says.

– Before Chur.

– That's a long story.

– We've got time, he says.

– You ask too many questions, Mike, she says.

– You've never been to Nice?

– Many times, she says.

– You don't have a brother in Genoa?

She laughs.

– I told you, she says. You're making a mistake.

– I don't think I am, he says.

The train starts to slow down. A sign announces Bad Ragaz.

– I followed you to Genoa, he says. I found your brother. He told me you'd gone to Milan. In Milan your friends said you'd gone to Sils Maria. To the Villa Serafina. I followed you there.

– Quite an adventure, she says.

On the platform, more travellers, with suitcases and backpacks.

The train stops.

– And then? she says.

– Then?

– There was music, he says. A big phonograph on a table. A chaise-longue. And you. Dead.

– Dead? she says, opening her eyes wide. Well well.

– At first, he says, your eyes were closed. And then you opened them. And then you closed them again.

The train starts to move.

– Then there was a scream, he says.

– A scream?
– Such a scream.
– I screamed? she says.
– So I realised you weren't dead, he says.
– I wasn't? she says.
– No, he says.
– You're not being very clear, she says.
– I'm trying, he says.
He is silent.
– Go on then, she says.
He examines her face.
– Was I dead then or wasn't I? she asks.
– I don't know, he says.
– There's a big difference, she says.
– Yes, he says.

She seems suddenly bored, turns away from him and looks out of the window.

– There were three men, he says. At the window. They were looking into the room.

He stands up suddenly.
– Come with me, he says.
– Come where?

– They're on the train, he says. The three men. In my compartment.

– Here? she says. In your compartment?
– I'll show you, he says. Come.

She stands up. He steps back to let her pass in front of him, then takes her arm and propels her ahead of him down the train.

3

He opens the compartment door to let her through.

– Well? she says.

– It's empty, he says.

– You're sure it's the right one?

He points to his briefcase and raincoat on the rack.

– Yours? she asks.

– Yes.

She sits down at the window facing the engine. He sits down opposite her.

– Charlie, he says.

She looks at him.

– Please, he says. Tell me what happened.

– What difference would it make if I said I was Charlie? she asks.

– Difference? he says. What do you mean difference?

She is silent, looking out of the window at the narrow lake along which the train is now running.

– It's going to snow, she says.

– It can't snow, he says. It's almost summer.

– It can and will, she says. We're in the mountains here.

– They took a knife out of my briefcase, he says. And a coil of rope. Green rope.

– Who did?

– The two guards, he says. On the landing at the Villa Serafina. They emptied it out on a little table they pulled out from behind them. Or rather one of them did. The one with the cudgel.

– Cudgel? she says.

– I saw them again at the railway station in St. Moritz, he said.

– You don't fool with the police here, she says.

– Charlie, he says. Do you know something?

– What?

– Now I've found you I'm never going to let you go.

She is looking out of the window.

– It's starting to snow, she says.

– Did you hear what I said?

– Yes, she says. I heard you.

– And what do you say?

– Never is a big word, she says.

– I mean it.

She is still looking out of the window.

– We are approaching Zürich, she says.

– Charlie, he says. What are you going to do?

– Do?

– Now. When we get to Zürich.

– I am going to a hotel with you, she says.

– What? he says.

– I am going to a hotel with you, she repeats. We will spend the night.

– Charlie, he says.

– I told you, she says, smiling at him. Johanna.

– As you wish, he says.

– There is the lake, she says. Isn't it grand?

She stands up.

– Come on, she says. It's time to go.

– I lost my suitcase, he says, standing up and reaching for his things on the rack.

She has taken a brush out of her bag and is brushing her hair, neck bent.

– I left it at the Nietzsche-Haus, he says.

– Who cares about your suitcase? she says, putting the brush back inside her bag.

– I need to buy pyjamas, he says.

– Pyjamas? She starts to laugh.

– And a toothbrush, he says.

– What do you want a toothbrush for when you have me? she says.

– That's true, he says.

He follows her out of the compartment and down the carriage corridor.

The train enters the station.

VII GIGUE

1

Outside the station it is snowing hard. The large flakes fall silently in the windless air.

No cars. No buses. A few pedestrians slowly crossing the station square in black and white. An old silent film.

– I can't believe it, he says.

– Come, she says. I want to dance.

– Dance? he says.

– Come.

– I can't dance.

– Come, she says, taking his hand.

– I can't, he says. I promise you. I'm hopeless.

She guides him out into the soft and silent square.

– My briefcase, he says.

– Damn your briefcase, she says.

– But –

– No buts, she says. Forget your briefcase. Forget your pyjamas. Forget your toothbrush. OK?

– OK, he says.

There he is dancing in a station square, dancing in the snow.

– My dear, he says as she whirls him round. How much I love you. Now I've found you again I'm never going to let you go.

2

In the big bed in the overheated hotel room he says:

– What happened in the Villa Serafina?

– All you ever do is ask questions, she says.

– I need to know, he says.
– Why?
– Charlie, he says. Please.
She is silent in the bed beside him.
– Please, he says.
She nestles up against him, licks his ear.
– Come on top of me, she says. Right on top.
At the climax she says:
– Ha ha. Ha ha, then immediately falls asleep.

3

He wakes to find her dressing in the morning half-light.

– What is it? he says.
– Go back to sleep, she says.
– But what are you doing?
– I have to go, she says.
He sits up.
– Go? he says. Go where?
– To see my boyfriend.
– Your boyfriend? he says. What are you talking about?
– I told you on the train, she says.
– Told me what?
– That I was coming to Zürich to see my boyfriend.
– Then what are you doing here with me?

She sits on the chair, easing her feet into her shoes with a helpful finger.

– Charlie, he says.
– Johanna, she says.
– You can't do this to me, he says.

She stands up and goes into the bathroom, leaving the door open.

– You came to Zürich to see him? he says.

– I told you, she says.
– Then what are you doing here with me?
– I like you, she says.
– Then forget about him.
– I can't, she says. He's my boyfriend.

She finishes putting on her make-up, stands at the bathroom door.

– You're coming back here? he asks.
– No, she says.
– Why not?
– I can't.
– Why not?

She puts on her coat.

– I'm not letting you go, he says.

She moves to the door.

– Charlie, he says.
– Please, she says.
– You're really going?
– Yes.
– Who is he?
– Goodbye, Mike, she says at the door.
– But what about us? he calls out.

But she is gone.

4

London. Night.

As he approaches the house he looks round for any Karims lurking in the shadows, but the street, at that hour, remains stubbornly empty.

On the landing he stoops to insert the key in the lock.

He pushes open the door and feels for the light switch. As the entrance hall lights up he closes the door behind him.

He puts his briefcase down by the coat-rack, hangs up his coat, goes through the flat switching on the lights.

All seems to be as he left it.

He goes into the kitchen, runs the cold tap, fills a glass, drinks.

He puts down the glass, goes into the bedroom.

He walks to the window and draws the curtains, then crosses to the bed and switches on the bedside light.

He returns to the door and switches off the overhead light.

He returns to the bed and, suddenly weary, sits down.

On the rug by the bed, his slippers, the toe of one against the instep of the other, waiting for his feet.

– Ah well, he says, and, his feet still on the floor, lies back across the bed and closes his eyes.

The End

NOTE

Many thanks to Michael, Andrew and Maren at Carcanet, and to Tamar and Steve, for making this book the beautiful object it is.

Remember also that perhaps the best time of your life, of which you have really never talked to anyone freely, were those eight months in a village about two years ago where you thought you'd burned all your bridges, where you confined yourself to that which was beyond all doubt, where you were free, without letters, without the five years of correspondence with Berlin, in the shelter of your illness, and when at the same time you didn't have to change but only to engrave ever more firmly the old contour, the old narrow contour of your nature (after all, your face under the grey hair has hardly changed since your sixth year).

Franz Kafka

CONTENTS

PREFACE

One day in the summer of 1917 the writer Franz Kafka woke up to find his mouth full of blood. Diagnosed with TB, he left Prague the following month and went to stay with his youngest sister Ottla, who was trying to make a living on a smallholding in the Bohemian countryside some fifty miles north-west of Prague. There, on sick leave from the insurance office in which he worked, far from his overbearing father and his friends, he settled down to try and make sense of what had just happened to him. It is there he wrote the series of over a hundred little pieces which we know as the 'Aphorisms' or the 'Zürau Aphorisms'. But these form only part of a feverish bout of activity in which he filled two of the little octavo notebooks he had taken with him with writing of all kinds, some of it among the best work he ever did.

Those months, the only extended period of time Kafka spent away from his native city apart from a brief period in Berlin and in successive sanatoria at the very end of his life, form a singular unit, a bracket in his normal existence. By April Kafka had accepted that the office would not grant him the permanent retirement he craved, felt that he had exhausted his initial intense desire to start his life afresh by facing up to his demons, and reached a kind of truce with his illness. By May he had returned to Prague and resumed his old life. It is with those eight months in Zürau that this book is concerned.

Rosalind Belben, Stephen Mitchelmore and Bernard Sharratt read an early draft of the book and made many helpful comments. To all three, many thanks.

For them, as for me, and, indeed for two of the greatest modern critics, Walter Benjamin and Maurice Blanchot, Kafka is more than just another interesting writer; he is a setter of

standards of integrity and a constant source of nourishment, as well as one of the acutest diagnosticians of the difficulties and paradoxes involved in writing in our times. There is always a place for another attempt to grapple with his greatness and his elusiveness.

Gabriel Josipovici
Lewes, January 2024

PROLOGUE: AUGUST 1917

The Blood

On the twenty-ninth of August 1917 Kafka wrote to his favourite younger sister Ottla: 'One night, some three weeks ago, I had a violent fit of coughing and spat up a stream of blood. It was about four in the morning. I wake up and am surprised to feel in my mouth an unusual quantity of saliva, I spit it out and then, for some reason, put on the light, weird, it's a clot of blood. And so it starts. *Chrlení*. I don't know if I've spelt it correctly but it expresses well that eruption out of the throat. I thought it would never stop. How could I close the jet when I hadn't been the one to open it? I got up, I walked up and down the room. I went to the window. I looked out, I returned – still the blood, finally it stopped and I fell asleep, I actually slept better than I had for a long time.'

Even here, when attempting to describe the greatest crisis in his life, the moment when his own death suddenly loomed up before him, he cannot help being waylaid by the words he reaches out for in order to convey to his sister what has happened. *Chrlení* in Czech means to vomit or spit out and Kafka clearly felt that its onomatopoeic qualities made it more appropriate than the German *speien* or *spucken*. We know from his diaries how aware he was of the inadequacy of German, the common medium of expression amongst assimilated Jews in the Austro-Hungarian Empire, to express his most fundamental feelings, such as his relations to his mother, but this is one of the rare times Kafka ventured into Czech, the language of the people. Perhaps it springs into his mind because, as he was to write to Milena three years later, describing just this episode (a touch he does not communicate to Ottla), the maid, coming into his room in the morning and

seeing the blood, exclaimed: '*Pane doktore, s Vámi to dlouho nepotrvá*' (Mr Doctor, you don't have long to go.)

He immediately went to see his doctor, Dr Muhlstein, who reassured him, saying it was most likely the result of a cold, and nothing to worry about. This, however, did not satisfy his close friend Max Brod, who insisted he see a specialist, Dr Gottfried Pick. While noting from the X-rays that he had a slight darkening of the upper lungs, Pick thought this might not imply tuberculosis, and that even if it did that wasn't really anything to worry about. He might if he wished take a few months of sick leave and spend it somewhere in the country and of course come back to him for a check-up, but that was just precautionary.

Kafka, however, was not convinced. He sensed that what had happened to him was life-changing. Reiner Stach, Kafka's most recent and thorough biographer, suggests that Kafka was being less than candid with his sister, his friends and his doctors, hiding that he had actually spat blood before the fatal day. He bases this, I imagine, on a remark Kafka makes in a letter to Milena written in 1920 in which he suggests that there had been an earlier episode, not at home but at the swimming baths: '... and suddenly, at the Municipal Swimming Baths, towards the month of August (it was warm, it was a fine day, everything bar my head was magnificently normal) I spat up something red'. Did Kafka forget this and only remember it much later? Did he not feel it was significant enough to mention in the light of the violent torrent of blood that had poured forth from his throat on that mid-August morning? Did he perhaps imagine it when he came to write about it to Milena? Whatever the truth of the matter, there is no doubt that he felt, after the 11 August episode, and in spite of the reassurances of the doctors, that he had reached a decisive moment in his life.

Writing to Felix Weltsch on 22 September, he speaks of Dr Muhlstein's repeated reassurances and only reluctant

acceptance that 'there was tuberculosis of both left and right lungs, which however would clear up fairly soon': 'It is as if he had wanted to shield me with his broad back from the Angel of Death which stood behind him' he writes, 'and now he gradually steps aside. But neither he nor it (alas!) frightens me.'

He had always fretted at his office job as an insurance lawyer in the Prague-based Workers' Accident Insurance Institute, though we know he was highly regarded by his colleagues, and his recently published 'office writings' confirm that he took the job extremely seriously and turned his considerable intelligence, empathy and linguistic gifts to trying to better the lives of factory workers throughout Bohemia. But now, though he was still only thirty-four, he decided that he would use his condition to seek permanent retirement.

This was not the only dramatic change in his life which he had immediately felt the flow of blood would entail. It was, he sensed, both sign and proof that he must bring to an immediate end his five-year, mainly epistolary relationship with Felice Bauer, the Berlin-based friend of Max Brod to whom he had twice been engaged – a relationship he increasingly felt had no future. This, however, was a far more problematic cutting-off than with the office. What Kafka's diaries and the six-hundred page volume of his letters to Felice show, letters that have been poured over by scholars and have even elicited a full-length study by Elias Canetti, is that Kafka, from his adolescence on, was caught in a terrible double-bind: only marriage, he felt, would propel him into the life his fellow human beings seemed to inhabit, make him feel part of the community of men and make of him a serious adult like his father, while bachelorhood would be a clear and visible sign to himself and to all around him, especially his father, of his failure in life. On the other hand becoming like his father was the one thing he knew in his bones he did not want, the thing that would once and for all destroy the person he was, and tolling the death-knell for

his literary ambitions. These contrary emotions, both of them fundamental to his being, were never resolved, but throughout the years 1912–17 the struggle between them dominated his life. For when it came to it he could not commit himself to Felice and marriage, and retreated in terror lest by doing so he destroy himself; yet he could not give her up either, lest by doing so he destroy his only chance of escaping the solitude and, he felt, the pointlessness of a bachelor's existence. Poor Felice, an intelligent Jewish woman who was, however, caught in the bourgeois limitations of the time, struggled in vain to make him overcome his hesitations, as confused as everyone else by his impossible vacillations. For him, then, the sight of the blood gushing from his throat that August morning brought with it the sense that marriage was now out of the question and that therefore the struggle had been definitely settled. Yet, as we will see, even at this juncture, he could not quite let his decision be final – in his own mind at least.

It did more. In a bizarre turn which troubled both Ottla and the friends to whom he confided it, Kafka saw, or persuaded himself that he saw, in the blood a symbol of his relations with Felice. Here is how he put it in a wildly convoluted account in the very letter to Ottla in which he announced the terrible news: 'These last days I have once more suffered atrociously from my old madness, last winter, as a matter of fact, has constituted the sole major interruption of this torment in five years. It's the greatest struggle which has been imposed on or more precisely entrusted to me, and a victory (for example in the form of marriage, F. in this struggle is perhaps the only representative of the probably good principle), I mean a victory bringing with it a loss of blood just about supportable would have had in my private world history something Napoleonic. But it seems that I must lose the struggle in this manner. And in fact, as though the finishing bell had sounded, I sleep better, not much better, it's true; since that night at four o'clock in the

morning, especially the headaches which drove me mad have completely ceased... This then is the situation of this spiritual disease called tuberculosis...'

What exactly is he telling Ottla? That for the past five years he has been engaged in a struggle with himself, or rather with a 'probably' good and evil principle within himself, a struggle in which Felice is 'perhaps' the representative of the good principle, and the goal of which is marriage? Had he had to shed blood in this struggle but the outcome been the triumph of the good principle, marriage, this would have felt like a truly Napoleonic victory. But though blood has indeed been shed, the result appears to be the triumph of the evil principle and the disappearance, with the blood, of all hope of marriage. In this scenario the blood he has shed, the result of his TB, is both the reason for the triumph of the evil principle and the material evidence of the battle that had been raging within him for the past five years.

By 1920, when he is telling his new lover, Milena, about what happened and his feelings at the time, he is much clearer: 'I am morally sick; the problem with the lungs is only an overflow of the moral illness. I have been ill for four or five years, since the time of my first two betrothals [He had twice been engaged to Felice and twice broken it off]... What the three betrothals [after Felice he had briefly got engaged to Julie Wohryzek but the encounter with Milena had put an end to that] have in common is that everything was my fault, indubitably my fault; I was responsible for the disaster that befell my two fiancées and – to speak only of the first... simply by not being able to become for her (who would probably have sacrificed herself, had I desired it) gay, calm, decisive, capable of becoming a husband...'

But to Brod, in mid-September, from Zürau, he writes a letter in which his anguish and confusion are palpable. He begins by describing his present condition: 'All the things

I'm supposed to be eating surround me in abundance and goodness (only my lips lock themselves against them, but that always happens in the first days of any change) and freedom, freedom above all. However, there is still the wound of which the lesions in the lungs are only the symbol. You misunderstand it, Max, to judge by your final words in the hallway, but perhaps I also misunderstand it and there is no understanding these things (the same would be true of your inner affairs [Brod was in the midst of a marital crisis and had sought advice from Kafka]) because there is no seeing it whole, so turbulent and ever-moving is the gigantic mass which yet at the same time never ceases to grow. Misery, misery, but what is it but our own natures? And if the misery were ultimately to be disentangled (perhaps only women can do such work), you and I would fall apart.'

Clearly he is struggling to understand the terrible thing that has befallen him, but the very openness with which he writes to Brod, using the letter not so much to explain as to explore his condition, allows thoughts and obsessions to appear that he had kept hidden from Ottla. He goes on: 'I am constantly looking for an explanation of this disease, for I did not seek it. Sometimes it seems to me that my brain and lungs came to an agreement without my knowledge, "Things can't go on this way", said the brain, and after five years the lungs said they were ready to help. But if I choose I might say that put in these terms the whole thing is totally wrong. The first step to insight. The first step on that stairway which culminates in a made-up marital bed as the reward and meaning of my human existence (which however would then have been well-nigh Napoleonic). The marriage-bed will never be made up, and I, that is my destiny, will never leave Corsica behind me.'

The passing reference to Napoleon in the letter to Ottla is here, a month later, fleshed out. To fulfil a 'Napoleonic'

destiny he would have had to get married, but he has shrunk back from that and will remain a Napoleon too frightened of the world even to leave his native island. Napoleon haunted Kafka's imagination (as it did that of so many artists in the century that followed Waterloo) rather as Hamlet's father did his, his extraordinary ability to act decisively a permanent rebuke to those who come after. In 1920, unable to sort out the best way of getting to see Milena in Vienna, mired in railway timetables, he writes to her that he feels 'a little as Napoleon should have felt had he, in making his plans for his Russian campaign, known exactly how it would all end'.

Napoleon is only one of a series of figures who act as a constant reproof to Kafka for the way he is leading his life. Another is Abraham, whose story in Genesis he wrestles with as had Kierkegaard before him, imagining him, in a later letter, as too overwhelmed by household worries to obey God's injunction to sacrifice his son on Mount Moriah. Here, though, the very description of the 'destiny' Kafka has, through his pusillanimity, allowed to pass him by, shows clearly why he has in fact acted as he has. 'The first step in that stairway which culminates in the made-up marital bed as the reward and meaning of human existence' suggests less the crowning of a hero than the setting of a victim on a sacrificial altar, and if this was the image Kafka had in mind of the reward and meaning of human existence it is no wonder he could not commit himself to it.

To Felice he writes in a rather different tone. In his first letter to her after the experience of 11 August, a letter only written on 9 September, he begins by explaining his long silence: 'Here is the reason for my silence: 2 days after my last letter, precisely 4 weeks ago, about 5am, I had a haemorrhage of the lung. Fairly severe; for 10 minutes or so it gushed out of my throat; I thought it would never stop. The next day I went to see a doctor, who on this and several subsequent occasions

examined and X-rayed me; and then at Max's insistence, I went to see a specialist. Without going into the medical details, the outcome is that I have tuberculosis of both lungs. That I should suddenly develop some disease did not surprise me; nor did the sight of blood; for years my insomnia and headaches have invited a serious illness, and ultimately my maltreated blood had to burst forth, but that it should be of all things tuberculosis, that at the age of 34 I should be struck down overnight, with not a single predecessor anywhere in the family – this does surprise me. Well, I have to accept it; actually, my headaches seem to have been washed away with the flow of blood. Its course at present cannot be foreseen; its future development remains a secret; my age may possibly help to retard it. Next week I am going to the country for at least three months, to Ottla in Zürau.' He adds that he wants to retire from the insurance office, 'but for my own good they think it would be best not to let me', and that he is keeping all this from his parents for the time being so as not to add an extra anxiety to their lives. And he concludes: 'So this is what I have been keeping secret [from you] for 4 weeks. "Poor dear Felice" were the last words I wrote; is this going to be the closing phrase to all my letters? It's not a knife that stabs only forward but one which wheels round and stabs backwards as well.'

There is a sense of enormous relief here, which Kafka must have sensed, for with his last sentence he tries, with a typically powerful image, to make Felice aware of the pain that he too is feeling at this announcement, apparently, of their final separation. (I say 'apparently' because Kafka is a master of the question-mark, the sign that all is still up in the air, that nothing is resolved.)

It is, as we will see, not quite final, and from Zürau, after she has been to see him there, he writes her a long letter which sounds much more like those to Ottla and Brod, telling her of

his symbolic reading of the blood and trying to make her aware of the infinite complexity of his emotions. It is unlikely that this in any way assuaged her grief, anger and bewilderment.

Ottla

Ottla (Ottilie), born in 1892, was the youngest and the most independent-minded of Kafka's three sisters, and the one he felt closest to. Some time before 1914 she had fallen in love with a non-Jewish law student, Josef David, a liaison she was keeping from her parents. Though she had served (extremely ably) in the Kafka haberdashery store in central Prague, she had set her mind on studying agronomy and eventually running a farm in the country. Such dreams of working on the land were in the air at the time, fuelling both Zionism and Soviet ideology. But for their father, Hermann Kafka, 'the country' was the site of poverty and despair, precisely that from which he had managed through his own single-handed efforts to escape and set up as the owner of a successful store in Prague, one of the great cities of the Austro-Hungarian Empire. This was for him the pinnacle of ambition, a sign that he had finally left the *shtetl* behind him and could give his children the chance to make their way in the world of the German speaking Austro-Hungarian bourgeoisie. Hence his appalled reaction to his son's mingling with the Yiddish actors who had visited the city in 1911–12 and his friendship with their leader Yitzhak Löwy, and the bitter and cutting proverb he had hurled at him then: 'He who sleeps with dogs picks up fleas'. One can imagine his response to the thought of losing his daughter as a valuable assistant in the store and having her speak of her dream of farming the land. Stach explains how, by a strange twist of fate, the rash husband of her older sister Elli, Karl Hermann, allowed Ottla to fulfil her dream.

After losing money in a failed asbestos factory he had bought a fifty-acre stretch of land in the village of Zürau in north-western Bohemia, from where he originated, but this too was failing and seemed likely to go the same way as the factory. Ottla, who was known as a young woman of great energy and considerable practical acumen, now suggested she take it over and see if she could make it work. In that way she would fulfil her ambition, have a chance to see Josef David when he came home on leave without arousing her parents' suspicion, and make a go of a family financial enterprise, something her father could not dismiss out of hand. In April 1917 she set out to turn her dream into reality.

Kafka was full of admiration. Here was his younger sister not only standing up to their father but actually translating that rebellion into concrete action. From being the wiser older brother he had now become her admiring acolyte. He had been planning to visit her in Zürau that summer, even before the events of 11 August. On 28 July he wrote: 'I won't come tomorrow but at the beginning of September for ten days, if that's all right with you.' With the onset of his illness, and having obtained three months' leave from the Institute, it was natural that he should think of Zürau. This, however, horrified his friends and family (he had merely told his parents that he had been granted compassionate leave by the firm because he was exhausted). He was crazy to bury himself in a nondescript village, far from any doctor, said Brod, his closest friend. What would happen if he had a recurrence of his haemorrhage? And what would he do there all day long? Far better, if he felt he had to get away from the city, to go to some picturesque spa like Merano, or, better still, to a sanatorium where he would be properly looked after and given the best possible help on the road to recovery.

Kafka was adamant. Perhaps, like Thomas Mann as he wrote *The Magic Mountain* (published in 1925 but set in the

immediate pre-war period), he sensed that a TB sanatorium was far more likely to be the end than the curing of him; but more because he had already planned to visit Ottla and wanted to be, in this moment of crisis, with the only member of his family with whom he could talk freely in the confidence of being understood, and because simply prolonging a summer visit to his sister was less of a break than a stay in Merano or a sanatorium would be. Whatever the reason (and he himself was probably not entirely clear as to his motives as he struggled to grasp the enormity of what had happened to him) he stood firm. Brod and his father could rail as much as they liked, he was determined to go. And as to doctors, Zürau was within easy reach of Prague and he would be able to go back and see Dr Pick at any time, while his friends would be able to come and visit him – he was in fact looking forward to playing host to them. On 12 September he boarded the train for Michelob, the nearest station to Zürau, a hundred or so kilometres away. There Ottla would be waiting for him with a horse and cart for the final leg to Zürau.

The Author

On 7 July Kafka had written to Kurt Wolff, his publisher, in Leipzig: 'Dear Herr Wolff, I am most happy to hear from you directly once again. I had an easier time of it this winter, which in any case is now well behind us. I am sending some of the better work of this period, thirteen prose pieces. It is a far cry from what I would really like to do. With cordial regards, sincerely yours F. Kafka.'

The idea that Kafka was a solitary genius, uninterested in publishing his work, is entirely wrong. He was a driven writer who, like most writers, desperately wanted his work to be published and recognised. He was, however, a stern, many

would say an absurdly stern, critic of his own work, and would only allow it out into the public sphere if he felt it had some value, even though, as this letter makes clear, he rarely felt that he had done what he had hoped to do.

In the autumn of 1912 and the early months of 1913 he had written the first of the stories he felt able wholeheartedly to acknowledge: 'The Judgement', 'The Stoker' (which became the first chapter of the unfinished novel *Amerika*) and 'The Metamorphosis'. Even as he was writing them, a slender volume of very short pieces, all he felt he could salvage from his early work was in the process of publication under the loose title *Betrachtung* (*Meditation*), but it was with 'The Judgement' that he sensed he had found his voice. He confided to his diary on 23 September 1912: 'This story, "The Judgement", I wrote at one stretch on the night of 22 to 23 from 10 o'clock in the evening until 6 o'clock in the morning. My legs had grown so stiff from sitting that I could hardly pull them out from under the desk. The terrible strain and joy, how the story unfolded itself before me, how I moved forward in an expanse of water... How everything can be risked, how for all, for the strangest ideas, a great fire is prepared in which they die away and rise again... The confirmed conviction that with my novel writing I am in the disgraceful lowlands of writing. Only in this way can writing be done, only with such cohesion, with such complete opening of the body and the soul.'

He followed those three stories a year later with 'In the Penal Colony' and then, whether because war had broken out in Europe, his struggle with himself over Felice and the question of marriage had sapped his energies, or that after those extraordinarily fertile few months it was inevitable that he would hit a fallow stretch, he ceased for a while to write anything he considered fit for publication.

Kurt Wolff published 'The Judgement' and then 'The Metamorphosis' on their own, but Kafka had hoped he

would see his way to bringing out the three stories together under the title *The Sons*. Wolff had also talked of bringing 'In the Penal Colony' out on its own but that seemed to have come to nothing. The war made all publishing more difficult, though Wolff was expanding, but not in a direction that would make him more sympathetic to Kafka's work. Popular novels were what people wanted and what the publisher was prepared to give them, not puzzling and disturbing short stories by a little-known author. Yet by the end of 1916 and through the early part of 1917 Kafka began once again to produce pieces he was satisfied with – or as satisfied as he ever was with his own work. Brod, ever trying to promote his friend's work, persuaded Martin Buber to publish two of these, 'Jackals and Arabs' and 'A Report to an Academy' in his new journal, *Der Jude*, the first in the October and the second in the November issue. In one of the new octavo notebooks he had started to use Kafka recorded his feelings on seeing his work in print: 'Always take a deep breath after outbursts of vanity and smugness. The orgy while reading the story in *Der Jude*. Like a squirrel in a cage. Bliss of movement. Desperate about confinement, the mad persistence, feeling of misery despite the calm exterior outside. All this both simultaneously and alternatingly, a sunray of bliss still lingering in the excitement of the end.' In December, Brod's wife Else read 'A Report to an Academy' out loud to the members of the Club of Jewish Men and Women in Prague, as Brod reported to Kafka. All this had the unfortunate effect of linking the stories specifically to Jewish issues, but Kafka was not concerned with this. The idea that his work was being read by strangers clearly brought him just that sense of mingled happiness and alarm that engulfs most writers lucky enough to find themselves in that situation.

And Wolff, who had retreated into silence for two years, was suddenly interested again. On 3 July he had written to Kafka saying that Max Brod had drawn his attention to the new

work he was doing and that he would, as always, be interested in publishing it. It is to this letter that Kafka responded on 7 July, sending him the new stories. On 20 July Wolff wrote that he found them 'extraordinarily beautiful and accomplished', and this led Kafka, on 27 July, to write back that he would of course leave the format of the book entirely up to him. 'At the moment,' he added, 'I am not concerned with royalties. After the war, however, that would change entirely. I will give up my job (giving it up is really my most intense hope), will marry and move away from Prague, probably to Berlin. To be sure I will not depend entirely on the proceeds of my writing. Nevertheless I – or the deep-seated bureaucrat inside me, which is the same thing – have an oppressive fear of the future. I do hope that you, dear Herr Wolff, will not quite desert me, provided of course that I halfway deserve your kindness. In the face of all the uncertainties of the present and the future a word from you at this point would mean much to me.'

Wolff's response was more positive than Kafka could ever have dreamed. On 1 August he wrote back: 'As far as your plans for the future are concerned I wish you all the best from the bottom of my heart. It is my sincerest pleasure to assure you that both now and after the war is over you will receive continuous material support; we will certainly have no trouble working out the details.' For the first time in his life Kafka's dream of devoting his life to writing without the need of an office job to keep him alive was being underwritten by his publisher. This was not just a wonderful solution to his financial worries but an affirmation from the outside that his work had some value. On 20 August he wrote back: 'Dear Kurt Wolff. Rather than disturb you once again during your vacation I waited until today to thank you for your last letter. What you said in it concerning my anxieties was extremely kind and for the moment totally suffices me.' He suggested 'A Country Doctor' as the title for the new book (it is the

title of one of the stories in it) and listed a possible table of contents. Wolff must have replied promptly because on 4 September Kafka wrote again. He began by saying that he was thrilled with the type size the publisher was suggesting and that he presumed 'the handsome format of *Meditation* will be used'. However, he went on, 'perhaps there is some misunderstanding over "The Penal Colony". I have never been wholehearted in asking for it to be published. Two or three of the final pages are botched, and their presence points to some deeper flaw, there is a worm somewhere which hollows out the story, dense as it is.' Always honest, both with himself and with others, as to the paradoxes involved in writing and publishing, he went on: 'Your offer to publish this story in the same manner as the *Country Doctor* is of course very tempting and excites me so much that I am ready to drop my defences – nevertheless please do not publish the story, at least for the present. If you stood in my place and saw the story from my viewpoint you would not think I was being over-scrupulous in this matter. Besides, should my powers halfway hold out you will receive better work from me than the "Penal Colony".'

The letter ends, however, with news that flatly contradicts the confident announcement of imminent marriage and a possible move to Berlin in the letter of 27 July: 'My address from next week on will be : "Zürau, P.O. Flöhau in Bohemia."' And he goes on: 'The disease which for years now has been brought on by headaches and sleeplessness has suddenly broken out. It is almost a relief. I am going to the country for a longish while, or rather, I must go. With cordial regards, sincerely yours, F. Kafka.'

The Village

'No electricity, no running water, no paved streets. No coffeehouses, no movie theatre, no bookstore, no newsstand. No postoffice, no telephone in the village.' So Stach describes the place Kafka arrived at on 12 September 1917. He goes on: 'Kafka found himself on a small teeming planet, unfathomably far from the urban hustle and bustle on Wenceslaus Square… and just as far from the dimly lit sterile world of the Workers' Accident Insurance Institute, in which nothing moved spontaneously.' Zürau, on the other hand, 'was populated by an extensive family of all kinds of living creatures that got up at the crack of dawn, each drowning out all the others, the three hundred and fifty human residents among them.' At sunset all grew quiet again, for there was no electric light and anyone who did not want to sleep needed to light a petroleum lamp, and petroleum was expensive.

In his keenness to emphasise the contrast between the conditions Kafka had lived in all his life and what he was now to experience Stach, though, perhaps underestimates the ways in which in the early twentieth century the countryside infiltrated even the most sophisticated modern European city: the stench of the abattoirs, the carts of the pedlars, the dray horses, the markets with their slaughtered chickens and geese, the birds and the flies – still to be found in London and Paris even after 1945. Moreover, though Kafka was a city boy through and through – he famously wrote to his friend Oskar Pollack: 'Prague doesn't let go… The old crone has claws. One has to yield, or else' – it's not true that he had had no experience of the country. Amongst the extraordinary set of letters he wrote to Pollack in 1902, when he was nineteen, and

which are as excited and passionate as any he was later to write to Felice or Milena, are two from Liboch, a village on the Elbe, twenty-five miles north of Prague, where he had obviously been spending part of the summer. The second especially, dated autumn 1902, is almost ecstatic: 'It's a strange time I've been spending here,' he starts, 'and I needed a strange time like this, in which I lie for hours on a vineyard wall and stare into the rain clouds which don't want to leave here, or... go through fields which now lie brown and mournful with abandoned ploughs, but which all the same glisten silvery when in spite of everything the late-afternoon sun comes out and casts my long shadow (yes, my long shadow, maybe by means of it I'll still reach the kingdom of heaven) on the furrows. Have you noticed how late-summer shadows dance on the dark, turned-up earth, how they dance physically? Have you noticed how the earth rises toward the grazing cow, how trustfully it rises? Have you noticed how rich, heavy soil crumbles under too delicate fingers, how solemnly it crumbles?'

That was in his dreamy and idealistic youth, with the whole of life to look forward to. Now, fifteen years later, a sick man weighted down with many troubles and anxieties, he knew it would be different. Yet he had made his decision and his spirits were buoyant: 'O beautiful hour, masterful composure, overgrown garden', he jotted down in his diary on 15 September, the first entry since his arrival. 'You turn out of the house,' he goes on, 'and on the garden path the goddess of happiness drifts towards you.'

These early entries are extraordinarily moving in their brevity: 'Majestic apparition, prince of the realm', he jots down, though what the apparition was, bull or horse, we will never know. A space and then: 'Bulldogs five. Phillip, Franz, Adolf, Isidor, Max'. No full stop, another space, then the enigmatic: 'Not so.' A space again, then the last entry of that day: 'The village square abandoned to the night. The wisdom of the

little ones. Predominance of the animals. The women – cows moving across the square with extreme naturalness. My sofa over the land.' A Chagallian Kafka, drifting over the fields and meadows on his flying sofa?

Yet the next entry, three days later, consists only of the bitter comment: 'Tear everything up.' Does this refer to the entries of 15 September? To the many fragments found in his diaries and notebooks? Or to his past life? 'Tear everything up.'

By 19 September he seems to have settled onto a more even keel and we begin to find again that disconcerting clarity of vision in his descriptions which makes his diaries and letters often so funny as well as so painful to read: 'The cat is playing with the goats. The goats resemble: Polish Jews. Uncle S[iegfried]. E[rnst] W[eiss], I[rma].' But then he allows himself, for the first time since his arrival, to voice disquiet, a sense of the utter incomprehensibility, for him, of the world in which he now finds himself: 'Distinct but similarly stern unapproachability of the overseer Hermann (who left today without dinner or goodbye…), of the young lady, of Marenka [one of Ottla's farmhands]. Fundamentally constricted in their presence, as in front of the animals in the stable when one instructs them to do something and they astonishingly obey. The case is more difficult here only because they so often seem approachable and completely understandable for a moment.'

In his letters Kafka is more guarded, unconsciously tailoring each to its recipient. To Brod, the one from whom nothing is withheld, he is prepared to confess his weaknesses: 'Dear Max, I did not get to writing the first day because I liked everything so much here; besides, I did not want to exaggerate as I would have had to do – thus giving the devil his due. However, today everything is already looking natural, my inner weaknesses (not the disease, of which I know almost

nothing as yet) are asserting themselves, from the farmyard across the way come an assortment of Noah's Ark sounds, an eternal tinsmith hammers his tin. I have no appetite and eat too much; there's no light in the evening, and so on. But the good still hugely predominates, as far as I can see: Ottla is literally bearing me up on her wings through the difficult world, the room (although it faces northeast) is excellent, airy, warm, and all this in an almost completely quiet building; all the things I am supposed to be eating surround me in abundance and goodness.'

To another close friend, Oskar Baum, the blind Prague writer and music teacher: 'At present I am feeling quite content and starting my new life with a measure of confidence. Yesterday at lunch a counterpart of mine sat opposite me at table. A real tramp. Sixty-two years old and has been tramping the roads for ten years. His face above the well-groomed imperial is clean and rosy. Sitting at the table he looks like a retired medium-grade civil servant. He has sustained himself for ten years, except for a short spell of work, entirely by begging. For instance he was on the road all last winter in the same clothes he is wearing now (except for a waistcoat, which is now too warm to wear, so he has sold it), yet he has no serious rheumatism or any other kind of sickness. Only in the last few years he has felt a bit muddled in his head… Several times he has had a chance to marry, but his mother, who lived until he was fifty-two, had always advised against marriage… Nowadays he tramps the roads… He tramps about without any particular plan (he has a map to be sure but it doesn't show the villages), and so often travels in a circle. It doesn't matter, people hardly ever recognise him when they see him again.'

One can sense Kafka empathising with this figure, as he does with the hens and goats, but also how he sees in this man a dangerous warning of where his instincts might take him. To the philosopher Felix Weltsch he writes on

22 September: 'My life here has been splendid, a least in the fine weather we've had so far. To be sure my room isn't sunny, but I have a marvellous spot for sunbathing. A hillock or rather a little plateau in the centre of a broad semi-circular valley, which I have taken over. There I lie like a king, surrounded by undulating hills... Because of the favourable lie of the land hardly anyone sees me, which suits me very well in view of the complicated positioning of my reclining chair and my semi-nudity. Only rarely do a pair of protesting heads appear at the edge of the plateau and shout: "You, shove off that bench there! [*Gehns vom Bänkel runter*]." More radical shouts than that I cannot understand because of the dialect. Perhaps I will become the village idiot, for the present one, whom I saw today, seems to live in the neighbouring hamlet and is already old.'

In Prague, whether with his family or his friends, Kafka had always felt alien, a condition reinforced by his profound sense that both his father and his closest friend, Max Brod, imagined they understood him perfectly. A diary entry on 2 February 1920, as part of a series of short pieces in which he explores his life in the third person, gives us a glimpse of this: 'He remembers a picture that represented a summer Sunday on the Thames. The whole breadth of the river was filled with boats, waiting for a lock-gate to be opened. In all the boats were gay young people in light, bright-coloured clothing; they were almost reclining there, freely abandoned to the warm air and the coolness of the water. They had so much in common that their convivial spirit was not confined to the separate boats, joking and laughter was passed on from boat to boat.' (Scholars now believe he is remembering 'Boulter's Lock, Sunday Afternoon', an oil painting by the British artist Edward John Gregory, painted in 1895 and frequently reproduced in magazines of the time.) He goes on: 'He now imagined that in a meadow on the bank – the banks

were only faintly suggested in the picture, the gathering of boats overshadowed everything – he himself was standing.... He naturally had a great desire to join in, indeed he longed to do so, but he was forced to admit to himself that he was excluded from it, that it was impossible for him to fit in there; to do so would have required such great preparation that in the course of it not only this Sunday, but many years, and he himself would have passed away, and even if time here could have come to a standstill it would still have been impossible to achieve any other result; his whole origin, upbringing, physical development, would have had to be different.' And he concludes: 'So far removed, then, was he from these holiday-makers, and yet for all that he was very close to them too, and that was the more difficult thing to understand. They were, after all, human beings like himself, nothing human could be utterly alien to them, and so if one were to probe into them one would surely find that the feeling which dominated him and excluded him from the river party was alive in them too, but of course with the difference that it was very far from dominating them and merely haunted some darker corners of their being.' There must then have been something profoundly attractive in feeling now that his difference from those around him was at last, in this village, out in the open, as visible to all as the tramp or the village idiot.

There were times, however, when village life became too much for him, despite his determination to tell himself and his friends that this was everything he wanted, and his unease spills over into his letters to those in Prague waiting for news: 'I am quite satisfied with my life here, as Max may already have told you,' he writes to Baum. 'However, the peace and quiet which you especially asked about is not to be found here either and I will give up looking for it in this life. My room, to be sure, is in a quiet building, but across the way is the only piano in northwest Bohemia, and a large farmyard, in which various

animals outdin each other [*einander überschreien*]. Almost all the neighbourhood teams drive by my window early and the geese pass me on the way to their pond. But the worst are the two hammerers somewhere in the neighbourhood. One hammers on wood, the other on metal. They are tireless, especially the first, who works far beyond his strength. He is wearing himself out but I have no pity for him when I have to listen to him from six o'clock in the morning. If he actually stops for a little while it is only so the metal hammerer can take the lead. In spite of this and in spite of some other things I have no wish to return to Prague, not at all.'

One reason for this was Ottla. He writes to Brod: 'I live with Ottla in a good minor marriage, not on the basis of the usual violent high currents but of the small windings of the low voltages. We run a fine household, which all of you, I hope, will like. I will try to put some supplies aside for you, Felix and Oskar, which isn't easy; there is not much food around here and the many family mouths to feed have priority.' We are, it must be remembered, in the third year of the war, and food is very scarce. People in the cities of Europe would go foraging in the countryside, but it was of course better if they had a relative living and farming in the country. Ottla and her brother, to judge from his letters, were always trying to get food to their family and friends; even an egg was welcome. But it is the first sentences here which are the most interesting. Kafka was no tramp or village idiot. Strange as it may sound to those who know only his fiction and his diaries, he was a social animal, with many friends and never happier than when reading his own works out loud to them or introducing a reading by his actor friend Yitzhak Löwy to the Writers' Circle in Prague. But he did need solitude for his work, and his horror of marital life lay largely in the fear that this essential solitude would be lost forever, which, he sensed, would be nothing less than a form of suicide.

Living with his sister Ottla, who made no demands on him, and whom he liked and admired, was a kind of solution – a 'good minor marriage' as he puts it. She was busy with the farm (it seems he took it on himself to take charge of the garden of their house and indeed enjoyed working there) and he was left on his own for much of the time, but she was also always there, a vital, totally unselfish support in his hours of need. What Felice thought of the arrangement is another question.

Felice

As soon as she learned what had happened, the blood, the diagnosis and Kafka's disappearance into the country, she determined to go and see him. In one of the first letters to Brod from Zürau Kafka writes: 'F. has sent a few lines saying she is coming. I don't grasp her, she is extraordinary, or rather I do grasp her but cannot hold her. I run all around her, barking as a nervous dog might tear round a statue, or, to present an equally true but converse picture, I gaze at her as a stuffed animal head mounted on the wall might look down at the person living quietly in his room. Half-truths, a thousandth of a truth. All that is true is that F. is probably coming.'

There is panic in these lines. It's as if an animal has tried to hide away from a predator only to discover that the predator had nosed out his hiding-place and was approaching. Except that as far as the world was concerned she was not that at all but a woman lovingly concerned with her sick fiancé. Kafka recognised that this was indeed the case and loathed himself for feeling that the first image was the truer one – or rather, that the two coexisted. So he was horrified by his reaction, which made him, in his own eyes, inhuman, a dog or worse – a stuffed animal head.

As far as Felice was concerned they were still engaged to be married. She needed to see him to make sure he was being well looked after and to find out where the sudden eruption of the blood had left their relationship. Kafka's first letter to her after his diagnosis, though he did not say as much, seemed to suggest that he felt that it signalled its end, but was that not his usual way of dramatizing everything? Yet she cannot have failed to reflect that, however passionate his letters throughout their five-year courtship, there had always been something in him that balked at any eventual marriage. After all, he had already broken off their engagement once. No doubt her mind was in turmoil. She sent a telegram to say that she was coming and, after travelling for a day and a night to get from Berlin to Prague, arrived in Zürau on 20 September.

We do not know how the reunion went. Stach suggests that though she may have come to offer a sick man support and to make sure he was comfortable in his temporary shelter she found him looking surprisingly well and with no desire to discuss the practical details of his situation or to listen to her lecture him about the need to boil the milk and eat regular meals. He had made his decision and was already far away from her. This sounds convincing and is clearly based on his diary entry for 21 Sept: 'Felice was here, travels 30 hours to see me, I should have prevented it. As I imagine it she bears, primarily because of me, an extremity of unhappiness. I myself don't know how to compose myself, am completely emotionless, equally helpless, think of the disturbance of some of my comforts and as my only concession playact somewhat. In details she is wrong in defence of her supposed or even real right, but on the whole she is an innocent woman condemned to severe torture. I have done the wrong for which she is being tortured and moreover wield the torture instrument. – With her departure (the carriage with her and Ottla drives round the pond, I go straight to head them off and come close

to her once again) and a headache (earthly remnant of the play-actor) the day ends.'

The rest of the entry consists only of a page-long account of a dream about his father, and the entry for the next day contains just the one word, 'Nothing'. And there is nothing in the diary for the next two days, not even 'nothing'. However, Stach's assertion that the blood had forced Kafka to make up his mind about Felice once and for all is unduly simplistic. Kafka rarely made up his mind 'once and for all', and one of his diary entries for 25 September shows that he had not given up the idea of marriage: 'Not entirely reprehensible to have children as a tubercular man', he writes. 'Flaubert's father tubercular. Choice: Either the child's lung fizzles out (very nice expression for the music the doctor puts his ear to the patient's chest to hear) or the child becomes Flaubert.' He was so taken with this that he repeated it verbatim in a letter to Brod in early October.

The letter he wrote to Felice on 30 September, however, is bleak in the extreme. After saying he had received her letters but had put them by, unwilling to read them, that his mother had visited for a day and that he had finally got round to reading them, he goes on: 'The way you saw me this time is how I have seen myself for ages, only more clearly, which is why I can explain what you saw: As you know, there are two combatants within me. During the past few days I have had fewer doubts than ever that the better of the two belongs to you. By word and silence, and a combination of both, you have been kept informed about the progress of the war for 5 years, and most of the time it has caused you suffering. Were you to ask if I have always been truthful I could only say, with no one else have I suppressed deliberate lies as strenuously or, to be more precise – more strenuously than I have with you.' He is, he says, by nature 'a mendacious creature', one who does not 'strive to be good, to answer to a suggested tribunal.'

Rather, he tries in an underhand way 'to be pleasing to everyone'. Then in a manner typical of him, he presses down on this as though trying to understand himself as much as to make her understand: 'Indeed (here comes the inconsistency) to become so pleasing that in the end I might openly act out my inherent baseness before the eyes of the world without forfeiting its love, the only sinner not to be roasted. In short, my only concern is the human tribunal, and I would like to deceive even this, and what's more without actual deception.'

What he had described in the diary as 'play-acting', a way of responding to her accusations or even to her accusatory presence, and which he had concluded was punished by the headache he was left with on her departure, is here described as 'mendacity', the response of one who wishes both to 'act out his inherent baseness' and to ask the world to love him. In writing to her, then, what had in the diary remained a puzzling and probably reprehensible response is here, in the letter to her, condemned openly. He is 'the only sinner not to be roasted'. But the suspicion has to be that even this breast-beating is itself a form of play-acting, and so we – and Kafka – go round the closed circle of hell once more. As we will see, this nexus of emotions and attempts at analysis remains central to what Kafka writes and thinks about for the next few months – and is in fact merely an intensification of feelings that had always been with him.

Here, though, he goes on with his attempt to explain to her what he had already tried to explain to Brod: two forces are battling within him and she represents the force of good while the evil all comes from within him: 'You are my human tribunal. Of the two who are at war within me, or rather whose war I consist of – excepting one small tormented remnant – the one is good, the other evil. From time to time they reverse their roles, which adds to the confusion.... Until very recently, however, despite reverses, it was possible for me to imagine

that the most improbable would happen (the most probable would be eternal war), which always seemed like the radiant goal, and I, grown pitiful and wretched over the years, would at last be allowed to have you.' And now he presents her with the fruit of his thoughts about his illness which he had been brooding on over the past six weeks: 'Suddenly it appears that the loss of blood was too great. The blood shed by the good one (the one that now seems good to us) in order to win you, serves the evil one. Where the evil one on his own would probably or possibly not have found a decisive new weapon for his defence the good one offers him just that. For secretly I don't believe this illness to be tuberculosis, at least not primarily tuberculosis, but rather a sign of my general bankruptcy. I had thought the war could last longer but it can't. The blood issues not from the lung but from a decisive stab delivered by one of the combatants.... It is tuberculosis, and that is the end. Weak and weary, almost invisible to you when in this state, what can the other one do but lean on your shoulder here in Zürau, and with you, the purest of the pure, stare in amazement, bewildered and hopeless, at the great man who – now that he feels sure of universal love, or of that of its female representative assigned to him – begins to display his atrocious baseness.'

And he concludes: 'Please don't ask why I put up a barrier. Don't humiliate me in this way. One word like this from you and I would be at your feet again. But at once my actual or rather, long before that, my alleged tuberculosis would stab me in the face and I would have to give up. It is a weapon compared to which the countless others used earlier, ranging from "physical incapacity" up to "my work" and down to my "parsimony" look expedient and primitive.' He concludes: 'And now I am going to tell you a secret which at the moment I don't even believe myself... but which is bound to be true: I will never be well again.'

Canetti, in the fascinating little book he wrote about the Kafka–Felice correspondence, called this 'the most painful [letter] that Kafka ever wrote to her'. He found the whole passage about the blood false and self-serving; the plain truth of the matter was that Kafka had long ceased to love her and was using his TB diagnosis as a way of telling her this once and for all, while at the same time trying to exculpate himself with a weird mythology of blood, battle and courts of law. Stach too finds it distasteful: 'His letter,' he writes, 'is awash in sparkling images aimed at an imaginary audience and paying no heed to the woman it is addressed to, who has just as much stake in the matter as he.'

What riles both Canetti and Stach is that Kafka copied the passage about the blood word for word both in a letter to Brod and into his diary. Surely then this is literary flummery and anything but genuine. But that is to misunderstand what Kafka was going through and what his whole relationship with Felice entailed. The sense that he had never been honest, that he had always been a hypocrite and a liar, had always performed before the world in order to win its admiration but that inside he was hollow – all that had been with him since his earliest memories. His impulse to write was, he had felt, that which would at last free him from this web of deceit – and yet was it not itself perhaps the ultimate deceit? As for Felice, had he ever been in love with her? Had she not always embodied for him an idea of love and marriage that was deeply ingrained in him, the idea his parents represented? The struggle he attempts to describe, in this letter and elsewhere, was in effect a struggle between his conviction that he would only be truly human if, like his father, he married and raised a family, and his equally strong conviction that his father was an arrogant bully and that only by living a quite different kind of life from him, giving free rein to his need to write, would he be able to hold his head high and feel he had done what he had

been brought into the world to do. Felice was the unfortunate victim of this struggle and Kafka felt deeply that the option she represented was the 'good' one, though he now recognised that he felt equally deeply that it was not an option he could take up. The blood and the consequent diagnosis was both a confirmation of the nature of the struggle and a sure sign that the 'evil', selfish option of solitude and writing had, against his better judgement, won out. The only part of the letter that possibly sounds meretricious is the paragraph that begins: 'Suddenly it appears that the loss of blood was too great. The blood shed by the good one… in order to win you serves the evil one.' Here a medieval literary notion of shedding one's blood in order to win the loved one seems to have intruded, though even here it is possible to imagine Kafka feeling that he had for five years metaphorically shed blood in his great battle with himself to persuade himself to take the plunge and get married, and that this was indeed blood shed in a noble cause, which was now literally manifesting itself and thus, by a supreme irony, turning into the weapon that would allow the 'evil one', the one who wished to deny her, to triumph, for it finally made marriage impossible.

There can be no doubt then that Kafka was telling both himself and her that their long-drawn-out affair was at an end, and that he was sheltering behind his TB to make this clear to both of them. But we fail to understand what was going on in those Zürau months if we do not realise that Kafka is writing as much in order to understand what is happening to him as to extricate himself from an affair he knew was over.

I Did Not Seek It

Behind every remark Kafka makes in those months, in diaries, notebooks and letters, lurks the inescapable fact of his illness.

We cannot understand anything he says or writes in this period unless we recognise that everything is coloured by his memory of the blood gushing out of his mouth that August morning and the subsequent diagnosis.

Tuberculosis or consumption as it used to be called, for the disease seemed to consume the victim slowly but inexorably, was to the nineteenth and early twentieth century what cancer has become for us today: a disease that seems to be everywhere and yet is largely invisible, which strikes at random and is often fatal. Keats, Chekhov, Katherine Mansfield and D.H. Lawrence are among its most famous victims. In literature, there is Henry James's Ralph Touchett in *Portrait of a Lady* and Hans Castorp in *The Magic Mountain*, Thomas Mann's epic exploration of the disease. Part of TB's peculiar eerie quality was that, as with cancer, those first diagnosed with it felt just the same as they had always felt and, sometimes, even healthier, and yet lodged in their minds was the inescapable thought that somewhere inside them something was happening that would eventually kill them. Death, which we all know we will eventually have to face but spend our lives trying to avoid thinking about, is, with these two diseases, suddenly there before us and can no longer be avoided. 'Whether my condition is better than it was I have no idea', Kafka writes to Baum in early October. 'That is to say I feel as well now as I did in the past. Up to now I have never had an illness so easy to bear and so restrained, unless it is this very quality that is sinister – which perhaps it is. I am looking so well that my mother, who came here on Sunday did not recognise me at the station.... In two weeks I have gained one and a half kilograms (tomorrow I have my third weighing).'

He had not told his parents about the blood or the diagnosis. As far as they were concerned he had gone to stay with Ottla 'for a rest', and he warned his friends to be careful not to give his secret away. But to all of them he repeated

versions of what he says here to Baum: he feels well, perhaps better than ever before, and he is putting on weight. But it is the very discrepancy between how he is feeling and what he believes is happening to him that is so bewildering and that leads him to seek desperately for an explanation. To Brod on 5 September, that is, before leaving for Zürau, he writes: 'It was very good that I went to the doctor and without you I surely would not have gone. By the way, you told him I was irresponsible, but on the contrary, I am too calculating and the Bible tells us what the fate of reckoners will be. But I certainly am not complaining, less than ever today. What is more, I predicted it myself. Do you remember the open wound in "A Country Doctor"?'

That story, written the previous year, tells, in a hallucinatory first-person, of a country doctor called out to a lonely farm where he is shown a boy lying on a bed, 'gaunt, without any fever, not cold, not warm, without a shirt'. It is hot in the stuffy room, the doctor's fur coat is taken off and he is offered a glass of rum. As he approaches the bed the boy heaves himself up and throws his arms round his neck, whispering in his ear: 'Doctor, let me die.' The parents cluster round, awaiting the doctor's verdict. He lays his head on the boy's breast and this confirms his feeling that there is nothing wrong with him and that the best thing would be to get him out of bed at once. He says this to the parents and is ready to put on his coat again but, feeling that everyone in the room is waiting for something more, goes once again to the bed, 'and this time I discovered that the boy was indeed ill. In his right side, near the hip, was an open wound as big as the palm of my hand. Rose-red, in many variations of shade, dark in the hollows, lighter at the edges, softly granulated, with irregular clots of blood, open as a surface mine to the daylight.' On closer inspection, he discovers that there is even more: the open wound is crawling with worms, 'as thick and as long as my little finger'. The poor

boy is clearly beyond help. Meanwhile the room has been filling with people and events now take an even stranger turn. The family and the village elders strip the old country doctor of his clothes, singing all the while, carry him to the bed and lay him down next to the boy, then leave the room, shut the door and the singing stops. A strange dialogue ensues: 'I have very little confidence in you', the boy whispers in his ear. 'Why, you were only blown in here, you didn't come on your own feet. Instead of helping me you're pressing me down on my deathbed.' The doctor apologises and the boy retorts: 'Am I supposed to be content with this apology? Oh, I must be, I can't help it, I always have to put up with things. A fine wound is all I brought into the world, that is my sole endowment.' But now it's time to leave. The doctor quickly collects his clothes, fur coat and bag, the horses are ready: 'I didn't want to waste time dressing: if the horses raced home as they had come I should only be springing, as it were, out of this bed into my own.' He hurls himself into the gig and shouts: 'Gee up!' to the horses, 'but there was no galloping; slowly, like old men we crawled through the snowy wastes,' while the 'new but faulty song of the children' echoes behind him: 'O be joyful, all you patients, / The doctor's laid in bed beside you.' 'Never shall I reach home at this rate', he concludes. 'Naked, exposed to the frost of this most unhappy of ages, with an earthly vehicle, unearthly horses, old man that I am, I wander astray.'

Kafka was so taken with this story that when on 20 August he wrote to Kurt Wolff about his new collection he proposed 'A Country Doctor' as the overall title, with the subtitle 'Short Tales', though he wished the title story to come second, after 'A New Advocate' – perhaps to indicate that he was not simply calling the collection after the first story but wished 'A Country Doctor' to cast its shadow over the whole. His invocation of the story in his letter to Brod, however, like

his insistence to him and to Felice that the vomiting of blood on 11 August and the subsequent diagnosis of TB were but the symbols of a long-standing struggle – with his angels, with Felice – should be seen as a desperate attempt on Kafka's part to try to make sense of things. With no visible sign of his possibly terminal condition apart from the occurrence of 11 August he reaches out to whatever he can get hold of, to visible, tangible evidence that he is indeed terminally ill. 'My attitude toward the tuberculosis today,' he writes to Brod in the mid-September letter I have already quoted from, the one in which he talks about the marital bed awaiting him at the top of the stairs, 'resembles that of a child clinging to its mother's skirts.... I am constantly seeking an explanation of this disease, for I did not seek it. Sometimes it seems to me that my brain and lungs came to an agreement without my knowledge. "Things cannot go on in this way", said the brain, and after five years the lungs said they were ready to help.'

Nowadays we all recognise the fallacy of blaming oneself for the onset of a possibly terminal illness, and the dangers of seeing illness as a metaphor. Sometimes a causal connection is indeed found between what one has been in the habit of doing, smoking in the case of cancer, having unprotected sex in the case of AIDS; but most often doctors warn us not to waste time and energy interrogating our past life. Nevertheless, such blame, such a search for a cause, is a natural result of our need to understand what is happening to us when there is no physical evidence of the disease. It is this that forms the substance of Susan Sontag's meditation on cancer in *Illness as Metaphor* (where she develops the parallels between cancer in the twentieth and TB in the nineteenth century). The stories Kafka tells himself and others in the wake of the sudden blow that was the vomiting of blood and the subsequent diagnosis of TB are simply a richer and more complex set of examples.

What Sort of a Surplus?

But then ever since he had begun to be aware of himself Kafka had been in the habit of interrogating himself, of trying to understand why he was so different from others, why he, the only son, was so different in every way from the child his dominant father had hoped for. The late *Letter to His Father*, which is much more than a letter, an extended attempt at autobiography rather or a long howl of pain at what he felt he had suffered at the hands of his father, and which was never sent, is proof enough of that. And his diaries, though they only start in 1910, when he was well past his twenty-fifth year, give us glimpses of the child Kafka was and of his place within the family. 'Once I planned a novel in which two brothers fought each other, one of whom went to America while the other remained in a European prison', he recalled in his diary on 19 January 1911. 'I only now and then began to write a few lines, for it tired me at once. Thus, one Sunday afternoon, when we were visiting my grandparents and had eaten the especially soft bread spread with butter that was always customary there, I wrote down something about my prison. It's quite possible that I did this mostly out of vanity and by shifting the paper about on the tablecloth, tapping with the pencil, looking around at the group under the lamp I wanted to tempt someone to take from me what I had written, look at it and admire me. It was chiefly the corridor of the prison that was described in the few lines, above all its silence and coldness… Perhaps I had a momentary feeling of the worthlessness of my description, but before that afternoon I had never paid much attention to such feelings when among relatives to whom I was accustomed (my timidity was so great that the accustomed was enough to make me half-way happy). I sat at the round table in the familiar room and could not forget that I was young and called to great things out of this

present tranquillity. An uncle who liked to make fun of people finally took the page that I was holding only weakly, looked at it briefly, handed it back to me without even laughing and said to the others, who were following him with their eyes, "The usual stuff", to me he said nothing. Though I remained seated and bent as before over my now useless sheet of paper, with one thrust I had been banished from society, my uncle's judgement repeated itself in me with what amounted almost to real significance and even within the feeling of belonging to a family I got an insight into the cold space of our world, which I had to warm with a fire that I first had to seek out.'

If he was twelve or thirteen at the time when the incident occurred then he still remembered it in all its excruciating detail fully fifteen years later. The story he is writing is itself clearly related to his condition, a prisoner in the cold and silent corridors of a European prison while his 'brother' has escaped to the freedom of 'America'. And lest we be inclined to side with him he points out that perhaps he is only writing this story and writing it so publicly out of vanity, wanting someone to take the page from him and, after reading it, heap him with praises, confirm for him that he is indeed 'called to great things', to a destiny which will allow him to escape the prison, to find his America. However, even then a part of him is convinced that the description he has been engaged on is worthless, so that we have to think that it is perhaps the very vanity of the enterprise that has landed him in prison in the first place.

Remember what he had said to Felice? All he really wanted was to please everybody. 'Indeed,' he had gone on, 'to become so pleasing that in the end I might openly act out my inherent baseness before the eyes of the world without forfeiting its love, the only sinner not to be roasted. In short, my only concern is the human tribunal, and I would like to deceive even this, and what's more without actual deception.'

Whether in love or in writing, the two central areas of his affective life, he avers, has never been concerned with the truth but only with making himself admired and liked by others.

The ambiguities and contradictions only grow as the little scene moves to its climax. The judgement of society arrives, but instead of confirming him in his great destiny it only returns him to a grey uniformity that makes the whole episode a scene not of triumph but of shame. 'The usual stuff.' Nothing is said to him directly, not by the uncle, not by the rest of the family, but that silence is worse than any criticism, which would at least involve an engagement with the piece, with him. It confirms the child in his sense that he, with all his hopes and wishes, simply *does not exist.* In the cold space of the world to which those three words have banished him he recognises that, even though he is here in the bosom of his family, from now on if he is to fulfil what he senses he has it in him to fulfil, he will have only himself to rely on.

Yet only two years after putting all this down on paper he hit at last upon the means to do just that. 'The Judgement', the first story he felt was really 'his', begins, like this anecdote, with the protagonist writing, though now he is writing to a friend far away who has escaped the prison he himself inhabits, of life with his old bedridden father, to congratulate him on his engagement. It ends with the father rearing up from the bed, suddenly a mighty figure of authority, and condemning him to death by drowning for having been 'a devilish human being', a judgement Georg proceeds to carry out.

Terrible as the story is, the writing of it gave him enormous joy: 'The fearful strain and joy, how the story developed before me, as if I were advancing over water... How everything can be said, how for everything, for the strangest fancies, there waits a great fire in which they perish and rise up again.' There is no hint here of suspicion that he might be fooling himself, that his writing was mere vanity, driven by the desire to show

off. The pleasure the writing gives him is proof of its quality and authenticity. But of course the feeling cannot last. It must be sought for and fought for again and again. And, as Virginia Woolf attests in her own diaries and as Eliot was to put it later, 'ridiculous the waste sad time before and after'. This is the time when doubts creep in, doubts not only about quality but about the nature of the feeling – is it the one and only good he feels it is here, or is it but another attempt to act out his own baseness and get the world to admire him for it?

On 15 September 1917 Kafka made the first diary entry in a new notebook. It was also the first entry he had made since arriving in Zürau. 'You have as far as this chance exists at all,' he writes, 'the chance to make a beginning. Do not waste it. You won't be able to avoid the filth that wells up out of you, if you want to penetrate. But don't wallow in it. If the lung wound is only a symbol, as you claim, symbol of the wound the inflammation of which is called Felice and the depth of which is justification, if this is so, then the medical advice too (light air sun rest) is symbol. Take hold of this symbol.'

The months he intends to spend in Zürau, away from the literary bustle of Prague, away from the Institute, away from his family (apart from Ottla, who is 'on his side') were never intended, as he had suggested to his employers as well as to everyone else, as a kind of rest cure, albeit an eccentric one. They were, rather, a chance to sort his life out, to make a new beginning necessitated by the onset of his illness. And he enjoins himself, as he rarely does in his diaries: 'Do not waste it.' This is followed by the sound advice: face up to whatever horrors your unconscious throws up, but do not wallow in it – he knows himself well. Yet he follows this with the by now familiar trope of 'the lung wound' as only a symbol, a term which immediately swallows up Felice, who is here seen as the thing that merely inflamed an existing existential wound. And what does 'the depth of which [is called] justification'

mean? That he has been using the wound to justify himself in the eyes of the world and even of his own? But what does that mean? And is it a coincidence that the term 'justification', *Rechtfertigung* in German, is a central pillar of Lutheran theology? At the time, as we will see, Kafka was avidly reading the theological works of his friends Brod and Weltsch, heavily imbued with Protestant thought, Jews though they were, as well as those of philosophers and theologians, Christian and Jewish, like Martin Buber, Ernst Troelsch and Kierkegaard. For the moment it is enough to focus on the first part of the entry: You have the chance to make a beginning. Do not waste it. But don't wallow in it.

Four days later, on 19 December, he is beginning to take stock. We have a set of jottings on a variety of subjects: on 'the wound'; on his constantly changing moods; on the fact that it is a week since he arrived. It is here that he remarks on the resemblance of the goats in the village to Polish Jews, including his uncle Siegfried and his friend Felix Weltsch. But then comes an entry which is going to be central to an understanding of everything he writes during his winter in Zürau: 'Always incomprehensible to me that it is possible for almost anyone who can write, suffering pain, to objectify the pain, so that I, for example, suffering unhappiness, my head perhaps still burning with unhappiness, can sit down and communicate to someone in writing: I am unhappy. Indeed, I can even go beyond that and in various flourishes, depending on my talent, which seems to have nothing to do with the unhappiness, improvise on it simply or antithetically or with a whole orchestra of associations. And it is not at all a lie and does not still the pain, is simply a merciful surplus of powers at the moment when the pain has actually visibly used up all my powers to the bottom of my being, which it scrapes. But then what sort of a surplus is it?'

Kafka is at his diary, doing what he needs to be doing: writing. He is in despair at the thought of the illness that has

so unexpectedly struck him; at his failure with Felice; at the thought of how little, at thirty-four, he has done with his life. He writes this down. He is driven to write it down, in spite of his wretchedness, or perhaps because of his wretchedness. And as he does so he realises that he could embroider on it, 'and in various flourishes, depending on my talent, which seems to have nothing to do with the unhappiness improvise on it simply or antithetically or with a whole orchestra of associations.' And as he writes it down this sentence itself becomes an example of just such rhetorical flourishes. He proceeds, pressing hard on the thought, 'it is not at all a lie and does not still the pain [*es ist nicht Lüge, und stillt den Schmerz nicht*].' It is, he concludes, 'simply a merciful surplus of powers [*einfach gnadenweiser Überschuss der Kräffte*] at the moment when the pain has visibly used up all my powers'. But then, he asks, and this is the question he will go on wrestling with for the rest of his stay in Zürau, 'what sort of a surplus is it'?

We have seen him accusing himself vis-à-vis Felice, of play-acting and hypocrisy, and in the next entry in the diary will note: 'Yesterday letter to Max. Mendacious, vain, theatrical.' But here he is not examining how he acts before others, either face-to-face or even through the medium of letters. He is examining something obviously related to this but much more mysterious, especially to someone whose life is devoted to writing and to writing as a way of speaking the truth, someone who has always used his diary as a way to the truth – about himself, about others, about the world. And yet here he comes up against the utterly mysterious disconnect between what he feels and what he writes, for as he writes down: 'I am unhappy', something happens. He finds that he can embroider on this, improvise on it, even enjoy himself in the doing of this, and it is not a lie and it does not still the pain. Yet his ability to do this is itself a minor miracle, 'a merciful surplus of powers' when he had seemingly been emptied of all power.

This looks superficially like Edgar's 'The worst is not so long as we can say "This is the worst"' in *King Lear*. But that is a true and fairly straightforward observation: there are degrees of degradation and horror, Edgar says in a play which is devoted to charting precisely this, and if we can still speak and express ourselves we have not yet reached the bottom. Kafka's remark is much more troubling. Perhaps, it suggests, there is no such thing as a bottom so long as we are alive.

The clarity of his thinking is almost frightening here. He recognises that '[i]t is not at all a lie' and yet that 'it does not still the pain'. But it is also, he feels, as he goes on testing it, 'a merciful surplus of powers' just at the moment when he seems to have had all power drained out of him. It is as if the very thing he is talking about, the awareness of the gap between some sort of inchoate feeling and the writing down of that feeling, here reasserts itself, for the next sentence cancels the 'merciful', suggesting it simply slipped in in the wake of that 'surplus', and asks: 'What sort of a surplus is it?' In other words, is it beneficient, merciful, or the final ruse of a malevolent deity?

When he accused himself in his dealings with Felice or Brod of hypocrisy or play-acting he came down firmly on the side of a negative interpretation of his actions. What is striking here is his recognition of ambivalence and complexity. But then his best stories up till then had recognised precisely that. In the last story he had published, 'In the Penal Colony', the officer, having explained the function of the dreadful punishment machine to the explorer, comes at last to 'the most important thing', the way the machine writes the sentence on the body of the condemned. He spreads out between them the sheets of paper with instructions from the former Commandant: "The explorer would have liked to say something appreciative, but all he could see was a labyrinth of lines crossing and recrossing each other, which covered the paper so thickly that it was difficult to discern the blank spaces between them,

“Read it,” said the officer. “I can’t,” said the explorer. “Yet it’s clear enough,” said the officer. “It’s very ingenious,” said the explorer evasively, “but I can’t make it out.” “Yes,” said the officer with a laugh, putting the paper away again, “it’s no calligraphy for school children. It needs to be studied closely. I’m quite sure that in the end you would understand it too. Of course the script can’t be a simple one; it’s not supposed to kill a man straight off, but only after an interval of, on average, twelve hours; the turning point is reckoned to come at the sixth hour. So there have to be lots of flourishes around the actual script; the script itself runs around the body only in a narrow girdle; the rest of the script is reserved for the embellishments.’ No wonder the machine goes wrong and with a life of its own destroys the officer before the eyes of the horrified explorer. In so doing it brings out the paradox of the machine: meant to make the accused feel in his own body the justice of the punishment, it only helps to bring out that language can never be ‘true’ or ‘just’, that it will always contain flourishes.

The word Kafka uses here is *Zieraten – viele Zieraten*, many decorations, adornments, while the word he uses in the 1917 diary entry is *Schnörkeln*, flourishes, curlicues, but the sense is the same: what was plain has been embellished and in the process rendered suspect. But is the notion of an original plainness not a delusion?

Yet it is not really language that is at issue here, but rather what it is that is essential to the self. At the end of the first story Kafka fully acknowledged, ‘The Judgement’, which I discussed above, Georg Bendemann, sentenced by his father to death by drowning, rushes down the stairs, crosses the street, ‘driven toward the water. Already he was grasping the railings as a starving man clutches food. He swung himself over, like the distinguished gymnast he had once been in his youth, to his parents’ pride… called in a low voice: “Dear parents, I have always loved you, all the same,” and let himself drop.’

Here what had once been his parents' pride, and by implication his own, his gymnastic prowess, a detail strictly unnecessary to the story, turns out to have been the very sign of the arrogance that leads to his downfall. He had innocently rejoiced in it as a youth, but as his father says as he sentences him to death: 'Till now you've known only about yourself! An innocent child, yes, that you were, but still more have you been a devilish human being!' In the same way the innocent child writer of the scene with the uncle now, much later, as Kafka looks back on it, may not have been so innocent after all, may have been harbouring the desire all along to be admired, to be praised. Yet (as we go round the circle once again) was he not perhaps innocent after all, seeking only to give expression to the fire we all have within us?

Into this nexus of guilt and innocence, of the flourish as an expression of the real self and the flourish as a way of showing off, we have to put the tall and awkward Kafka's early preoccupations with gestures, which are evident everywhere in his writings and in his drawings. In an extraordinary letter to Pollack, written when he was nineteen, in December 1902, he suddenly comes out with a story he is sure his friend doesn't know, 'because it's new and is hard to tell'. It concerns Shamefaced Lanky and Impure in Heart. 'Shamefaced Lanky had crept off to hide his face in an old village, among low houses and narrow lanes. The lanes were so small that whenever two people walked together they had to rub against each other... and the rooms were so low that when Shamefaced Lanky stood up his big angular head went right through the ceiling and without his particularly wanting to he had to look down on the thatched roofs.' Now, 'One day before Christmas Lanky sat stooped at the window. There was no room for his legs inside so he'd stuck them out of the window for comfort, there they dangled pleasantly. With his clumsy, skinny, spidery fingers he was knitting woollen socks for the peasants. He had almost spitted his grey eyes on the knitting needles, for it was already dark.' In to see him comes Impure in Heart, the

smooth-talking city slicker. 'Lanky gaped. The guest smiled. Lanky began feeling ashamed. He was ashamed of his height and his woollen socks and his room.' Impure in Heart turns his eyes towards the ceiling, 'and the words emerged from his mouth. Those words were fine gentlemen with patent-leather shoes and English cravats and glistening buttons… And as soon as those little gentlemen were out of his mouth they stood up on tiptoe and were tall; they then skipped over to Lanky, climbed up on him, tweaking and biting, and worked their way into his ears.' Impure in Heart talks and talks, about himself, his clothes, the city, and as he talks he sticks his pointed cane into Lanky's belly. At last he is done. He smiles. 'Lanky grinned and politely led his guest to the plank door. There they shook hands.'

So much of later Kafka is there: the awkwardness, the embarrassment at his size, the gestures, the confrontation with an enemy in a closed room which may not be a confrontation with an enemy at all but merely a social exchange. But while the visitor has no problem with words and merely uses gestures to reinforce what he is saying, Shamefaced Lanky has no words to counter his aggression with, only gestures, awkward gestures which both express his sense of shame and exacerbate it. In a late diary entry (24 January 1922) Kafka writes: 'Childish games (though I was well aware that they were so) marked the beginning of my intellectual decline. I deliberately cultivated a facial tic, for instance, or would walk across the Graben with arms crossed behind my head. A repulsively childish but successful game. (My writing began in the same way.…)' Once again he chooses, when he thinks about it, to interpret his need to write in the worst possible light. He will often do this, it is his fall-back position. What is striking about the September 1917 entry is that he remains open, ends with a question. The curlicue, the gesture, the act of writing, expresses a mysterious surplus – but what kind of a surplus is it?

OCTOBER

Again Felice

The end of September and the start of October saw Kafka still tormented by the Felice dilemma, still feverishly mining the metaphors of wound and war in the hope of finding some sort of resolution. 'In peace you make no progress, in war you bleed to death', he jots down in his diary in the kind of compact formula he is beginning to favour. In other words, while all apparently goes well no progress can be made, nothing can be resolved or properly understood, while in a crisis progress will indeed be made but it will result not in resolution or understanding but in death. 'Way to the woods', he writes a few days later, attesting to the need we most of us have to mark some new or pleasurable event by putting it down in words. And then: 'You have destroyed everything without having actually possessed it. How do you intend to reassemble it? What powers remain to the wandering spirit for this greatest of tasks?'

To Felice, in what is the last of the letters to her that we have, written almost a month after her visit, he wrote, going back over that visit: 'You were unhappy about the pointlessness of your journey, about my incomprehensible behaviour, about everything. I was not unhappy… I was tormented but not unhappy; I did not feel the whole tragedy as much as I saw it, recognised it and diagnosed it in its immensity…; and in this knowledge I remained relatively calm, my lips shut tight, very tight.' He goes on to confess his familiar failing of 'probably' playing a part, putting on an act, and half-heartedly tries to excuse himself by saying the spectacle before him was so hellish 'that one was bound to try to help the audience by introducing some diverting music; it did not succeed, as it hardly ever does,

but it did take place.' Rarely have the convolutions of shame and guilt in the relations between lovers been articulated with such horrifying precision. He ends with news about his physical condition and a forthcoming visit by Max when he gives a lecture in a nearby town. There may be other exchanges between them and they will meet up again for the last time in Prague at the end of December, but here the volume of Kafka's letters to her ends.

His attempt to explain his apparently unnatural response to her evident distress in terms of happiness and unhappiness was triggered by a letter from Brod which cut him to the quick, in which his friend accused him of being 'happy in your unhappiness'. Kafka in fact cites the offending passage at the start of the letter to Felice. To Brod he writes on 12 October that he cannot understand how he could say such a thing not as a mere statement or with regret but as a reproach. Don't you realise what this means? Kafka asks. It brands the mark of Cain upon the forehead of the accused and implies that 'he has fallen out of step with the world…, that no clear call can reach him any longer and so he cannot follow any call with a clear conscience'. Brod suggests by this accusation, he says, that he is both play-acting and self-satisfied, that he is wallowing in sorrow, and that this is not a mere attitude but an essential component of his nature. Knowing him as he does how can Brod speak in this way?

But of course this violent reaction, which goes on manifesting itself in the subsequent letters to Brod, is caused by Kafka's own fear that it might be true. Indeed, as we have seen, the accusation of play-acting is one he often levels at himself – hence his attempt, in the letter to Felice, to differentiate it from Max's. It is of course in the nature of things that no one can finally adjudicate on this.

Village Life

Meanwhile Kafka was settling in to his life in Zürau. 'This village life is lovely and remains so', he writes to Weltsch. 'Ottla's house is located on the Ringplatz, so when I look out of the window I see another cottage on the opposite side of the square, but right behind that the open fields begin. What could be better in every sense for breathing?' In his diary he describes his day: 'Feeding the goats, field tunnelled by mice, digging potatoes ("How the wind blows up our arses"), picking rosehips, farmer Feigl (7 girls, one of them short, a sweet look, white rabbit on her shoulder), in the room a picture of Kaiser F.J. . . . The boys who hasten across the vast fields on the hill in the evening in pursuit of the feeding scattered cattle herd and at the same time must keep yanking around a young tethered bull that refuses to follow.'

If the farmers seem a race apart, 'noblemen who have escaped into agriculture' he describes them as, the many animals in the village feel strangely familiar. Though Kafka was a city boy he always seems to have had an extraordinary empathy with animals of all kinds, especially the lowliest and the seemingly most repulsive. His most famous story, 'The Metamorphosis', gives an insect a voice and a conscience without ever letting us forget its physical characteristics, and the new collection Wolff was considering included a story about jackals and Arabs which succeeds in entering imaginatively into the world and feelings of the jackals in a quite startling way, while the heart-rending story of the performing ape, Red Peter, does the same for the world of the great apes. In a letter to Brod's wife Elsa, who seems to have sent him a photo of a cabaret performer she has recently seen, he writes: 'In comparing [W.] to a pig I mean no insult. Have you ever looked as carefully at a pig as at W.? It is amazing. A pig's face is a human face, in which the lower lip is folded down over the chin; the upper lip, without affecting

the eyes and mouth, is folded up to the brow. With this snout-face the pig actually grubs the ground. We take that for granted and it would be an amazing pig who did not do so, but of late I have often seen the creature from close up, and you must believe me when I say that it is even more amazing that the pig does so. You would really think that just for testing purposes it would be enough to poke at the thing in question with a foot, or to smell it, or if necessary to sniff at it from close quarters – but no, this will not do, and the pig does not even try but throws his snout right in, and if he has plunged into something horrid – all around me are the droppings of my friends, the goats and the geese – then he snorts with delight. And – this above all reminds me of W. – the pig's body is not dirty, the animal could even be called fastidious (though this is not the kind of fastidiousness you would want to embrace). He has elegant, delicately stepping feet, and the movement of his body seems to flow from a single impulse. Only his noblest organ, his snout, is hopelessly piggish.' And he concludes: 'So you see, dear Frau Elsa, we in Zürau also have our "Lucerna" [the cabaret where W. was performing] and I would be so happy if I could repay you for the picture of W. by sending you a ham from our piglet. But in the first place he doesn't belong to me and in the second place the animal gains weight so slowly, for all the good living, that to our (mine and Ottla's) joy, it will be a long time before he can be slaughtered.'

So much of Kafka is here: the ability to look as few writers have; the ability to express what he sees in all its rich complexity, taking his time and allowing the elements to unfold in the required manner; the sly humour, never far away; the empathy and refreshing lack of distinction between animals and men; and the evident pleasure he takes in his little vignette, so much at odds with his agonising over the moral validity of writing and the constant fear that he is writing not to tell it as it is but to show off.

As the conclusion reveals, food was on everyone's mind in this, the third year of the war. Kafka and Ottla must have been constantly receiving requests from family and friends for eggs and meat and other farm produce, and doing their best to meet these, though they all too often have to admit that food is scarce even on a farm.

In his early letters to his friends, too, Kafka badgers them to come out and visit him, stressing how easy it is to get to Zürau from Prague: 'The trip can be made as a day's outing', he writes to Oskar Baum, 'or for a longer while since my room has two excellent beds', and he himself can sleep in Ottla's room, while he might be able to provide them with milk 'and what goes with it' to take back to the city. However, in typical Kafka fashion, he immediately qualifies this: 'Nevertheless I cannot advise you wholeheartedly to come. During the first week and perhaps still in the second it was different. Then I wanted to have all of you here… But now, in the third week of my stay things are different and I no longer know what point there would be in inviting you.' While he himself is settling down happily enough, he says, he is beginning to see that 'there are things that no one could possibly like, even you two, obliging as you are.' Among these 'may be myself'. To Brod, on 12 October, he is more explicit: 'Don't misunderstand my fear of visitors. I would not want people to make a long trip, at considerable expense, to come in this autumnal weather to this village which is bound to strike a stranger as dreary, to this household of ours which a stranger is bound to find mismanaged, rife with little inconveniences and even unpleasantness, and all simply to see me – who am sometimes bored (a state that is not the worst for me), sometimes oversensitive, sometimes fretting over a letter that is supposed to come or has failed to come or is threatening to come, sometimes calmed by a letter I have written, sometimes immoderately concerned about myself and my own comforts, sometimes inclined to spit myself out as utterly repulsive, and so on.'

What Kafka does not say is that he wants the time for himself and that though he enjoys the company of his friends and genuinely misses them he is becoming more and more conscious of the imperative he had laid down for himself at the start of his sojourn in the village: 'You have, as far as this chance exists at all, the chance to make a beginning. Do not waste it.'

The Reader

He had always been an avid reader, but there is a new critical edge to his comments on the books and authors he is reading in these early October letters and in his diary, a new sense of testing what he is reading against some ultimate standard and usually finding it wanting. '*Das Neue Geschlecht* [*The New Generation: A Programmatic Essay Against Metaphor*] by Tagger,' he notes in his diary for 23 September, 'wretched, loud-mouthed, agile, experienced, well-written in places, with faint shivers of dilettantism. What right does he have to show off?' Theodor Tagger, a German-Jewish playwright, is long forgotten, but the adjectives Kafka uses to condemn him are illuminating. They form a little anthology of what Kafka most hated in the books he read – and sought to banish from his own writing: 'loud-mouthed', 'agile', 'experienced', 'well-written'. He tells Brod he has read his translation into German of the libretto of Janáček's *Jenufa* with great pleasure but questions the German at one point: 'Isn't that the sort of German we have learned at the lips of our unGerman mothers?' In another letter he thanks him for sending his story 'Radetzky March' ('everything you send me gives me great pleasure'), but then proceeds to raise serious questions about it, questions we frequently see him raising about his own work in the diaries. Of course, he says, it could not be expected to make the same impression as when Brod read it aloud to him, 'but something

is missing. Is the cutting to blame? That can't be. After rapture, hate rears up, but no one has seen it growing. Perhaps there is not room enough inside the story for the antithetical twist to develop, perhaps not enough room even in the heart.'

On 8 October he notes: 'Dickens's *Copperfield* ("The Stoker" sheer imitation of Dickens, the planned novel [*The Man Who Disappeared*, also known as *Amerika*, of which his story "The Stoker" was to form the first chapter] even more so. Suitcase story, the delightful and charming young man, the lowly jobs, the beloved country estate, the dirty houses, among other things, but above all the method. My intention as I now see was to write a Dickens novel, only enriched by the sharper lights I would have taken from the time, and the duller ones I would have found in myself.)' And then, the devastating critique: 'Dickens' richness and the unreserved powerful onrush, but as a result of this passages of horrible weakness when he wearily stirs what he has already achieved into a jumble. Barbaric the impression of the strengthless whole, a barbarism that I, thanks to my weakness and the wiser for my epigonism [Kafka uses the word "epigone" – *mein Epigonentum* – which the shorter OED glosses as "one of a succeeding (and less distinguished) generation"], have avoided. Heartlessness behind the style overflowing with feeling. Those blocks of coarse characterisation, which are artificially applied to every person and without which Dickens would not be capable of even once hastily climbing up his story.' And he ends with a thought about his Swiss contemporary Robert Walser (Kafka liked to keep up with what was being written around him): 'Walser's connection with him in the blurring of abstract metaphors.'

Has there ever been a more just account of Dickens? One that recognises the weaknesses that are (as in Wordsworth) inseparable from the strengths? Like Eliot and Virginia Woolf, Kafka understands certain writers so well because

he is a writer himself. The reason why he is not, like them, recognised as a major critic, is because he never wrote a critical essay in his life. But embedded in his diaries and letters are the most wonderful insights, and views on books and writers which, even if one does not always agree with them, always make one think.

Writer and Author

On the same day as Kafka dismissed Theodor Tagger in his diary he also commented on his own work: 'I can still have temporary satisfaction from works like "Country Doctor", provided that I can still achieve something of the sort (very improbable), but happiness only if I can raise the world into the pure, true, immutable.' That last clause had been a refrain from the earliest letters and diary entries. What he is after in his writing, he notes in January 1911, is 'a description in which every word would be linked to my life, which I would draw to my heart and which would transport me out of itself.' In November of that year he dreams of being able one day to write something 'large and well-shaped from beginning to end', feeling that the story would then be able to detach itself from him 'and it would be possible for me calmly, and with open eyes, as a blood relation of a healthy story, to hear it read.' That such a dream is not fantasy but capable of realisation is proven for him by 'The Judgement', which seemed, as we have seen, at least in its immediate aftermath, to fulfil all his expectations. But by and large, if he is harsh on Dickens or his contemporaries and friends, Brod and Werfel among them, he is much harsher on himself. Even with 'The Metamorphosis' and 'The Stoker', which followed hard on the heels of 'The Judgement' in the great spurt of creative energy of the winter of 1912–13, and the writing of which brought him

much joy and the sense that he had at last come into his own, he feels that there are many weak passages: 'In high spirits because I consider "The Stoker" so good,' he writes in his diary on 24 May 1913. 'This evening I read it to my parents, there is no better critic than I when I read to my father, who listens with the most extreme reluctance. Many shallow passages followed by unfathomable depths.' Yet when he rereads 'A Country Doctor' he admits to thinking it rather good (though, being Kafka, he has to add that the satisfaction is 'merely temporary'), and hopes to achieve 'something of the sort' in the future, though – that extraordinary phrase – 'happiness only if I can raise the world into the pure, true, immutable [*falls ich die Welt ins Reine, Wahre, Unveränderliche heben kann*].'

On 19 October he describes his reaction to reading his own story, 'Jackals and Arabs', in the October issue of Martin Buber's new journal, *Der Jude* (the Red Peter story, 'A Lecture to an Academy', was to appear in the November issue): 'The orgy while reading the story in *Der Jude*. Like a squirrel in a cage. Bliss of movement. Desperate about confinement, the mad persistence, feeling of misery despite the calm exterior outside. All this both simultaneously and alternatingly, a sunray of bliss still lingering in the excitement of the end.' Both stories formed part of the collection Kafka had offered to Kurt Wolff under the title 'A Country Doctor'. He has obviously received his copy of *Der Jude* and he reacts as any author would to seeing his work in print, with surprise and pleasure, not having remembered that what he had written was so good, but also with unease and even dismay, not having realised it was, in places, so bad. Very few authors, though, feel their work as viscerally as Kafka and express their reaction with such physical intensity – 'bliss of movement', 'desperation about constriction', 'filth of the end'. To read this helps one understand what his writing meant to him, how every sentence, every word even, worked upon not just his mind or

his ears but his whole body. Kafka was a writer, subject to the ups and downs, the pride and the embarrassments every writer feels when faced with what they have written in the privacy of their rooms suddenly enters the public domain. Except that with him the feelings appear to be much more extreme than with other writers. I am tempted to say that this is a mark of how much finer a writer he is than most of us, but I wonder if that's true.

A glimpse, though, of Kafka the author, is provided by a letter to Brod at this time. It seems that Brod had been shown a letter Felix Weltsch had written to Kafka about a conversation he had had with Kafka's old law professor at university. 'He praised you to the skies as a writer', Weltsch had written. 'His mother-in-law at a spa heard from another lady about a writer named Franz Kafka whose works one absolutely had to know. She asked for the book and received it. As a consequence the Professor read four pages and was enthusiastic: "I certainly must know him if he has a doctorate from us."' So many myths surround Kafka and his work, quite a few of them propagated by his own diaries and letters, that it is refreshing to find ourselves face to face with an experience that is both banal and (for the author) always pleasing: that an utterly unknown person in a far-away town thinks about you as 'a writer… whose works one absolutely had to know'. Suddenly you step out of the bubble of your own dreams and self-criticism and get a glimpse of how the world sees you, never mind that the world consists of one lady in a spa town and your old professor. What is important is that it has evoked a reaction out there, beyond your ken.

Kafka responds to Brod with typical grace and modesty: '"That book" of mine might actually be worthwhile. I too would like to read it. It is sitting somewhere in the heavenly bookshelves. But that a seventy-seven-year old lady should ask to have the book for a birthday gift (perhaps for her

great-grandson: "I am but small, my gift is small..."), that my book should cause the family blood of the Clemenceaux to race [Zukerkandl, his old professor, was a distant relative of Georges Clemenceau, the French Prime Minister], that the Hofrat deigns to speak of it without adding a reprimand (a circumstance that undoubtedly proves how deeply contemptuous he is of the whole thing), all this – it is too much, that is the trouble.'

The Little Octavo Notebook

Early in October Kafka had said to Brod: 'I'm not writing. What's more, my will is not directed towards writing. If I could save myself... by digging holes I would dig holes.' (A photograph in the second volume of Beckett's letters shows the Irish writer, back bowed, the image of depression, doing just that in the bare garden of his little country retreat in Ussy). On 15 October he jotted in his diary: 'Kunz and wife, on their fields, on the slope opposite my window.' The next entry, dated 21 October, consists only of two brief comments, one on the weather, the other on the village dogs. There is nothing till 6 November, where we find just the two words: 'Sheer incapacity'.

Clearly the early euphoria brought about by leaving Prague and its problems behind him and settling down in the cultural isolation of the countryside had evaporated, to be replaced with an ever-growing sense of gloom and despair. The next entry, on 10 November, seems much more positive: 'I have not yet set down the decisive [*das Entscheidende*] in writing. I am still flowing in two branches. The work waiting is immense [*ungeheuerlich*].' This is immediately followed by a long description of a dream. The next entry is dated a year and a half later, 27 June 1919.

If this was all we had we would be forced to conclude that 'sheer incapacity' had triumphed over the dream of accomplishing the 'immense work' he felt was awaiting him. But fortunately among the material Max Brod saved from the destruction of his papers that Kafka had instructed him to carry out upon his death were a number of little unlined octavo notebooks, suitable for carrying around in a jacket pocket. Kafka had bought and begun using these in the autumn of 1916, in Prague, when he was finding refuge in Ottla's tiny one-room hideout in Alchemists' Lane in the Old City and working there while she was out. In Zürau, in the middle of October 1917, he seems to have turned to one of these and begun to use it both as a diary, replacing the quarto notebooks he normally used, and as a notebook in which to jot down thoughts, fantasies, fragments of fiction and indeed anything that came into his head and needed to find expression on paper.

Of course the diaries he had been keeping from 1910 on had also consisted of much more than notes on how he had spent the day. It was there he had scribbled the aborted beginnings of many stories and the whole of some, like 'The Judgement', which he would go on to publish with only minor corrections. But what Brod designated as the third and fourth octavo notebooks and which are now described in the scholarly literature as Octavo Notebooks G and H, are something else. Notebook G starts with an entry for 18 October 1917 and ends with one dated 28 January 1918, while the first date of Notebook G is 31 January and the last 28 February, though a large number of undated pages follow. These two notebooks thus contain the bulk of the writing Kafka was engaged on during his winter in Zürau, and they show that he had at least begun to engage in the 'immense work' he talked about in his old diary by 10 November.

Why did he switch from the quarto to the octavo notebooks in the middle of October? Did the smaller format

make it feel even more secret than his secret diary? Did the change of format, the brand new little notebook, represent that decisive change in his life and habits he had come to Zürau to seek? Or was it simply that he could take them on his walks in the country around Zürau? And why, given all this, did he go on, albeit only sporadically, writing in the old diary? We will never know. What is clear from Octavo Notebook G is that the floodgates had opened to another bout of intense writerly activity *and* that in these months he seemed to be moving towards a new form of extreme compression.

Everything, we can now see, had been preparing him for this: the blood; the break with Felice (clear to him if not to her); the encouragement of Kurt Wolff; the imminent publication of two recent stories in an important new journal; and of course the move to Zürau itself. Octavo Notebooks G and H bear witness to it all.

18 and 19 October

On 18 October, then, Kafka jotted down in the new notebook: 'Dread of night. Dread of not-night. [*Furcht vor der Nacht. Furcht vor der Nicht-Nacht.*]' *Nicht-Nacht* sounds like one of those word-creations Celan was to come to favour but which is unusual in Kafka, but otherwise the comment does not seem very different from many of the diary entries, and its brevity suggests that the octavo notebook will, like the diary, soon peter out. But what follows on 19 October is three pages of the most varied and remarkable writing. Instead of noting how he is feeling there is a new attempt to use what he is feeling as a way to an understanding of what it is we are, both as a species, 'man' and as twentieth-century beings, 'modern man'. That too, though, was hardly absent from his earlier writings, but it found expression not in discursive prose

but in fiction. What is new here is the melding of fiction and discursive prose in extremely compact pieces. Whether we call these parables, aphorisms or thoughts is irrelevant. They are what they are and have to be approached in full recognition of their uniqueness, their strangeness – and their unevenness.

The 19 October entries begin with an unpromisingly obscure remark: 'Senselessness (too strong a word) of the separation of what is one's own and what is extraneous to the spiritual battle'. As we will see, much of what follows has to do with the limitations of psychology and self-searching and with the need to see oneself not by looking inwards but by trying to grasp what kind of animals we are. Anthropology, we might say, not psychology. Sometimes this is explored in the abstract terms of the philosophical language of the day and sometimes in brief flashes of imagery and fiction. Here the opening remark is followed by what seems like an attempt at scientific rigour but which appears to us now, a century on, to be mired in the jargon of the times, with its unquestioning use of terms like 'the absolute' and 'the One': 'All science is methodology with regard to the absolute. Therefore there need be no fear of the unequivocally methodological. It is a husk, but not more than everything except the One (*dem Einen*).' This leads to a longish paragraph which brings him back to his own case, though, unlike what we find in the letters to Felice and to Brod, he is still trying to universalise it: 'We are all fighting a battle. (If, attacked by the ultimate question, I reach out behind me for weapons, I cannot choose which of these weapons I will have, and even if I could choose I should be bound to choose some that don't belong to me…).' I cannot fight this battle all on my own, he goes on, and if I ever thought I could I would soon be disabused. He carries on with the battle image for a while before concluding: 'There is no one who fights an independent battle.' Is this vanity? he asks himself, and answers: 'Yes, but also a necessary encouragement, and one in accordance with the truth.'

At this point he abandons the attempt at argument with an abrupt Wittgensteinian: '*Ich irre ab*', I'm on the wrong track. So he starts again: 'The true way leads along a cable stretched not high in the air but just above the ground. It seems designed more to trip one up than to be walked along. [*Der wahre Weg geht über ein Seil, das aber nicht in der Höhe gespannt ist, sondern knapp über dem Boden. Es scheint mehr bestimmt stolpern zu machen als begangen zu werden.*]'

This, unlike the previous, jargon-laden passage, is difficult to understand not because we are unsure how to take individual words such as 'the One' and 'the absolute', but because the image is both resonant and mysterious. Yet before trying to unpack it we need to understand a few things about how it has normally been presented to us. The waters have been muddied by a series of extraneous circumstances, most of Kafka's own making.

In the early part of 1918, still in Zürau, he seems to have begun to read back over the two octavo notebooks and to do something unusual for him, who was usually so indifferent to the state of his jottings: he took a large number of sheets of blank paper (very precious at this stage in the war), cut them in half and then in half again, creating a stack of over a hundred tiny pages, numbered them and began to copy out short passages from the notebooks, one to each page. Some he changed slightly as he copied them, some he crossed out once he had copied them, but left in the pile. Three years later, in 1920, he made some additions to these, so that even then he clearly thought of the stack as a distinct entity, yet he never gave them a title, never attempted to show them to anyone, so far as we know, or to try to get them published. When Max Brod started to put his friend's unpublished work before the public, in the late twenties and thirties, he began with the unfinished novels, *The Trial* and *The Castle*, and, in line with his view of Kafka as a secular saint, gave this small collection, when he got round to the shorter works, the title: 'Reflections on Sin, Suffering,

Hope and the True Way', as it was translated into English by Ernst Kaiser and Eithne Wilkins. Since then the collection has been known as *The Aphorisms* or *The Zürau Aphorisms*, and been translated countless times into English. Recently Reiner Stach, Kafka's most recent biographer, has brought out an edition keeping one 'aphorism' per page, as Kafka had done, and with a facing page commentary. This has been translated into English (wisely keeping Kafka's German as well) by Shirley Frisch, who also translated Stach's biography.

The problems begin with the first 'aphorism', which Kafka copied onto the first of his numbered sheets when he came to extrapolate these brief passages from the two octavo notebooks. Whether in the interests of brevity or because he read it as a sort of note to himself, unconnected with the two sentences that follow, Kafka dispensed with the opening sentence: '*Ich irre ab*'. Stach, in his edition, tells us that Kafka had in fact originally written one sentence, 'The true way leads along a rope stretched not high in the air but just above the ground', but added the second, 'It seems designed more to trip one up than to be walked along' to the octavo notebook before inscribing it onto sheet one. (Actually Kafka wrote *Dratseil*, cable, which he later changed to *Seil*, rope, a slight but significant difference.) But to anyone reading the notebook it seems evident that the '*ich irre ab*' of the start of the paragraph is directly linked in both thought and wording to the sentence that follows. The English translation of the entire paragraph in the notebook by Wilkins and Kaiser and then by Frisch in the commentary in the Stach edition, has 'I digress', which cuts it off from what follows. On 19 October 1917, however, Kafka had as yet no thought of a collection of aphorisms or thoughts or however one chooses to refer to them, and all the dictionaries I've consulted give '*irren*' as 'go astray, wander', a meaning not decisively altered by the prefix 'ab'. 'To digress', on the other hand, is '*abschweifen*' in both Collins and the Oxford Duden.

The two terms are thus far from interchangeable. To digress is to wander from the true path when one is clear what that path is and is able to return to it; to wander or stray suggests that one is lost, as Dante found that he was lost at the start of the *Commedia*: '*mi ritrovai per una selva oscura, / che la diritta via era smarrita* [I found myself in a dark wood for the straight way was lost]'. Once we translate correctly as 'I've gone astray', 'I've lost my way', we can read the whole paragraph as it needs to be read, as a whole, not a note to himself ('I digress') and then a new thought, but a single thought about ways and ends. Kafka notes that he has lost his way amidst the abstractions he has been employing, and the image of a battle, and the words '*ich irre ab*', I've got lost, then lead him into another train of thought: that there is *no* clear way, and so the idea of being lost does not imply an opposite being found. The very idea that there might be a clear way is itself perhaps the primal lure. The cable which seems to be there to guide us in fact only serves to trip us up. Whether this implies a malign deity who (unlike Dante's God, who makes sure there is a guide to bring the erring pilgrim back to the true way) takes a perverse pleasure in tripping up the eager human, or a critique of the very notion of a way posited by those anxious for a meaning in their lives is not, at this moment, clear. What is clear to us now and probably was to Kafka as he read through those entries months later is that there is a world of difference between the turgid philosophising of 'All science is methodology with regard to the Absolute' and the fresh and suggestive image of the cable or rope – actually more of a little fiction than a (static) image, though one which seems to disintegrate as one tries to imagine it, leaving behind only a powerful sense of unease. I think this is generated by the seeming certainty of the notion of '*the* true way' and the questioning of that with the image of the cable/rope – not so much a Hansel and Gretel aid as a mischievous impediment to any advance. The entire collection of little

thoughts is thus set under the sign of the error of thinking that there is such a thing as 'the true way' and yet the recognition that however much we try to avoid it we always find ourselves thinking in terms of a 'way'.

That day, though, in mid-October 1917, he leaves the thought and turns to his feelings on reading his 'Jackals and Arabs' story in *Der Jude*, which I've already quoted. This is followed by a long paragraph in which he seems to be using the rereading of the story to help him confront the future: 'Weakness of memory for details and the course of one's own comprehension of the world – a very bad sign.' And he returns to a thought, central to him, the need to feel the whole story in your body for it to succeed: 'How are you going even to touch the greatest task, how are you going even to sense its nearness, even to dream its existence, even plead for its dream, dare to learn the letters of the plea, if you cannot collect yourself in such a way that, when the decisive moment comes you hold the totality of yourself collected in your hand like a stone to be thrown, a knife for the kill?' And then one of those lovely enigmatic yet earthy Kafka conclusions: 'However, there is no need to spit on one's hands before clasping them.'

On 12 November he will return to the image of the stone in the hand, but complicating and enriching it, as we will see. Here he leaves it and, in a further long paragraph, turns to another thought, one which had been troubling him, as we have seen, since he first arrived in Zürau: 'How is it possible to think of something unconsoling?' The very act of writing, he had felt as he wrote in his diary on 19 September, transmutes a feeling into something else. To write 'I am in despair' does something strange to that feeling of despair, brings into play an unexpected aspect of the self, one which finds energy in the writing, makes of it something other than a simple description. Is the same true of thinking? Kafka had been reading Pascal's *Pensées* that summer, and they had evoked a powerful response.

On 2 August he wrote in his diary: 'Pascal arranges everything very tidily before God makes his appearance, but there must be a deeper, uneasier scepticism than that of a man cutting himself to bits with – indeed – wonderful knives, but still, with the calm of a butcher. Whence this calm? This confidence, with which the knife is wielded?' The confidence comes with Pascal's belief in God, but if one is trying to think through what it means to exist in the world without the comfort of the belief that God created it, how to do it without the thought itself somehow acting as a kind of God? This is the dilemma Nietzsche had struggled with in his later writings, but there is no evidence that Kafka had read such works as *The Twilight of the Idols*, or indeed any of Nietzsche at all. 'You must put yourself aside,' he says here, 'and somehow grasp this simply by recognising the problem.' But, he adds, 'that then really means having pulled oneself up by one's own hair'. And this leads to the observation that 'descriptive psychology is probably, taken as a whole, a form of anthropomorphism, a nibbling at our own limits. The inner world can only be experienced, not described.' We cannot use psychology to grasp how we stand in the world, for it only reflects back to us ourselves and the world as we imagine them, not as they are: 'Psychology is impatience'. Which leads to the thought that '[a]ll human errors are impatience, a premature breaking off of a methodical procedure, an apparent fencing in of what is apparently at issue'.

This last sentence he was to copy out later as 'aphorism' number two in his little projected anthology. There is nothing really new here, for it had been a long-held belief of Kafka's, linked to the idea that a story or even just a description of his had been a failure simply because he did not have the patience to allow it to emerge into its fullness in its own time. What is new is the attempt to face this head-on, to generalise it and thus free it of the self-laceration evident in earlier entries.

And, having jotted it down, he moves on again, that day, to one final thought, mysterious and seemingly unconnected but which, as we will see, opens up a rich field of exploration in the days to come: 'Don Quixote's misfortune is not his imagination, but Sancho Panza.'

20 and 21 October

The next day, still in bed, he jots down some further thoughts about patience and impatience: 'There are two cardinal sins from which all others derive: impatience and indolence. Because of impatience they were expelled from Paradise, because of indolence they do not return. But perhaps there is only one cardinal sin: impatience. Because of impatience they were expelled, because of impatience they do not return.' Here, though, unlike the previous thought on the subject, we are suddenly plunged into a theological universe, a deeply Christianised reading of the first chapters of Genesis, with its talk of cardinal sin and expulsion from Paradise. Hebrew theology makes little reference to those chapters, though its mystical undercurrents are naturally fascinated by them. It is with St. Paul and St. Augustine that they take on a central importance in the West, with Adam and Jesus and Eve and Mary playing central roles in the Christian view of the unfolding of history. Yet in the circles in which Kafka moved, Jewish thought was deeply imbued with Christian and especially with German Protestant theology.

The passage about the two cardinal sins was to become the third of the 'aphorisms'. It is followed, in the octavo notebook, by a paragraph which finds another image for the impossibility of humans being able to understand who and what they are, since they cannot escape their human vantage point: a train meeting with an accident in a tunnel, where the light at the

beginning of the tunnel can no longer be seen, the light at the end is a mere glimmer, but all around is the chaos and confusion of the accident. 'What should I do? or: Why should I do it? are not questions to be asked in such places.'

This is followed by an extraordinary and seemingly unrelated little vignette: 'Many shades of the departed are occupied solely in licking the waves of the river of death because it comes from our direction and still has the salty taste of our seas. Then the river rears up in disgust, flows the opposite way and washes the dead back into life. They, however, are happy, sing songs of thanksgiving and stroke the indignant stream.' In Book XI of the *Odyssey* the souls of the departed are drawn to the blood of the sacrificial sheep Odysseus has poured into a newly-dug trench, and, by drinking the blood, regain the ability to see and converse with the living. There is no blood in Kafka but instead the river of death, with 'its salty taste of our seas', to which the shades of the departed are drawn compulsively. But then the story takes a totally unexpected and very Kafkaesque turn, as the river itself is given life, rearing up in disgust either at the constant lapping of the shades or at the idea that it still contains traces of the seas of the world above, and it starts to flow backwards, washing the dead back into life. They are delighted at this, says the story (*sie aber sind glücklich*), sing hymns of thanksgiving and – how Kafka visualises, empathises – 'caress the indignant stream [*streicheln den Empörten*].'

We feel as though we should experience this as a story of human triumph over death, a little like the stories of heroes who go down into the underworld to rescue their friends from death. But actually we don't, and the reason is, I think, because the return of the departed to this world after they have died feels – is made by Kafka to feel – profoundly unnatural. The shades who lap at the river are like starved dogs lapping up what they shouldn't, and the vivid though always silent

responses of the river give us the sense that it has been forced against its will and against all natural laws to turn back, and no caresses by the resurrected humans, and no number of hymns of thanksgiving sung by them will appease its anger. Yet a paraphrase of the little story as: 'Human beings should accept death as natural' would lose almost everything, like paraphrasing *Hamlet* as: 'Don't procrastinate'.

Kafka was to copy this out into his new little anthology on the page numbered 4. It is followed, in the notebook, by 'aphorisms' number five and six, more obviously aphoristic and far less resonant. The first, 'Beyond a certain point there is no return. That point is to be reached', is one of those admonitions to himself couched in generalising language that he has been jotting down since his arrival in Zürau. The second, which begins 'The decisive moment in the development of mankind is everlasting', shows, in contrast to the little story of the river of death, how weak are Kafka's attempts at dealing with the thoughts and feelings which beset him in the philosophical language of his day and how counter-productive is the attempt to formulate things in short and pithy fashion in the tradition of Pascal's *Pensées* and La Rochefoucauld's *Maximes*.

'Evening walk to Oberklee', he then notes, before resuming his musings on how his situation can give him insights into the human condition. One of these he thinks well enough of some months later to add to his growing pile of numbered thoughts (seven): 'One of Evil's most effective means of seduction is the challenge to battle. It is like the battle with women, which ends in bed.' If we can swallow our distaste for the second sentence, which merely repeats a trope common in central European intellectual circles at the time, it raises interesting questions. It is not all that far, at one level, from Wittgenstein's consistent attempt, in his later writings, not to engage in arguments with other philosophers, living or dead, for such fights, he suggests, give us the impression that

we are getting somewhere when we are simply going round the same old circles. But the remark is also interesting when we recall that one of Kafka's recurrent images is of a struggle with someone or something, as though the imagining of such a struggle was just a way of getting started.

The next day, Sunday 21 October, he returned to his diary notebook for some reason, and noted there: 'Beautiful day, sunny warm windless'. He then remarked how 'most dogs bark senselessly, even when someone is approaching in the distance, but some, perhaps not even the best watchdogs but reasonable creatures, walk up to the stranger, sniff at him and bark only when there's a suspicious smell'. There is nothing here to tell us that that day was to be one of the most productive of his entire stay in Zürau. For that we have to turn to the octavo notebook.

After noting again '*Im Sonnenschein* (in the sunshine)', he adds: 'The voices of the world becoming quieter and fewer', but whether that is cause for mourning or rejoicing we are not told. A space, and then comes a two-page piece that Brod extracted and titled 'A Common Confusion' when he included it in his selection of stories, *The Great Wall of China.* Like the title story, this one is about never reaching your goal despite infinite patience and pains, and, as in his innumerable variations on this theme, Kafka manages in very few words to convey the sense of a lifetime's struggles and frustrations. This brilliant little piece would be enough to fill most writers' day, but not Kafka's, not on this October Sunday. Another space and he returns to exploring how cunningly 'the Diabolical' tempts one by pretending to be 'the Good', perhaps thinking of himself and Felice, and then for the first time in the notebook comes a piece with a title: 'A Life'. It appears at first to be an autobiographical fragment but then slowly reveals itself to be a nightmarish fiction: 'An evil-smelling bitch, producer of countless litters, already decaying in places,

though in my childhood she meant everything to me, who follows me faithfully all the time, whom I cannot bring myself to beat but instead retreat from step by step, unable even to stand her breath; yet she will drive me, unless I determine otherwise, into the corner that I can already see looming up, where she will decompose wholly upon me and along with me, with the purulent and wormy flesh of her tongue – is this an honour for me? – upon my hand to the very end.'

According to Stach, Kafka first wrote *Hund*, a male dog, but after completing the piece he changed it to *Hündin*, a bitch, and added the phrase 'producer of countless litters'. When he came to transcribe it he retained the title but then crossed it out. It appears on sheet 8, which was later changed to 8/9, which suggests that he might have destroyed a sheet. Stach also mentions that Brod left it out when he published the reflections, as he called them, and suggests that this was because he found the contents repulsive. But it could also be because he felt that they did not belong there, and indeed, why would Kafka have selected it for inclusion when other passages, closer in tone to the other 'aphorisms' were not? In the octavo notebook it stands out as being neither general and impersonal nor having the mysterious resonance of the best of them. The feeling it conveys is one of horror at the sight of a suffering sentient creature clinging to one, but which one is unable to help. Is it a grotesque reimagining of his relations with Felice? But then it recalls 'A Country Doctor' and both stories could be seen, among other things, as attempts to imagine what it means to be composed of flesh and blood and how for every thought, no matter how repulsive, there is a form.

Having written this, Kafka went out for an evening walk, noting laconically: 'Evening on the way to Zarch'. He then returned to his notebook, first to try and develop his thoughts on good and evil and then, to crown the day, produced one of those striking meditations on one of the monuments of European

culture which are such a feature of his later writings. Two days earlier, as we have seen, he had ended his notebook entry with the enigmatic remark that 'Don Quixote's misfortune is not his imagination but Sancho Panza'. We are to imagine him pondering on this on his evening walks, and now he sits down and turns the whole thing round, centring it not on Cervantes' hero but on his squire: 'Without making any boast of it,' he writes, 'Sancho Panza succeeded, in the course of years, by devouring a great many romances of chivalry and adventure in the evening and night hours, in so diverting from him his demon, whom he later called Don Quixote, that his demon thereupon set out in perfect freedom on the maddest exploits, which, however, for the lack of a preordained object, which should have been Sancho Panza himself, harmed nobody. A free man, Sancho Panza imperturbably followed Don Quixote on his crusades, perhaps out of a sense of responsibility, and had of them a great and edifying entertainment to the end of his days.' [tr. Willa and Edwin Muir, modified.]

In this version of or meditation on Cervantes' great novel there is only one person, split, as Kafka felt himself to be split, into two, a living person moving as we all do from birth to death, and a demon whose name is Imagination, who does not know what time or death mean and fills the mind of the living being with the wildest fantasies. And such demons are not harmless. Unless a conduit can be found for them, they will destroy the living. With a great deal of effort Sancho Panza finds just such a conduit, gives him the name of Don Quixote, and, having thus rendered him harmless, allows him free rein. Cervantes, who is never mentioned, is thus seen to have found a way of dealing with the agonising struggle which has been tearing Kafka apart, not by suppressing his demon but by writing a story about this struggle, giving it a local habitation and a name.

22 and 23 October

The next day he is up at five, or it may be that he has not slept at all. Still thinking about Don Quixote, he finds a darker interpretation, imagining the Don's fight with the windmills (the imagination's fight with reality) as suicide: 'The dead Don Quixote wants to kill the dead Don Quixote' he notes. However, in order to do so 'he needs a place that is alive [*eine lebendige Stelle*],' for which he searches 'ceaselessly and in vain'. But then Kafka finds his fantasy spinning out of control: 'The two dead men, inextricably interlocked and positively bouncing with life, go somersaulting away down the ages.'

'Morning in bed', he next notes, but this is no retreat into depression, for there he seems to have jotted down what he later extracted as the tenth of his 'aphorisms', a kind of counter to the Don Quixote fantasy. A man, A, 'very puffed up [*sehr aufgeblasen*]', imagines he is 'very far advanced in goodness' whereas in fact 'a great devil has entered into him, and the countless smaller devils are coming along to serve the great one'. Kafka must at this point have got up and gone about farm business, for he next notes: 'In the evening went to the forest, moon waxing, confused day behind me. (Max's card.) Sick stomach.' The card was probably informing him of the details of a trip Brod and his wife were planning to the nearby town of Komotau, where they had been invited to a Zionist literary event which Kafka planned to attend, the three of them then setting out for Prague the next day. We have seen Kafka's ambivalent feelings about seeing his Prague friends, both wanting to (he was in some ways a very sociable being) and also, especially now that his whole *raison d'être* for isolating himself in the country was starting to bear fruit, feeling that this was the last thing he needed or wanted. No wonder Max's card troubled him.

Nevertheless he ended the day with one more little meditation, later to be selected for inclusion in the anthology, on sheet 11 (then renumbered 12 by him). This one moves away from what has gone before, though it's not difficult to see that he is still trying to find ways of expressing the fact that there are as many worlds as there are people inhabiting them and that we must therefore never take our own perspective as 'the right one': 'The different views one can have, say, of an apple: the view of the little boy, who has to crane his neck to get just a glimpse of the apple on the table-top, and the view of the master of the house, who takes the apple and freely hands it to his companion at the table.' Wallace Stevens also wrote about the fallacy of taking one view of a situation as the true one, but 'Thirteen Ways of Looking at a Blackbird' is a poem that opens you to the richness and complexity of the world and our perception of it, while Kafka's feels very different. This is a little family drama, such as we find elaborated in the *Letter to His Father*. The child here peeps over the edge of the table, longing for the apple he sees there, just as the 'master of the house' (a terrible term for the father), takes it and hands it to his guest, totally ignoring the gazing child.

'Early morning in bed', he notes the next day. And then there follows one of Kafka's most fascinating and thought-provoking interrogations of the rich store of narratives that have come down to us out of the past. This time, as with the little story of the River of Death, he goes back to Homer, to the story of Odysseus and the Sirens. Kafka's take on this is two pages long, interrogating the episode with relentless attention. Though Brod gave it a title, there is none in Octavo Notebook G. It begins in Kafka's best lawyerly manner: 'Proof [*Beweis*] that inadequate, even childish measures, may serve to rescue one from peril'. A new paragraph provides the example: 'To protect himself from the Sirens Ulysses stopped his ears with wax and had himself bound to the mast of the ship.' This is not how Homer tells it. His more realistic story

describes how Ulysses, keen to hear the Sirens sing, had himself bound to the mast of the ship so that he would not be able to respond to their call and go to his death, and put wax in the ears of his crew so that they would not hear and so would row on. But who is to question so authoritatively presented an account as Kafka's? It was well known, he goes on, that such things were of no use whatsoever, that the song of the Sirens could pierce through everything and the longing of those who heard them would be such that it would have broken far stronger bonds than mere chains. But Ulysses, though he might have heard of this, did not think about it: 'He trusted absolutely in his handful of wax and his fathom of chain, and in innocent elation [*in unschuldiger Freude*] over his little stratagem sailed out to meet the Sirens.'

Now Kafka adds a new element: 'The Sirens have a still more fatal weapon than their song, namely their silence.' It is conceivable – though it has never happened – that someone might escape their singing, 'but from their silence certainly never'. And indeed, when Ulysses approached them that day, 'these potent songstresses' did not sing, whether because they thought only their silence would vanquish him or because – one of those delightful, unexpected, Kafka details – 'the look of bliss on the face of Ulysses, who was thinking of nothing but his wax and his chains, made them forget their singing'. But Ulysses 'did not hear their silence', he thought they were singing. And soon – another turn of the narrative screw – 'all this faded from his sight as he fixed his gaze on the distance, the Sirens literally vanished before his resolution, and at the very moment when they were nearest to him he knew of them no longer'.

And now Kafka adds a final twist. The Sirens actually no longer had any desire to draw him to destruction, 'All they wanted was to hold as long as they could the radiance that fell from Ulysses' great eyes.' Had they possessed consciousness they would have been annihilated at that moment, he says,

but as it was nothing happened, they clung to their rock and Ulysses sailed on.

The legal language returns to nail the story into place in the concluding paragraph: 'A codicil to the foregoing has been handed down.' Ulysses, 'it is said (*sagt man*)' was such a 'cunning fox' that 'perhaps he had really noticed, although here the human understanding is beyond its depth, that the Sirens were silent, and opposed the aforementioned pretense to them and the gods merely as a sort of shield'.

Readers of Homer have long commented on the lack of interiority in the narratives, and the more perceptive among them have understood this as a mark of their power. It was a staple of German Romantic thought that Homer and Shakespeare belonged to an earlier, more innocent age (and the adulation of Goethe often went with the idea that he too had somehow, even though he lived in a self-conscious age, managed to retain that Homeric innocence). In these pages of his Zürau notebook Kafka does not lament a lost time, he asks instead how we can find that innocence in today's critical age. He is not interested in the varieties of primitivism for which modern artists, faced with this dilemma, have often reached. Innocence is a wonderful thing, perhaps the essential thing for the storyteller and perhaps even for the human being, but, as Kafka's critique of Dickens suggests, reliance on that today can only lead to sentimentality and falsehood. More: it can lead to internal strife which can only be described as a form of suicide. What is needed is a way of appeasing the demons of self-consciousness, and one way, the way of Cervantes, is to let them have their way by means of a fiction which will include both the innocent Don and his down-to-earth squire. Homer, belonging to an older culture, could create an innocence which was yet full of cunning ('many-wiled [*polumetis*]' is his favourite epithet for Odysseus). We can no longer do that. Or perhaps we can. Perhaps Kafka's telling of this story allows him, for a moment, to inhabit that older world of the cunning/innocent Ulysses.

There is more in the notebook for that day, 23 October 1917. 'Afternoon,' he notes, giving us a glimpse of daily life in the village, 'before the funeral of an epileptic drowned in the well.' This is followed by a brief comment on how 'to know yourself' does not mean 'observe yourself', which is the admonition of the serpent, and this leads to a critique of psychology and of the 'make yourself the master of your actions' admonition, that staple of self-improvement manuals, which, he suggests, only reinforces our bondage to the serpent.

With that the extraordinary creative outpouring of those four mid-October days comes to an end.

Late October

On the 22 October Kafka had sent a postcard to Brod about his visit to Komotau, which had by then been rescheduled for the 27th. Kafka, it will be remembered, was to join Brod and his wife there and travel back with them to Prague. But he was getting cold feet: 'If it were not for your Komotau trip I would not be going to Prague yet, not for two weeks at least. It is not only the life here that is beneficial, but also its continuity, and that is what the journey would destroy.' Being Kafka, he goes on to say that though he is feeling perfectly well he is not eating and Dr Pick (his main reason for going to Prague) might insist that he leave Zürau, 'the best place for me', and move to a sanatorium. Besides, other reasons for going to the capital are to see his dentist and pay a call on the Institute, and the thought of both depresses him. Altogether what he sees in store for him is 'an exchange of freedom for servitude and sorrow'.

Such thoughts, no doubt, are what kept him from writing anything in the octavo notebook on the 24th, while the 25th begins unpromisingly: 'Sad, jumpy, physically unwell, dread of Prague, in bed'. There follows a page-long unresolved story

about a close-knit community, which ends: 'So they always stood by each other and even after death they did not desert the community but rose to heaven dancing in a ring. All in all it was a vision of the purest childlike innocence to see them fly. But since everything, when confronted with heaven, is broken up into its elements, they fell down with a crash (*stürzten sie ab*), veritable slabs of rock.'

He leaves this and starts a new paragraph: 'A first sign of understanding is the wish to die. This life seems unbearable, another unattainable. One is no longer ashamed of wanting to die; one begs to be moved out of the old cell, which one hates, into a new one which one must learn to hate. One is moved by a certain residual faith that, during transport, the master will happen to come along the corridor, look at the prisoner and say: "This man is not to be locked up again. He comes to me."'

Here it is again (it is never far away in these pages), the folly of hope that things will get better, the hope that one will not die – and the persistence of hope. Again it is left open whether this is a good or a bad thing. From the way the paragraph develops it appears at first as if the persistence of hope merely shows that the idea of the first sign of understanding having dawned is an illusion. We think it has, we think we are no longer ashamed of wanting to die, only to discover, when it comes to it, that we don't want to at all. But by this stage we have left the rather abstract opening sentence behind and begun to inhabit a person.

Kafka would copy this paragraph into the new anthology on the blank sheet numbered 13, no doubt feeling that his personal fears and anxieties had a universal significance. There are no more entries, either in the diary or in the octavo notebook for the rest of the month, which was no doubt taken up with the Prague visit, the first he had made since his departure a month and a half earlier.

A Good Deal of Swinishness

His lightning visit to the city did not go well. The dentist broke his tooth, his superiors at the insurance company were no more willing to grant him early retirement than they had been in September, and he missed seeing Felix Weltsch. 'On my return I found Zürau in no way disappointing', he writes to Weltsch, after excusing himself. 'But,' he goes on in characteristic Kafka style, 'this is not the moment to sing its praises as truth requires, for my stomach is slightly upset and there is some unfamiliar noise about the house, never before noted at this time of day, which bothers me as I occasionally try to reassess my resources (certainly a sensible thing to do). You see, from the start I brought a good deal of swinishness here from Prague, something I must always reckon with. Agricultural metaphors will always be useful out here.'

To Brod, as we might expect, he is more open: 'I don't want to make much of the suffering associated with the unlived life, for in retrospect this suffering seems (and has always seemed so at all the small stages along the way) all too unreservedly mild compared to the facts whose pressure it has had to withstand. Still and all it was often too great to be borne much longer, or if it was not too great, was too meaningless. (In these morasses the question of meaning is perhaps admissible).' From childhood on, he goes on, he had toyed with suicide, or 'perhaps not suicide but the thought of suicide'. What deterred him from this was not any sort of cowardice but the thought that 'you, who can't do anything, imagine that you can do this', and if you could you would no longer have to. Later, he continues in this long letter to

his friend, thoughts of suicide left me. 'What now lay before me, when I was able to think clearly, over and beyond the confined hopes, the lonely raptures, the swollen vanities (the "over and beyond" that I was able to achieve only very rarely, as rarely as staying alive permitted) – what lay before me was a wretched life and a wretched death. "It was as if the shame of it must outlive him" are more or less the closing words of my *Trial*.'

This catches wonderfully well the constant ambivalence at the heart of Kafka's work and thought in these years: my suffering is unbearable, my suffering is, in reality, trivial; there is no meaning to anything, but is meaning so important? I should end it all, but how could someone who has never been able to do anything be able to do that? And then, at the end, parenthetically, the moments of bliss, clearly connected to his writing, are flagged up and then immediately dismissed as 'swollen vanities', and the return to the central leitmotif: a wretched life, a wretched death, pinned down, as it seems, by the quotation of the shocking final words of his own novel. I say 'as it seems' because the introduction of the quotation immediately raises the spectre again of performance, rhetoric – but then is that, to return to the key passage in his diary from the beginning of his stay in Zürau, 'a merciful surplus of powers at moments when the pain has… used up all my powers to the bottom of my being'? And, if so, then 'what sort of a surplus is it?' Is it, as no doubt the writing of that sentence from *The Trial* was, a cause for 'lonely raptures', or merely 'swollen vanities'?

There are more surprises in store in this letter to Brod. In a rare admission he goes on: 'I now see a new way out, which in its completeness had so far seemed impossible and which I could not have discovered with my own resources (unless the tuberculosis is to be reckoned among my own "resources"). I have only seen this way, I imagine I have seen it, I have not

yet begun to take it. It consists in this, or would consist in this – that I not only privately by an aside, as it were, but openly, by my whole behaviour confess that I cannot acquit myself here.' It is not a question of changing, he concludes, but of accepting himself and thus 'finding a coherence where before there was only meaninglessness'. We never normally hear this sort of thing from Kafka. Has he taken to heart the upbeat messages of Christian and Jewish theologians and philosophers of which he was usually so sceptical? Does he really believe that his illness can act as a Virgil to his Dante, leading him towards the truth in a way that would have been impossible on his own? That he can 'accept himself' and 'find coherence' in his life where before there was only meaninglessness? Of course he wants to believe this, but one wonders if he really does believe it or is only trying it out in an effort to get himself to believe it. And he has in any case qualified it by saying he has only 'seen' the way, or perhaps only imagined he has seen it, and certainly not 'begun to take it'.

However, it would be wrong to imagine that the struggle with himself was all that his life consisted of at the time. Enclosed with the letter to Brod is one to Brod's wife Elsa, telling her he is happy for her to read his newly published story, 'Jackals and Arabs', in public in December, as she hoped to do, but please to avoid all mention of this in the papers. Moreover, if she feels the text contains 'something dirty' she is not to remove it, for in that case she would soon find that there was nothing left to read. Clearly 'something dirty' does not refer to pornographic content but to the repulsive nature of the story, which brilliantly conveys the desert jackals' thirst for newly shed blood, and perhaps also to weaknesses in the writing, and the injunction merely repeats Kafka's heightened awareness of his inadequacies as a writer. To Brod, in another letter, he says, in a typically convoluted way, that he doesn't feel he has anything to offer for a potential reading in Frankfurt: 'If

I sent it I would be doing so out of vanity alone. If I don't send it, it is also vanity, but not vanity alone, therefore something better.'

Kafka, though, was happy enough to inform Brod that Wolff had sent him a statement about the sales of his first volume, *Meditations*, though he commented anxiously that there was nothing from the publisher about the new volume, *A Country Doctor*, scheduled for that year. He was also clearly very interested in what was going on in the world of books. He asks Weltsch how his book is progressing, comments on what Brod sends him of his own work, talks of a public reading by Mann he has heard went very well, and dreams of Werfel. He is keen on his friends sending him books and journals – the *Jüdische Rundschau, Aktion, Selbtswehr* – a special issue on the Balfour Declaration. As this last suggests, he is keenly following political events, and the course of the war: the Austrian victories in the Alps, Allenby's entry into Jerusalem. And he is quick to correct Brod as to Lenin's real name.

He resumes his walks to the surrounding villages and regales his friends with anecdotes about village life: 'The goose pond outside my window is already freezing over now and then, the children are skating, and my hat, which the evening gale blew into the pond, had to be prised loose from the ice in the morning', he writes to Oskar Baum. 'One of the geese died of excessive stuffing… The goats have been to the billy (who seems to be a particularly handsome young fellow; one of the goats who had already been taken there had a flash of remembrance and ran back to him again all the way from our house), and soon the pig is going to be slaughtered without more ado.' To Brod he writes: 'Today a slaughtered goose lay outside in the rain looking like someone's dead aunt.'

In short, nothing was keeping him from his routine and his notebook.

A Frightful Mute and Mighty Race

Nothing, that is, except for one thing. This time not an importunate fiancée from Berlin but a creature he had not hitherto encountered. Here is how he described it to Weltsch: 'The first fatal flaw of Zürau: a night of mice, a fearful experience.' My hair is no whiter than yesterday, he goes on, but it was a gruesome experience. 'Here and there previously… in the night I had heard a delicate nibbling, once in fact I started out of bed all atremble and had a look round and the noise stopped at once – but this time it was an uproar. What a frightful mute and mighty race this is! Around 2am I was wakened by a rustling around my bed and from then on the rustling did not stop until morning. Up the coal box, down the coal box, across the room they ran, describing circles, nibbling at wood, peeping softly while resting, and all along there was that sense of silence, of the secret labour of an oppressed proletarian race to which the night belongs. To preserve my sanity I decided that the noise was concentrated around the stove, which stands at the other end of the room. But it was everywhere and it reached its peak when a whole swarm of them leapt down together somewhere. I was completely helpless, could feel nothing in my whole being to cling to. I did not dare get up, light the lamp. All I could manage was a few shouts with which I tried to intimidate them. So the night passed. And in the morning my disgust and misery were such that I could not get up but remained in bed till one o'clock, straining my ears to hear what one tireless mouse was doing in the wardrobe, either finishing the work of the night before or getting a start on the next night's assignment. Now I have taken a cat (which I secretly hated all along) into my room, and must often shoo her away as she tries to jump into my lap (writing interrupted); if she makes a mess I must go and fetch the maid from the ground floor; when she (the cat) is good,

she lies by the stove while at the window one early riser of a mouse scratches unequivocally. Today everything is spoiled for me here, even the good coarse smell and taste of the farm bread is mousy.'

Soon news of Kafka's mouse adventures had spread among his friends – as he perhaps intended. On 24 November he wrote to Brod: 'Plenty of leisure time but oddly enough none for letter-writing. Since the plague of mice, which you may have heard about (long interruption: I had to paint a box and a pot), I've really not had a room (that is, with the cat, but only with her, I can just about spend the night there). But I am in no mood to sit there and hear rustling, sometimes behind the basket, sometimes at the window (one hears every claw). There is also the cat; she is a very good little creature but I must always be on guard, while I am reading or writing, lest she jump on my lap, or be ready with the ashes when she makes her multiple messes, and that's a great bother. In short, I don't like being alone with the cat. With other people around it is less embarrassing, but then it's a considerable nuisance to undress in front of her, do one's exercises, go to bed.'

The vision of Kafka doing his exercises before going to sleep, embarrassed in front of the cat, and then getting into bed in his mouse-infested room deep in the Bohemian countryside is not one that would spring to the minds of most readers of *The Trial*, and yet it is not altogether unexpected. The child ashamed at the swimming baths before his powerful father and utterly unused to domestic animals might easily be embarrassed before the impassive gaze of this mouser. That of course does not stop it also being funny.

He moves on to other things, but returns to the mice towards the end of this long letter, showing just how obsessed he has become by them: 'If I still clung to the old principles – my time is the evening and the night – things would be bad with me, especially as the lighting is troublesome.

But since that is no longer so, since I am not writing at all, I don't have to strive for quiet, mouseless, brightly lit evenings and nights, though I don't dread them either. Instead I have the free morning hours to spend in bed (hardly is the cat put out in the morning when the little scratchings begin to be heard somewhere behind the wardrobe. My sense of hearing has become a thousand times sharper and has become more uncertain by the same proportions – if I rub my finger over the sheet I no longer know for certain whether I am hearing a mouse. But mice are not fantasies of mine, for the cat comes to me in the evening thin and is taken out in the morning fat), a few moments with a book (now it is Kierkegaard), towards evening a walk on the road, and this suffices me in my solitude. It is fulfilment enough and there is little need to complain.'

This image of Eastern serenity, already undercut by the account of the mice and the cat, gives way not exactly to a complaint but to the confession of another line of thought that has clearly been lying beneath all his protestations of satisfaction with his new rural life: 'Unless I were to complain,' he goes on, 'that it is humiliating to be cared for and surrounded by others who are working while I myself, without any visible sign of illness, am to all appearances incapable of any kind of decent work. Lately I tried to work just a little in the vegetable garden and keenly felt it afterwards.' 'Decent work' in this environment is work on the land. But that is not what Kafka had come to Zürau for.

If this is not writing then what is it?

If, on the other hand, by 'decent work' he meant fiction of the kind he had been producing for the past five years, then Kafka was not lying to Brod, though the volume of stories now with Wolff, which he insisted should open with

'The New Advocate' and which included 'Before the Law' and 'An Imperial Message', seemed to hover between fiction and parable in a such a way as to put into question any simple division between fiction and non-fiction. But if he was suggesting that he had simply stopped writing, then he was either lying or least being economical with the truth. For though in the month of November and for a good part of December Kafka's little octavo notebook did not fill up as quickly as it had in those hectic writing days of late October, on most days he was steadily adding to the little pieces he would later extract from his notebooks and which we know as the Zürau Aphorisms. By the end of the month he had moved from number 14 to 42. Clearly he was now firmly committed to a new, concentrated form of writing which would, he hoped, bring his personal feelings into line with more general philosophical, metaphysical and ethical concerns. But that what he had in mind or eventually realised was a 'treatise', as Paul North[1] suggests, seems to me to be going far too far.

On 3 November he jotted down in the octavo notebook: 'To Oberklee. Evening in room'. And then: 'If you were walking across a plain, had every intention of advancing, and still went backwards, then it would be a desperate matter, but since you are clambering up a steep slope, about as steep as you yourself are when seen from below, your backward movement can only be caused by the nature of the ground and you need not despair.' Neither the sentiment nor the manner of expression is new. Kafka admonishes himself not to take personally his failure to find 'the true path', or even to move forward in his life or his thought but rather to explore the possibility that this is perhaps the result of a false mindset, one that makes us

---

1 *The Yield: Kafka's Atheological Reformation*, Stanford University Press, 2015, *passim*.

think in terms of paths and goals. The problem is not Kafka or any other individual but 'the nature of the ground'. This is very close to the Wittgenstein of the *Investigations*. And yet the way he puts it, bringing in his size as a kind of measure (as we have seen from the early tale of Shamefaced Lanky, Kafka was always conscious of his thinness and tallness), and seeing himself from below as a poor creature trying to struggle up an almost vertical slope, as well as being the struggler on the slope, makes it far more of a little narrative or the record of a nightmare than Wittgenstein ever allows himself, for all his talk of ground and spades.

The only other comment in the notebook at this point is the mysterious: 'Best of intentions [*Guten Willen?*]. You couldn't stop your thoughts of Italy, you read P. Schlemiehl aloud.' Here Stach the biographer is helpful. He suggests that this probably refers to the girl Kafka had been very taken with in Riga on Lake Garda when on holiday there in 1913 and was still thinking of when, in Marienbad with Felice in 1916, one of their few happy times together, he read her Adelbert von Chamisso's story about a man who sells his shadow to the devil. If this is so, then what he seems to be hinting at here is that even at this moment he was thinking of another woman, that even 'with every intention of advancing' in his relationship with his fiancée he found himself falling backwards into the abyss of fruitless yearning for another, barely known woman. This is interesting and very possibly true, but it shows the dangers of moving directly from the life to the work. Kafka may have had such thoughts as he fashioned his little piece, but he was trying, in his 'aphorisms' and elsewhere in his octavo notebooks, to test how far his own life could illuminate the general predicaments of human beings in Europe in the modern era, and it is notable that he keeps the 'aphorism' about clambering up a steep slope (it became 14 in the projected anthology) separate from the painful memory.

There are no comments for 4 and 5 November, but on the 6th he produces two of his finest 'aphorisms', short, simple and resonant. The first is no doubt inspired by the walks he took that autumn: 'Like a path in autumn: scarcely has it been swept clear than it is once more covered with dry leaves.' *Wie ein Weg*. We are not told what is 'like' that path. He himself? His life? I'm not sure why but it seems to me that it would be much weaker if it started with: 'I feel like' or 'My life is like a path in autumn'. And the simplicity and brevity of it, almost but not quite a little glimpse of country life (that initial '*Wie*'), gives it a resonance missing from the greater length and complexity of the previous 'aphorism'. (I have to persist in putting the word in inverted commas because while it does not quite suit these pieces I have yet to find a term which does.)

The next is even shorter: 'A cage went out to catch a bird [*einen Vogel fangen*].' When Kafka came to copy this out onto sheet 16 of his little anthology he changed the last word to *suchen*, 'in search of'. Usually these changes barely alter the thrust of a piece, and not always for the better, but here the change of the one word immeasurably improves it. 'A cage went out to catch a bird' is a grim thought and there's an end to it; 'a cage went out in search of a bird' has the haunting, mysterious quality of the best of these pieces, for suddenly there is not a simple contrast between innocent victim and cruel world but both sides (as with the jackals and Arabs of his story of that name) are now identified with, felt for. We know cages are a bad thing, and it might be that this is a predatory cage, intent on grabbing a prisoner if it can; but we also know that a mother would go in search of her child to give it shelter, protection, so the cage here could also be a benign and caring thing, a protection and a source of comfort in an unpredictable world. All that in six simple German words: *Ein Käfig ging einen Vogel suchen*.

The 'aphorisms' come thick and fast in the next fortnight. 'Early morning in bed after evening spent gossiping', he notes

on 7 November. Then an injunction to himself to 'accept the coldness of the sword and the coldness of the stone', followed by what became 'aphorism' 17: 'I have never been in this place before: breathing works differently here and more dazzling than the sun shines the star beside it.' This brings out well how the first person in these little pieces is not Kafka but is not quite a generalised 'we' either. Even if we imagine he is talking about TB, that ailment only stands in for a spiritual lack of air. The effect of the first person is to make of this a challenge to the reader to enter the imaginative space of the piece. And what is this star that shines more brightly than the sun? Stach notes that a few weeks later Kafka jotted down in his notebook: 'Evil is the starry sky of the Good', while in a letter to Oskar Baum he was to refer to Kierkegaard as 'a star, but one that shines over a region that is almost inaccessible to me'. This is Stach's frequent method in the commentaries he appends to his edition of the 'aphorisms', but it rarely helps in individual cases. The reference to Kierkegaard, for example, is one of a number Kafka made to the Danish writer, all in the same vein: there is much to admire in him, much to feel close to, but in the end he inhabits a different world in his northern Protestant asceticism from that of the Jewish denizen of the dying Austro-Hungarian Empire. It is irrelevant to this piece. And as for the first quote, Kafka is not talking here about a starry sky but of a single star shining more brightly than the sun beside it. The piece, short as it is, is full of puzzles, but that does not mean that there are answers to them. It remains mysterious, though the mysteries feel more like puzzles unsolved than truths that can only be caught in his web of words, which is what is conveyed by the best of them.

There is nothing in either the diary or the octavo notebook for the following day but on 9 November, after noting 'To Oberklee', he jots down another little piece: 'If it had been possible to build the Tower of Babel without climbing up it, it would have been permitted.' This is the first of a long

series of reflections on the early chapters of Genesis, which in these years became a source of continual inspiration for Kafka, and he was to write about the Tower of Babel several times (in one version it becomes: 'We are digging the pit of Babel'). This version, though, which he later copied out into his new little anthology as number 18, only makes the rather banal point that the only reason the tower was destroyed was because men would use it as a way of reaching up to heaven, a point often made by the rabbis commenting on the text. In the Biblical story, the name of the tower suggests the Israelite belief that a city like Babylon, with its ziggurats, was a symbol of pride, of the idea that you could reach up into the sky and usurp God's power.

On 10 November, when Kafka for some reason returned to his diary for a couple of comments, in the little octavo notebook he merely noted 'Bed' and jotted down two further 'aphorisms'. The first, 'Don't let Evil believe you could keep secrets from it', one of many thoughts about the profound interconnection of good and evil and the difficulty of extricating the latter from one's life that pepper the notebooks; the second, quite different, and one of the most striking of the 'aphorisms': 'Leopards break into the temple and drink the sacrificial vessels dry; this is repeated over and over again; finally it can be calculated in advance and becomes part of the ceremony.' Is this a story or a parable? One thing it definitely is not is an aphorism in the accepted meaning of the word. But what exactly is it saying so enigmatically yet so authoritatively? Is it an anthropological observation or a comment on tradition? If the latter, is it to be taken as a good or a bad thing that the ceremony can now incorporate and thus render harmless the violent intrusion of the leopards? Is it an indictment of rituals or, on the contrary, a testament to their flexibility? Like so many of the most memorable of these short Zürau pieces, it goes on resonating for us a hundred

years after they were written precisely because they cannot quite be pinned down. And this not because they are nebulous, but because the little, half-glimpsed stories they tell keep us swinging from one perspective to another.

Having written these two pieces Kafka leaves a space and then adds: 'A good deal of agitation (Blüher, Tagger).' Hans Blüher was a notorious antisemite, author of the *Secessio Judaica*, and we have already seen Kafka's dismissal of Tagger's work in his diary. Clearly he is spending his days reading as well as dealing with mice, undertaking household tasks, walking the countryside and composing his short pieces.

There is nothing again the next day, but the entry for 12 November takes the same form as that for the tenth: a note about his condition ('Long time in bed, resistance [*Abwehr*, implying protecting oneself against something]', followed by more little pieces. On 19 October, remember, he had noted the need 'when the decisive moment comes [to] hold the totality of yourself collected in your hand like a stone to be thrown, a knife for the kill'. Now he returns to the image but gives it a new context that multiplies the ambiguities: 'As firmly as the hand grips the stone. But it grips it firmly only to fling it away all the further. But the path leads even into that distance.' *So fest wie die Hand*, like the earlier *Wie ein Weg im Herbst*, leads one to ask what the subject is: Life? My Life? Again, the precision which somehow does not clarify yet seems immediately understandable, drawing us into an ongoing inner dialogue. The German has *hält*, hold, and to hold firmly is to grip (Kaiser and Wilkins) or to grasp (Frisch). But is this the grip of anxiety or of confidence? Are we simply being told that in order to fling the stone far you have to have a firm hold of it? The *so* implies that this is not a simple observation of an act performed on a daily walk and the path (*Weg*) of the third sentence merely the route the walker is taking. And surely it would be more natural for

the walker to fling the stone to the side, into the fields or the forest, than straight along the path he is taking. And what are we to make of the *jene Weite*, that distance? 'But the path leads even into that distance. [*Aber auch in jene Weite führt der Weg.*]' This seems to suggest that however far you fling the stone there will always be a path leading to it. Suddenly the path does not seem benign but a form of imprisonment: you can never get away from it, can never send the stone free of you, however hard you try. We feel as we read these simple sentences that we are being told something that could not be said in any other way, but what exactly we are being told remains unclear. The physicality of the first part (we have all gripped a stone in order to throw it) comes up against the immateriality of the second (*Weite, Weg* – distance, way) and leaves us moved, yet uncertain as to why.

This is not the case with the next piece, which is only nine words long: 'You are the task. No pupil far and wide.' Again, each word is simple but we have difficulty making sense of how they fit together. And yet, the piece does not resonate as do the ones about the leopards or the stone. It remains abstract. What does the word 'task' (*Aufgabe*) signify here? And the word 'pupil' (*Schüler*)? Stach draws attention to 'you are' where we would have expected 'you have', but his comment that 'this has a hidden deeper meaning' takes us off on a wrong track, as so often with commentators on Kafka. The meaning is all on the surface, it is just a question of getting a handle on the piece, but how to do that?

I often feel, with these little 'aphorisms' as I do with some of Emily Dickinson's poems, such as:

Aurora is the effort
Of the Celestial Face
Unconsciousness of Perfectness
To simulate, to Us.

There's the sense, with both Dickinson and Kafka, that they know exactly what they are saying and that for them it's blindingly obvious, but for most of us, though we can guess at it, it remains opaque.

Clearly this 'aphorism' is connected to Kafka's feeling that what he has to do in his self-imposed exile in Zürau is to leave his previous life behind and start afresh. It has less to do with learning something than with re-orienting his whole being, but what such re-orientation entails is nothing less than the question of what life 'really' means, and that, naturally, is not forthcoming.

Another little 'aphorism' follows: 'From the true antagonist boundless courage flows into you.' This is easier to get a handle on for those familiar with Kafka. Many of the little fragments scattered throughout the diaries and notebooks have to do with fights, often with hand-to-hand combat, and in the larger unfinished works we could say that Josef K's antagonist in *The Trial* is the Court and K's in *The Castle* the castle authorities, and that problems arise and resolution cannot be achieved precisely because they are not 'true' antagonists but rather reflections of the protagonist. On the other hand, the first story Kafka fully acknowledged, 'The Judgement', does indeed pit the protagonist, Georg, against his father, and the story demonstrates how true an antagonist he is, all the more so as he had appeared at first to be nothing but a sick and dying old man. It seems as though the *agon* or trial of strength was the fulcrum on which Kafka's imagination turned, rather as the artist in his studio was for Picasso. If you can find a true antagonist, boundless strength will flow into you. The question is whether for modern man such an antagonist exists.

Does the next short piece help? It is almost as brief as the other: 'Grasping the good fortune that the ground on which you stand cannot be larger than the two feet covering it.' What difference would it make if the first word (the third in German – *Das Glück begreifen*) were absent? Clearly something has to be

grasped and such grasping is both necessary and difficult. Yet it's not an imperative, like 'Don't let Evil' etc., but a present participle (an infinitive in the German) and, like the words 'as' and 'like' in earlier 'aphorisms', what it does is to take us into an uncertain imaginative space where we seem to be overhearing a fragment of an inner conversation which has briefly surfaced. But what follows? Kafka repeats again and again, both in his diaries and notebooks and in his letters to Brod and Felice, that his great misfortune is that he has no solid ground to stand on – just as he has no tradition to rely on and no 'true antagonist' to wrestle with. Yet here he seems to be struggling with the notion that there is solid ground – but it is no larger than our two feet, which means that no two people share the same ground. But why is that considered good fortune? Or are the words ironic? Is this an assertion that psychology is all we have, that it will only keep reflecting the self we already know back to us, and that this is both a cause for relief and the source of all our anxieties and troubles?

The last of these 'aphorisms' composed on 12 November – but it's possible that he simply did not bother to date some of his entries – seems to continue the lines of thought of the last two: 'How can one take pleasure in the world unless one flees to it for refuge?' The last two words are added by both Wilkins and Kaiser and by Malcolm Pasley to help make sense of the piece. But even so it remains opaque because it is so abstract: what does 'pleasure' (*freuen*) mean here, what does 'the world' (*die Welt*)? And flees from where? Kafka cannot be saying that one must immerse oneself in the world, but then what is it he is saying? We sense that there is some sort of conflict between self and world, but without an image, a fiction, even a minimal one such as the path covered in autumn leaves, it fails to resonate.

The next date in the octavo notebook is 18 November, and the first entries are two more 'aphorisms' later copied out into the new little anthology. The first reads: 'There are countless hiding-places but there is only one rescue [*Rettung*], yet the

possibilities for rescue are as numerous as the hiding-places.' Kafka crossed this out after copying it later on sheet 26 of his little anthology, and in September 1920 he added (replaced it with?) 'There is a goal but no way, what we call a way is hesitation.' This is obviously part of his continuing struggle with the notion of a 'way', so much part of spiritual discourse, whether Christian or Buddhist. This, however, Kafka feels to be the problem rather than the solution, since it posits progress (advance along the path), which he does not believe corresponds to reality, either psychological or spiritual. But it seems to bear little relation to the thought of 1917, which is again both teasing and opaque. We are forced to ask, as so often with these pieces, what effort of the imagination is needed to make them cohere?

The next entry is opaque for another reason. Like other entries (5 and 43 for example) that he was evidently satisfied enough with to copy into the little anthology, it is too abstract for us to get any traction on it: 'To perform the negative is what is still required of us, the positive is already ours.' This is the language of countless books of philosophy and theology that were produced in the early years of the twentieth century, and only serves to remind us how different from that most of Kafka's work is, even when he is not at his best.

In the octavo notebook this is followed by a paragraph that seems at first to be describing a village scene Kafka had noted down, but which soon takes on a life of its own and becomes a recognisable Kafka story/fragment. This in turn is followed by two little pieces which might well have been included in the 'aphorisms' but weren't. The first is one of those gnomic but resonant sentences addressed both to himself and to us: 'You complain about the stillness, about the hopelessness of the stillness, the wall of the Good.' The second is another of those glancing references to the Bible, but this time to Moses and the burning bush in Exodus, not Genesis: 'The thornbush

is the old obstacle in the road. It must catch fire if you want to advance.'

Between 21 and 23 November there is a rush of thoughts connected with the notion of evil, nearly all in the new condensed style, but a couple of longer meditations as well. What became 'aphorisms' 28 and 29 read: 'When one has once taken evil (or Evil; since German nouns take capitals there is no way of knowing) into oneself it no longer demands that one believe in it'; and 'The ulterior motives with which you take evil/Evil into yourself are not your own but those of evil/Evil.' In October 1920 Kafka added a piece which does what the best of the compositions of 1917 do but which 28 and 29 signally fail to do: embody the feeling, or thought, in a memorable image or mini-drama: 'The animal wrests the whip from its master and whips itself in order to become the master, not knowing that this is only a fantasy produced by a new knot in the master's whiplash.' On that November day in 1917, however, he had to be content with his abstractions as he struggled to step outside himself and see himself/man from the outside. And, still pursuing this elusive goal, he adds four more sentences, each separated from the others by a gap: 'Evil is whatever distracts.' 'Evil knows of the Good, but Good does not know of Evil.' 'Self-knowledge is something only Evil has.' 'One method that Evil has is the dialogue.'

He is struggling with the thought that evil/Evil cannot be separated from thinking and expression, so that the very need to think things through is itself already a sign that evil has taken hold. Soon he is going to relate this to the stories told in Genesis 2–3, but at this point he merely notes it and follows it with a comment on 'the laws' and 'the law-giver', suggesting again that he is reading and thinking about Exodus as well as Genesis. Then comes the bleak 'In a certain sense the Good offers no comfort', which Kafka later crossed out after copying it onto sheet 30. This in turn is followed by two thoughts on

miracles, the second of which is itself a miracle of concision: '*Wer Wunder tut, sagt: Ich kann die Erde nicht lassen.* (He who works miracles says: I cannot *lassen* the earth).' Kaiser and Wilkins translate *lassen* as 'let go'. But what does this mean? Kafka, as is his way in these octavo notebooks, leaves it at that.

On the 23 November he returns to his old anxieties about the relation of writing to truth: does simply writing something down distort it? Does it help the writer or does it, by allowing him to imagine it is helping him, only keep him from reality? 'Distributing belief correctly between one's own words and one's own convictions', he admonishes himself. 'Not letting a conviction escape like steam in the very moment when one becomes aware of it. Not shifting onto the words the responsibility imposed by the conviction. Not letting convictions be stolen by words.' This is followed by two pieces that became 'aphorisms' 31 and 32, and which between them demonstrate how absurd it is to see these as a unit, so different are they in their mode of expression. The first drags to its conclusion in leaden philosophical prose, which Shelley Frisch does her best to render into English but which even she cannot redeem: 'I don't strive for self-mastery. Self-mastery means wanting to be effective at some random point within the infinite radiations of my spiritual life. But if I do have to describe such circles around myself I had better do so inactively, merely gazing in awe at the colossal complex and taking home with me only the invigoration that this sight provides *e contrario*.' The next, by contrast, is one of the gems of the collection: 'The crows maintain that a single crow could destroy the heavens. That is incontestable, but it proves nothing against the heavens, for heaven simply means the impossibility of crows.' This could be Wittgenstein, but he would never have included a phrase like 'That is incontestable [*Das ist zweifellos*]', which suggests a dialogue with himself; he would have set it down as a firmly held paradox for the reader

to work at. It is because Kafka seems to be letting us in to his own struggles to understand that the best of these little pieces are so unsettling.

The same contrast is to be found in the next two 'aphorisms', 33 and 34, though not quite for the same reasons. The first lacks resonance not because it is mired in 'philosophical' prose but because its use of Christian imagery and its mixture of homoeroticism and masochism feel strangely *fin-de-siècle*: 'Martyrs do not underestimate the body; they let it be raised up on the cross, and in this respect are in accord with their opponents.' The second compresses history and deals with modern life as well in twenty plain words: 'His exhaustion is that of a gladiator after the fight, his work was the whitewashing of one corner of a clerk's office.' This picks up a frequent Kafka theme of imagining we are making a heroic effort which will finally get us to where we want to be when in fact, looked at from the outside, we have barely begun. Mao's remark that even the Long March required a first step belongs to a different, optimistic, Kafka would say idealistic, world.

As November wore on, Kafka's production of these compressed thoughts showed no sign of diminishing. On the 24th or 25th came: 'Human judgement of human actions is true and void, first true and then void.' Only a family member can judge a family member, he notes in the next paragraph, but by the same token the judgement of a family member is meaningless. He tries a more compressed form of this: 'Only he who is a party can really judge, but as a party he cannot judge.' In other words, we need a true adversary, someone who both understands us and can judge impartially – but if he understands he will not be impartial, so where will we ever find a true adversary? Then comes a more personal thought, which starts out abstractly but veers at once into authentic Kafka territory: 'There is no having, only a being, a state of being that strives for its last breath, for suffocation.' Why did

he choose to include *this* in the little collection (on sheet 35) but not the previous two? The next thought as well seems too personal and biographical to be included, but it goes down on sheet 36: 'In the past I didn't understand why I got no answer to my questions; today I don't understand how I could believe I was entitled to ask. But I didn't really believe, I only asked.' Is the 'I' here, like Ulysses, innocent enough to ask when by all rational and even psychological accounts he would not be able to do any such thing? It doesn't quite feel like that. It feels more resigned to failure than oblivious even to the possibility of failure, which is how Ulysses is portrayed in the little piece about him and the Sirens. The difference between the two is minimal yet absolute, showing how slippery these little pieces are, how they are stabs in the dark for Kafka rather than perfectly turned thoughts handed out to his readers.

The next thought, returning to the question of being and possessing, contrives a remarkable transition from the abstract to the concrete, from the mind to the body: 'His answer to the assertion that, while he might perhaps have possessions, he had no being, was only a trembling and a beating of the heart.' Here we feel Kafka is getting close to his quarry: the answer to all those 'philosophical' questions about self and being and our place in the universe lies not in 'philosophy' but in our sense of suffocation or a fit of trembling. You may have, indeed perhaps should have, no being, but as long as you are alive you will be subject to trembling and have a heart that beats.

He returns to thoughts of celibacy and suicide, marriage and martyrdom, but swerves again to formulate what became 38: 'Someone [*Einer*] was astonished by how easily he was moving along the road to eternity; it was because he was dashing down it.' Wittgenstein put it more clearly if less pithily in *Zettel*, para. 456: 'Some philosophers (or whatever you like to call them) suffer from what may be called "loss of problems". Then everything seems quite simple to them,

no deep problems seem to exist any more, the world becomes broad and flat and loses all depth, and what they write becomes immeasurably shallow and trivial.' For Kafka, though, unlike Wittgenstein, the entanglement of life and of writing about life is always plain to see.

Now comes a wonderful little piece: 'The good walk in step. Without knowing anything of them the others dance around them, dancing the dance of the age.' Amazingly, he did not include it in the little anthology, but the composer György Kurtág, a great reader and a man of rare insight, made of it the first 'fragment' in his great musical homage to a fellow central European Jew, *Kafka Fragments* for violin and soprano. And he was right to do so, for it contains that combination of opposed elements set in play one against the other without the writer/ speaker revealing which side he favours that is characteristic of Kafka at his best. Are 'the good' here really the good, or is it that they simply consider themselves the good? In that case they are really 'the bad', the conformists, and it is the dancers we should admire. But they too seem to be conformists in their own way, dancing the dance of the age. Are we to take them as innocent fools then, or Hasidic sages – or both? Kurtág's setting preserves the ambiguity, indeed revels in it.

Kafka was not done for the day. He returned to his thoughts about the insidious ways of evil: 'It is impossible to pay Evil in instalments – and one never stops trying to do so.' Does this mean that one should pay all at once then? And how does one do that? By developing TB? In 1920 he added a long second section to this, ostensibly about Alexander the Great, which picks up on the many other places in the collection where the gap between ambition and achievement is shown to be unbridgeable, but which seems to bear little relation to the thoughts about evil. And then comes a thought which has since been made famous by Stevie Smith's poem, 'Not Waving but Drowning': 'The man in ecstasy and the man

drowning – both throw up their arms.' This is followed by a little ditty, reminiscent of the eerie songs Kafka introduced into 'A Country Doctor', the story which, we have seen, was much in his mind at the time:

Ich kenne den Inhalt nicht
ich habe den Schlüssel nicht
ich glaube Gerüchten nicht
alles verständlich
denn ich bin es selbst.
I do not know the contents
I do not have the key
I do not believe the rumours
all quite understandable
for it is myself.

We are to think of him on those cold autumn days, as winter began to set in and less and less work was possible in the fields, pacing his room, sitting scribbling at his desk, going out for walks, returning, sitting down at his desk again, free for the first time in his life of pressures from his father or his office, no longer struggling with thoughts of marriage and Felice, trying doggedly to get to grips with the disaster that has befallen him, committed now to putting his chaotic thoughts and feelings into this new compressed form he has discovered – and yet conscious all the while that there is a profound contradiction between what it is he is trying to articulate and the old maker's pleasure in finding the right words, the right form, while the attempt to see yourself as you really are can never succeed, for you can never step outside yourself, however hard you try. And that too becomes the subject for meditation, for expression.

On 25 November he jotted down two thoughts which he later copied into his new little collection – and then crossed out. The first is another meditation on the notion of 'the path (*Der*

Weg)': 'The path is unending, nothing can be subtracted, nothing added, and yet everyone applies his own childish yardstick to it.' Again he is pushing at the thought that how we see and feel our lives is quite other than how our lives 'really' are. This has nothing to do with any injunction to 'face the inevitable', but is rather an attempt to grasp what our life is, not through looking inwards but through looking at ourselves from the outside, as embodied social animals existing in time. The second thought makes use of biblical terms – Christian biblical terms – to get a handle on the same problem: 'It is only the concept of time that makes us call the Last Judgement by that name; it is actually a court martial.' A court martial, we are made to understand, that lasts for each of us as long as we live.

The next day finds him returning to a subject that had obsessed him from the start of his stay in Zürau, vanity, after which comes a gnomic and abstract sentence, later copied out as 41, and then crossed out. Clearly he found it difficult to know what to include in the little anthology and what to leave out, and that may be one reason why, despite all the attention he lavished on it, he never brought that project to a conclusion. The final entry for the day leaves all thoughts behind to note his condition: 'Afternoon. Letting the head full of disgust and hatred sink upon the chest. Indeed – but what if someone is throttling you?' The image of the head sinking onto the chest as a sign not just of despair but almost of petrifaction is one Kafka had long resorted to in order to convey moments of utter hopelessness. What is new here is the last sentence. Who would it be throttling you? God? Evil? Life personified?

He leaves it at that and the next entry, under 27 November, opens with the mundane: 'Reading newspapers'. As we have seen, Kafka was an avid reader of the papers and a keen follower of political and military developments. And these were tumultuous times for Europe and the Middle East. Not only had war been raging on the entire continent for three

years, but suddenly there was chaos in Russia as various factions of Left, Right and Centre struggled for dominance after the February Revolution and the flight of the Tsar, leading to huge German advances on the Eastern front. On 2 November the Balfour Declaration had transformed the situation in Palestine, though exactly how was not yet clear, and on 11 December General Allenby would enter Jerusalem at the head of British troops, a herald of the end of the Ottoman Empire. Quite a lot for the denizens, especially the Jewish denizens, of central Europe to take in.

Perhaps that is why the next entry in the little octavo notebook, dated '31 (perhaps 1.12.)' (there are of course only thirty days in November) concerns the coming of the Messiah: 'The Messiah will come as soon as the most unbridled individualism is possible in faith – as soon as nobody destroys this possibility and nobody tolerates that destruction, that is, when the graves open.' This, he goes on, is perhaps Christian doctrine, with its implication 'of the resurrection of the Mediator in the individual human being', yet it clearly resonates with him, for he develops it in one of those passages that suggest he is writing more in hope than in expectation: 'Believing means liberating the indestructible element in oneself, or, more accurately, liberating oneself, or, more accurately, being indestructible, or, more accurately, being.' But his heart is clearly not in this, for he ends with the paradox: 'Idleness is the beginning of all vice, the crown of all virtues.'

He may have gone for a walk to clear his head, for the next entries, still under the same date, consist of three of the most disturbing of the meditations in the little anthology, 43, 44 and 45. Gone is the Christian imagery and the attempt at philosophical analysis; instead we have three little dramas, starkly presented. The first is one of the most disconcerting products of those Zürau months: 'As yet the hounds are still playing in the courtyard, but their prey will not escape,

however fast it may already be charging through the forest.' The dogs are '*Jagdhunde*', hunting dogs, but the prey '*durch die Wälder jagt*', literally 'hunts through the forest', stressing the bond between the pursuer and pursued. And the 'as yet (*noch*)' with which it opens is magical. We can abstract from this and say it means 'we cannot escape our fate', but then we have lost everything. Kafka may be thinking of his illness or of his life in general, but the point is that what he conjures up is a central European world of hunting, slavering hounds, forests, and the terror of the prey.

The next little 'aphorism' stands back from such visceral images and presents us with one of those wry self-admonitions that are another of Kafka's modes: 'Ludicrous, the way you have girded your loins for this world.' In other words, no amount of self-protection – or bravado – will protect you from what the world has in store for you. The third combines rural imagery and address to the self to produce a slightly blurred impression: 'The more horses you put to the task the faster it goes – that is to say, not the tearing of the block out of the base, which is impossible, but the tearing of the straps and as a result the merry unencumbered journey.' We are back imaginatively in the world of 'A Country Doctor' and conceptually with the Wittgensteinian critique of those who suffer from a 'loss of problems', and go on their merry unencumbered journey. This is immediately followed by one of the leitmotifs of Octavo Notebook G, couched, as so often, in Christian imagery: 'The various forms of despair at the various stations on the road', and finally a stray thought which Kafka was to rephrase slightly when he copied it into the new little anthology on page 46 before crossing it out: 'In German "being" and "belonging to him" are designated in the same way, with *sein*.'

DECEMBER

Father, Mice, Cat

Nothing changed much for Kafka as winter set in. He went for his walks, observed village life, wrote long letters to his friends, struggled to understand, shaped his little 'aphorisms'. In Prague, though, something had changed. He had been feeling increasingly concerned about going on hiding his condition from his parents, and in mid-November asked Ottla on her next visit to let their father in on the secret, though keeping it from their mother. Ottla, in a letter to Josef David of 23 November, recounts how the news was received: 'Yesterday evening, soon after I arrived, at a moment when Mother was in the kitchen, I revealed to him why my brother had obtained his leave. I thought that if he didn't know the real reason Father would get cross when he perceived Franz doing nothing for so long. But I had never imagined that the news would make such an impression on him. He is worried and I have constantly to reassure him that in Zürau my brother has everything he needs and is in no danger.' This is fascinating because we invariably see Hermann Kafka through his son's eyes, and however much Kafka insists that his is bound to be a false and biased view his writing is so powerful, especially in the *Letter to his Father*, written two years later, that it is bound to colour our view of him – his constant assertion of his authority, his repulsive manners, such as cutting his fingernails at the dining table, his surreal threats such as 'I'll tear you to pieces like a fish', his rudeness to his staff, his rages. But here we see not only his children's fear of him ('I thought that if he didn't know the real reason Father would get cross when he perceived Franz doing nothing for so long'), but the terrible misunderstandings at the heart of this family drama

as they are at the heart of most family dramas. Hermann, who had always felt it to be his task to make sure his family was well-provided for and to leave the emotions to the women, is profoundly shocked to hear that his son has a potentially life-threatening illness and is immediately solicitous, worrying, as all Kafka's friends had worried, that retreating to this village in the middle of nowhere is hardly the most sensible move for an invalid. Enjoined to silence by Ottla, according to Stach he was not able to keep the secret from his wife for more than a few weeks, much to his son's disgust.

All that, however, was in faraway Prague. In Zürau Kafka had more pressing things on his mind. 'Dear Max,' he writes at the beginning of the month, 'Pure chance that I have not answered until today; other reasons are room, light, mice. But it is not a question of nervousness or adjusting from city conditions to village. My reaction to the mice is one of sheer terror. To analyse its source would be the task of a psychoanalyst, which I am not. Certainly this fear, like an insect phobia, is connected with the unexpected, uninvited, inescapable, more or less silent, persistent, secret aim of these creatures, with the sense that they have riddled the surrounding walls through and through with their tunnels and are lurking within, that the night is theirs, that because of their nocturnal existence and their tininess they are so remote from us and thus outside our power.' However, he goes on, and we can see before our eyes the transition taking place from terror at the mice, a terror which, as he recognises, has its seeds far back in his childhood, to pleasure in the story he is conjuring up for his friend: 'For the past few days I have found a quite satisfactory if only provisional solution. Overnight I leave the cat in the empty room next to mine, thereby preventing her from dirtying my room. (How hard it is to arrive at an understanding with an animal on this question. There seem to be only misunderstandings, for the cat knows, through blows and other explanations, that there is something undesirable about

taking care of her needs of nature and that the place for it has to be carefully chosen. So what does she do? Well, for example she chooses a spot that is dark, that will in addition show me her affection and will have other qualities she finds pleasant. But from the human side this spot happens to be the inside of my bedroom slipper. So here is another misunderstanding, and there are as many of these as there are nights and needs of nature.) This also averts the possibility of her jumping onto my bed. But I also have the reassurance that I can let her into my room should things get bad. These past few nights have been quiet, at least there were no unequivocal signs of mice. But it does not help one get to sleep to take over a portion of the cat's assignment and sit upright or leaning forward in bed with pricked ears and glowing eyes. But that was only on the first night. It is getting better now.' Kafka, though, cannot let the story go. Brod has suggested mousetraps, but he objects to this: traps exterminate the mice they kill, but what of the others? Cats, on the other hand, drive all the mice away by their mere presence, 'even by their mere excretions'. And he reverts to 'the first cat night, which followed the great mouse night'. 'To be sure,' he says, 'the room did not become "as still as a mouse", but none of them continued running around. The cat sat in the corner by the stove, depressed by the enforced change of place, and did not stir. But that was enough; it was like the presence of the teacher, there was only some chattering here and there in the mouseholes.'

This is going from paranoia to P.G. Wodehouse to paranoia and back to Wodehouse in a few sentences and with remarkable ease. And Kafka is aware of this: 'You write so little about yourself', he says to Brod when his story comes to an end, 'so I retaliate with mice'. And to Baum at the same time: 'What I wrote about the mice was only in fun.' Except that Kafka, being Kafka, cannot let it rest there. 'It would only become serious when you heard the mice. I hardly think any

writer or musician can sleep so soundly as not to hear them, or that any sensitive heart could not be overcome, if not by fear, at least by disgust or sadness. But that is only said in fun, since thanks to the cat I have not heard anything suspicious for quite a while.'

Friends and Foes

Mice were not the only thing on his mind that December. He was making efforts to help a local farmer find a family in Prague that would take in the farmer's eighteen-year-old daughter who wanted to spend three months there learning Czech and taking piano lessons. He was also busy reading whatever books and magazines his friends sent him. 'If you could recommend a well-printed and easily purchasable edition of Augustine's Confessions (that is the title, isn't it?) I would gladly order it', he writes to Weltsch before himself recommending Solomon Maimon's *Autobiography* ('an excellent book in itself, and a harsh portrait of a man haplessly torn between East and West European Judaism'). To Brod, who has sent him his play *Esther*, he writes that he has read it aloud to Ottla in a single session ('a feat of breath, wouldn't you say?', he adds, thoughts of his TB never far away) and is full of admiration for certain parts of it. But he then proceeds to criticise the rest, pulling no punches and concluding by saying he feels that 'certain wrong paths are followed' which, though they strengthen the play as a work of art, leave him feeling that 'they represent a sacrifice to art and are harmful to you'. An interesting observation that tells us a great deal about Kafka's own perpetual self-criticism, heightened, as we have seen, in these Zürau months. There is clearly a difference between taking one's art in a certain direction in order to be popular with the public

('a sacrifice to art'), and doing so to make it better, truer, but that difference is not necessarily obvious. Kafka is always on the look-out for the former in the work of himself and his friends because he has the unshakable conviction that it is a betrayal of the high calling of art ('a sacrifice to truth'?) and a form of self-aggrandisement and thus, ultimately, of self-harm. Yet however harsh his criticism of his friend, he always wants to remind him, as he does at the end of another letter: 'Max – I miss you… but the knowledge that you exist, that I have you, that letters come from you, gives me peace.'

He is just as forthright to those he hardly knows. To Josef Körner, the editor of the nationalist journal *Donauland*, who had praised him in its pages, talking of his 'noble and clear style' and calling *The Metamorphosis* his 'so far most accomplished work', and who had asked him for a contribution, he writes of how 'reading that praise produced in me an orgy of vanity but also an anxious feeling of having seduced you'. Then he gets down to business: 'You will surely allow me to speak frankly? *D.* strikes me as an unmitigated lie. It can have the best people connected with it, its literary department can be run, as you will no doubt run it, with vigour and the best of intentions. But the impure cannot be made pure, especially when it inevitably must go on pouring out impurities from its source. By this I do not mean to say anything against Austria, against militarism, against the war, for it is not any of these that repels me in *D.*, but rather the special mixture, the studied and outrageous mixture, out of which the magazine is concocted.'

There are three possible reasons for my associating myself with such a journal, he goes on in his most lawyerly fashion. The first is that you are one of the editors, but my respect for you should not be allowed to cloud my judgement; the second is that it might help me in my desire to avoid being called up, but that is highly unlikely anyway because I am a sick man; the third is the thought of possible remuneration, but at the

moment I do not need it. He ends, though, by reiterating his plea for Körner to send him an essay of his on Achim von Arnim, the German Romantic poet.

We have become used to Kafka being tough on himself and are inclined to view this as masochism, but the truth is that he was just tough on the world, and that included himself. Like his fellow Jews in the last days of the Austro-Hungarian Empire, Schoenberg, Krauss and Wittgenstein, he had what some might consider inordinately high principles and a very low tolerance threshold: a lie, any form of baseness, was for them not an isolated incident but a tear in the fabric of the world. Uncomfortable people to be with, no doubt, but at least no one could accuse them of being neither hot nor cold: they burned and they froze.

And Kafka at any rate was also the most caring of friends. In those cold weeks of November and December 1917 Brod's marriage was on the verge of collapse. In an all too familiar way he had fallen in love with a younger woman but could not imagine leaving his wife. Kafka was a sympathetic listener while insisting that he found it impossible to offer advice, for 'I believe such advice can only be given in the spirit of the get-a-grip-on-yourself pedagogy, which I only see as more and more impotent'. Yet he also spent time and effort writing to the aggrieved wife, Elsa, who had clearly written to him about Max. 'Your grief springs from love', he writes. 'But you have the true opportunities of love. You are looking for an advocate. But Max, when he is clearheaded, is your strongest advocate. You see (or at least you let your eyes drift that way) a possibly remote incidental as the main thing. You grow confused and thereby neglect calmly to be what you are.' However, he ends, 'I realise it is only too easy to spout principles at someone in distress. And you would be right, and every time I think about you this feeling shames me. But should shame make us keep silent or even lie? Especially in this, when we are both at one in our concern for Max.'

The Octavo Notebook Keeps Filling Up

And all the while the work in the octavo notebook went on. The struggle to find a form to contain the thoughts and feelings tearing him apart was over. In the month of November he produced roughly thirty of the pieces he would later copy out into the little anthology he was planning; in the period 1–20 December (after which he went to Prague till the end of the year) he produced another twenty-five or so, bringing the total for the period to more than half of the final 106. Though there are still a few occasional longer entries that don't get included in the anthology and the occasional comments on daily moods and events, the bulk of the entries in the octavo notebooks now consists of the 'aphorisms'.

On 2 December he begins with one of the longest of these, 'aphorism' 47: 'They were offered the choice between becoming kings or kings' messengers. As is the way with children they all wanted to be messengers. That is why there are only messengers, they charge through the world and, since there are no kings, call out their now meaningless messages to one another. They would gladly put an end to their miserable lives but don't dare do so because of their oaths of allegiance.' This is a variant on a familiar Kafka theme and would not be out of place in a volume of stories: in our world there is no source of authority, there are only opinions; no original story, only versions. It reminds us how artificial is the distinction between stories and 'aphorisms', a distinction which Kafka himself encouraged with his attempt to compile an anthology of his short Zürau meditations. But where Kafka is concerned there is no clear separation between novels, stories, parables, aphorisms, diary entries and even letters at times. They overlap and share characteristics; they are all part of the 'Kafka family'. What is charming about this particular example is the act of seeing as the outcome of a children's game what is elsewhere

seen as a Fall, and the phrase 'As is the way with children they all wanted to be messengers (*Nach Art der Kinder wollten alle Kuriere sein*),' which gives the whole thing a naturalness and a sweet innocence closer to fairy tale than any of the other pieces in the collection, despite the grim conclusion.

'Stormy night,' the next entry (4 December) begins, 'in the morning telegram from Max, truce with Russia.' Winter in the Bohemian countryside and world-shaking events. One of the main factors in the Russian revolutions of 1917 was the discontent of the common soldiers with an incompetent, smug and uncaring officer corps and Tsarist government, a discontent fomented by Germany in the hope that chaos in Russia would lead to a truce on the Eastern front. The implications for men of military age in Germany and the Austro-Hungarian Empire were of course enormous, and it is no surprise that Brod would want to apprise his friend of the fact that a truce with Russia had been agreed. But after noting this down Kafka returns to his totally apolitical thoughts: 'The Messiah will come only when he is no longer necessary; he will come only one day after his arrival, he will not come on the last day but on the last day of all (*Er will nicht am letzten Tag kommen, sondern am allerletzten*).' He chose not to include this in the little anthology but did include two further, briefer and more abstract thoughts (48 and 49): 'To believe in progress does not mean believing any progress has been made. That would not be belief.' And: 'A is a virtuoso and heaven is his witness.' This deploys a word unusual for Kafka, *Ein Virtuose*, suggesting a showman, and one, moreover, pleased with his showmanship, both notions carrying negative connotations for him. It compresses into ten words what *Don Quixote* develops over 600 pages and Kierkegaard's *On Authority and Revelation* over 250: that in our modern world where there is no central source of authority men can only claim to speak authoritatively by claiming to have had a personal revelation

from God – a claim rightly greeted with scepticism by those around them.

On 6 December he jots down: 'Pig-slaughtering (*Schweineschlachten*)', a central activity in the autumn in rural communities and one that takes a long time and is painful to watch for any city folk, as the many viewers of such a scene in Ermanno Olmi's *The Tree of the Wooden Clogs* will attest. And remembering Kafka's lifelong vegetarianism and his lovely portrait of Ottla's pig in his letter to Elsa Brod, we must wonder what feelings the single word suppresses. It is followed by the enigmatic: 'Three different things: looking at oneself as something alien, forgetting the sight, remembering the gaze. Or only two different things, for the third includes the second.' Again, a film can help us fill it out, this time Beckett's *Film*, in which our refusal to look at ourselves from the outside and our memory of what such a look entails is turned into painful slapstick. Kafka's remark, along with the next one, 'Evil is the starry sky of the Good', would have seemed to be strong candidates for the little anthology, but he chose not to include them, preferring the next, rather clumsy formulation: 'Man cannot live without a permanent trust in something indestructible, though both the indestructible element and also the trust may remain permanently concealed from him. One of the ways in which this lasting concealment can express itself is faith in a personal god.' The first part of this comes back to the central issue of the 'surplus', but what has a personal god got to do with it? He was still trying to get it right when he copied it into the anthology on sheet number 50, adding 'within himself' at the end of the final sentence before scratching the whole thing out. He then jots down another enigmatic phrase, 'Heaven is dumb, only echoing the dumb', followed in turn by what became 51 before itself being first rephrased and then crossed out: 'The snake was necessary. Evil can speak to man but cannot become man.'

It is one of many such thoughts: language, speech, the attempt to understand ourselves and our place in the world through introspection and philosophical/theological discourse – all that belongs to the Devil and is only a lure and a temptation. It is also the first of many entries dealing directly with the story in Genesis 2–3 of what in Christian theology is known as the Temptation and the Fall. In a letter to Milena written three years later, Kafka was to give a new twist to the old story and in the process confess his kinship with it: 'It's as though Eve,' he writes, 'having indeed plucked the apple from the tree (sometimes I believe I understand the Fall of Man as no one else), did so nevertheless only in order to show it to Adam – because she liked it. It was the biting into it that was decisive – the playing with it was, though not permitted, not forbidden either.'

8 December was to be a fruitful day for work in the notebook, though the first entry does not bode well: 'Bed, constipation, pain in back, irritable evening, cat in the room, dissension.' The dissension was presumably with Ottla, not the cat. However, a rich stream of thought follows, which was later copied out onto pages 52 to 58 of the little anthology. The first, 52, is one of the best-known, partly because it is so clear and partly because it is so pithy: 'In the struggle between yourself and the world, back the world.' Yet though it is clear, it is hard to fully take in. It had, however, been the central subject of Kafka's mature fiction, accurately describing both 'The Judgement' and *The Metamorphosis*. One could even say that discovering its centrality was what led to the breakthrough. The novel and its shorter forms, as we know them in the West, had always been written from the point of view of the protagonist, whether in the first or the third person (*Don Quixote* is a notable exception). The shock of 'The Judgement' is that though it starts like that, it ends quite otherwise: Georg's father rises up from his bed and condemns

him to death by drowning and Georg immediately carries out the sentence. In *The Metamorphosis*, the hateful insect that had once been Gregor is finally eliminated from the picture and the family can celebrate and return to life by taking a day out in the country. Yet in both stories what is taken as a just sentence by the protagonist can also be seen as an appalling travesty of anything we might call justice, and Blanchot has, rightly in my view, seen the final image of *The Metamorphosis*, of the young sister stretching out her body in joy as she runs in the countryside, as the ultimate horror of the story. Both stories thus raise questions about 52, questions that can only be raised by fiction, for it is only because we have invested emotionally in Georg Bendemann and Gregor Samsa that we can question the validity of the point of view of the survivor.

Fiction can do this – bring out how vital it is to back the world as well as how fraught with ambiguity such an attitude is – but discursive language can't. Perhaps this is why Kafka, after copying out the 'aphorism' in the anthology, crossed it out as well. The next sentence in the notebook, though, a version of the previous one, he let stand as number 53: 'One must not cheat anyone, not even the world, of its victory.'

He follows it with another thought: 'There is only a world of the spirit; what we call the world of the senses is the Evil (*das Böse*) in the spiritual world (*in der geistigen*).' He added a sentence to this when he came to copy it out as number 54, presumably to clarify, but it only muddies the waters further: 'What we call Evil is only a momentary necessity in our eternal development.' It obviously meant a lot to him, however, for in October 1920 he added another thought, which he clearly felt was related, but it remains opaque, lacking the resonance of 52. Is he really insisting on a Gnostic separation of spirit and flesh? And what on earth does 'our eternal development' mean?

He keeps struggling with this in the next two thoughts, the second of which became 56, but without making things

any clearer, to us or, obviously, to himself. Finally he gets to: 'For everything outside the phenomenal world language can only be used allusively, but never even approximately by way of comparison, since, corresponding as it does to the phenomenal world, it is concerned only with possession and its association.' This is almost Ayer-like in its stark division into what can and what cannot meaningfully be said, though the description of 'the phenomenal world' as 'concerned only with possession (*Besitz*)' is startling, but feeds in, as we will see, to Kafka's meditations at this time on the nature of the just society – meditations connected with his growing interest in the possible setting up of such a society in Palestine.

He is not finished for that day, though. There follows a thought about lying, simple and moralistic in a way Kafka almost never is, one of the few pieces which might legitimately be termed an aphorism or a *pensée*: 'The way to lie as little as possible is only by lying as little as possible, not by speaking as little as possible.' This, slightly emended, became 58 before being crossed out. The entries for the day then end with a longish paragraph meditating, Wittgenstein-fashion, on the way an ordinary sentence is to be understood: 'If I say to the child: "Wipe your mouth and then you'll have the cake", that does not mean that the cake is earned by means of wiping the mouth, for wiping one's mouth and the value of the cake are not comparable, nor does it make wiping the mouth a precondition for eating the cake, for apart from the triviality of such a condition the child would get the cake in any case, since it is a necessary part of his lunch – hence the remark does not signify that the transition is made more difficult but that it is made easier, wiping one's mouth is a tiny benefit that precedes the great benefit of eating cake.' Even here, though, the choice of example is telling: an instruction to a child by an omniscient adult who holds in his hands what the child desires and whose commands are probably felt by the child to be quite arbitrary,

though to the adult they are perfectly rational. In a small way it is as much a little drama of acculturation as anything Red Peter, the ape of 'A Report to an Academy', has to go through in order to survive in the world of men.

On 9 December Kafka notes: 'Annual fair yesterday'. The German is *Kirchweihtanz*, 'church consecration dance', which brings out the symbiosis of church and village that has existed in rural Europe since the Middle Ages. And it is perhaps this that leads him to one of his finest 'aphorisms', a meditation on tradition: 'A stair-tread that has not been deeply hollowed out by footsteps is, from its own point of view, merely something that has been specially assembled out of wood (*nur etwas besonders zusammengefügtes Hölzernes*).' When he came to copy it out as 59 of his little anthology he improved it by substituting *öde* for *besonders* (special). *Öde*, with its connotations of emptiness, hopelessness (English readers will have come across it as the word used to designate Tristan's desolation at seeing the empty sea in Wagner's *Tristran und Isolde*, as quoted by Eliot in *The Waste Land*, *'Oed' und leer das Meer'*) is a brilliant touch, suggesting as it does the spiritual emptiness of both those who hammer the new staircase into shape and of the stair itself – 'merely something that has been bleakly put together out of wood' is Pasley's inspired translation. However, after that he crossed out the whole thing, suggesting once again that he lacked any clear sense of what he was after with the whole project.

When he first wrote it down, though, what he was clearly after was finding a way to convey his sense of the loss of tradition in the modern world, thoughts perhaps brought on by his experience of the village fair. The result is the most Heideggerian of these pieces in its sense of sadness at the passing of a way of life that consists of daily repeated practices – though of course only Kafka could identify so easily and naturally with the poor modern staircase. It tells us a great

deal about Kafka's agonies over his own life and writing. What these lack, he feels, is the unthinking life-activity that produces the works of Homer, say, and this is not a lack that can be made good by will power and effort, since it is part of the fabric of modern life. When Kafka is at his best is when, as here, he catches both the loss and a sense of *what* has been lost. The word *öde*, which he hits upon when he is copying these pieces into the new little anthology, is so apt because it perfectly expresses what is already there, ghost-like, in the original formulation.

There follows a paragraph in which he wrestles with this in more orthodox fashion, talking about 'the soul' not being able to know itself, which is in turn followed by an unmemorable thought, strongly Christian in feeling, later inscribed as 60 in the anthology, and this time not deleted: 'Whoever renounces the world must love all men, for he renounces their world too. He thus begins to have some inkling of the true nature of man, which cannot but be loved, provided one is worthy of it.' Two more 'aphorisms' follow on the same lines, the first (61) crossed out after being copied into the anthology, while the second, more enigmatic, survives undeleted: 'The fact that there is nothing other than a spiritual world deprives us of our hope and gives us our certainty.' The use of the term 'a spiritual world', so prominent everywhere in the octavo notebook, is so frustrating because it is so nebulous. What did Kafka mean by it? Stach's notes in his edition of the 'aphorisms' do not help.

So those December days go by. The next entry, two days later, gives us a glimpse of the life Kafka was leading: 'Yesterday Senior Inspector. Today *Der Jude*. Stein: The Bible is a sanctum, the world a cesspit.' The Senior Inspector was Eugen Pöhl, Kafka's immediate superior at the Institute. Kafka had accompanied him to Vienna in 1913 to attend the Second International Congress for First Aid and Accident Prevention. Whether he had come to Zürau on a friendly visit

or to discuss Kafka's future is not known. All Kafka says, in a letter to Brod later in the month, is that he is 'on an extremely friendly footing' with him and that 'he has come here for a visit'. *Der Jude* was Buber's Zionist journal in which Kafka's two stories, 'Jackals and Arabs' and 'A Report to an Academy', were appearing. About Stein nothing seems to be known. Was he another visitor from Prague or a village resident? He is mentioned again as 'Nathan Stein' in the entry for 19 December, this time 'telling the peasant woman that the world is a theatre', so was he the village intellectual? Or the village visionary?

This glimpse of Kafka's daily life is followed by one those resonant remarks which spring out at us unexpectedly again and again from the octavo notebooks and only some of which he later incorporated into his little anthology: 'Art consists in being dazzled by the truth. The light upon the grotesque mask as it shrinks back is true and nothing else is.' Kafka, when transcribing it for his little anthology, changed it to 'Our art consists…', but whether it was human art or modern art or art created by Jews is unclear, and anyway does little to alter the meaning: art cannot speak directly of the truth, it can only show what the effect of seeing the truth has on the one who has seen it. Wise Sophocles knew this to be the case and explored it dramatically in his greatest play, *Oedipus at Colonus*, where Oedipus's apotheosis is twice removed from the audience, since the audience only learns of it from the messenger's account of his view of Theseus' face as *he* sees it happen. Art that pretends it can see the truth and tell it is a lie, but that does not mean we should forget about the truth; what good art will do is to show the blinding effect of truth upon the face of the one who views it – though whether 'the grotesque mask' is merely the contorted face of the one who has seen or an absurd mask put on as some sort of protection is not clear. Yet we, as we read the piece, can immediately grasp

it. As in all the best of these little pieces the effect lies in the choice of image or fiction and the words used to create that. It helps us understand not only much of Kafka but also of Eliot and Beckett and the early William Golding.

It is followed in the octavo notebook by a less resonant version of the same thought: 'Not everyone can see the truth, but he must be it.' He then returns to thoughts about Paradise, time and eternity which, after revision, became 64 (65 is either missing or Kafka misnumbered), followed by a meandering paragraph on the same theme, full of vague terms such as 'the world here and now' and 'the Beyond'. The next day he notes that he began Herzen's memoirs but was distracted by the arrival of several newspapers and journals. Then comes an entry which seems as resonant as any of the 'aphorisms' but which he chose not to copy into the anthology: 'He who seeks will not find, he who does not seek will be found.' The combination here of the ethical and the aesthetic is characteristic of the best formulations of the Zürau period, as well as describing to perfection the mechanism of the major novels. There, though, not seeking is never an option.

On 14 December he notes: 'Yesterday, today, worst days. What has contributed: Herzen, a letter to Dr Weiss, other things not capable of interpretation. Nauseating meal: yesterday, pig's trotters, today tail. Walk to Michelob through the park.' Why did Herzen, the exiled Russian revolutionary whose memoirs have been championed by innumerable thoughtful liberals, contribute to his gloom? Or a letter to the writer and doctor Ernst Weiss? After all, in 1914 Kafka had confided to his diary: 'A lot of time well spent with Dr Weiss.' And why was he writing to him now? The food is another matter. Kafka, as a vegetarian, always fastidious about what he ate, having to eat pork? But this was the third year of the war and, as we have seen, food was getting more and more scarce. In the middle of the countryside pig's trotters and tail

may have been the only things available. At least he could still walk it off.

There follows a longish paragraph, later incorporated into the little anthology on sheet 66. It reiterates the paradoxes he has been struggling with throughout the winter in dramatic terms not deployed before: 'He is a free and secure citizen of the earth, for he is attached to a chain long enough to give him access to all parts of the earth yet not long enough to allow him to go beyond the earth's borders. At the same time, however, he is also a free and secure citizen of heaven, for he is also attached to a heavenly chain similarly calculated. If he wants to go to earth the heavenly collar will choke him, if he wants to go to heaven the earthly collar will. Yet even so all possibilities are open to him and he is aware of this. Indeed, he refuses to attribute the whole thing to an error in the original system of chains.' All the Kafka hallmarks are there (though it is also an eerie foreshadowing of some of Beckett's later plays): the factual, precise language; the masochism; the construction of a machine from which there is no escape despite the fact that 'all possibilities are open'; indeed, the implications of that phrase is what is most terrible about the whole situation.

The next day he records getting a letter from Josef Körner and on the seventeenth he notes that he has replied – no doubt the fierce letter we saw him writing, giving his reasons for not wishing to contribute to Körner's jingoistic journal. There was also a letter from his mother, to which, again on the seventeenth, he also notes that he has replied. Otherwise, on that day, his only comment is: 'Empty days', and he follows this with an anecdote which he no doubt took from one of the papers he'd been sent and which has uncanny echoes of 'A Report to an Academy', his recent story of an ape who teaches himself to learn European ways in order to escape from captivity and make a decent life for himself: 'The Negro who was taken home from the World Exhibition and, having

gone mad from homelessness, in his village, surrounded by the lamentations of the tribe, with the most solemn face, by way of tradition and duty demonstrated the pranks that delighted the European public, who believed they were the rites and customs of Africa.'

This is in turn followed by the enigmatic remark: 'Self-forgetfulness and self-cancelling-out of art: what is an escape pretends to be a stroll or even an attack.' The word I translate, following Kaiser and Wilkins, as 'self-cancelling-out' is *Selbstaufhebung*, the abolishing of the self, and what I translate, for the sake of clarity, as 'pretends to be' is *vorgeblich*, a strange word made up by Kafka from *bleichen*, to bleach, from *bleich,* pale. So is Kafka repeating the time-honoured trope that the making of art leads the maker to forget or abolish himself, subduing his nature, as Shakespeare puts it, 'to what it works in, like the dyer's hand' (sonnet 111), or is he saying that it is merely an escape – an escape, moreover, that passes itself off as something much less reprehensible, a casual stroll in the park? He seems to start with the notion of the making of art as leading us away from the turmoil of the world, a way of at last being rid of the burdens of the self, but this is then turned on its head in the second part: here, art becomes a cowardly way of avoiding the world, made worse by the attempt to whitewash this as a stroll or an attack, depending, we imagine, on whether the art in question is sentimental and appealing or expressionist and aggressive. And that, as have seen again and again, is the burden of these months in Zürau and a question to which there is no answer.

A brief comment on his reading – van Gogh's letters – and then what was to become 67: 'He runs after the facts like a novice skater who also practices where it is forbidden.' Is this a criticism of his recent glut of reading, his attempt to catch up, in his self-imposed exile, on the latest writings on Judaism, Christian theology and politics? Or is he talking about his

writing? I had first taken it as the latter, meaning that he was mad to try to learn this art and unaware of the dangers, but *den Tatsachen,* the facts, now seems to me pretty unequivocal – unless of course he is thinking of the quest for meaning his fiction enacts as a quest for facts. But this is what Kafka's best fictions and images do to you: in a few plain and simple words they set your imagination going and refuse to provide it with a safe landing.

Christmas and the New Year: Prague

On 18 December the routine Kafka had established for himself in Zürau was shattered by a letter from Felice announcing that she was coming to see him. Her telegram or letter is lost and we only have his laconic entry for 19 December: 'Yesterday announcement of F's visit, today alone in my room, over there the stove is smoking, walked to Zarch with Nathan Stein.' He took three days to reply, suggesting they meet in Prague, not Zürau. Stach is surely right to suggest (*Kafka: The Years of Insight*) that, unlike earlier meetings in neutral territory away from Prague, such as Marienbad, 'Zürau now represented Kafka's actual and thus highly vulnerable life, while Prague was more neutral territory.' He would have had to visit the capital in any case because he needed to sort out his future both with the Institute and with the military authorities. For, surprising as it might seem that a sick thirty-four-year-old was due to be called up, this was indeed the case unless Kafka could convince the authorities of the seriousness of his condition. He writes to Brod: 'A letter from F, who announces her arrival at Christmas, although we had earlier agreed on the senselessness, even the harmfulness of such a journey. For various reasons not worth listing, then, I shall probably – though I was not due there

until after Christmas – be coming to Prague this Saturday, towards evening.'

Until then he returned to his notebook. 'What is more cheerful than the belief in a household god', he noted, and went on in a dense, almost Hopkinsesque attempt to pin down the feeling: 'There is an under-through-beneath-true-knowledge and a childish-happy rising up [*Es ist ein Unten-durch unter der wahren Erkenntnis und ein kindlich-glückliches Aufstehn!*].' Frisch, in her translation of Stach's edition of the 'aphorisms', renders the last phrase as 'and a childlike happiness arising from it', which is probably closer to what Kafka had in mind, but however one tries to English it there is no getting away from the fact that it is an extraordinary sentence in anyone's book, and even more so in Kafka, whose instinct is to use the most ordinary and often bureaucratically cold language to express even his most outrageous fantasies. It suggests that the thought of a household god aroused in him an extraordinarily intense feeling of joy – even if it is a joy whose source he knows is lost to us today. Perhaps unwilling to commit such raw emotion even to the privacy of his notebook, he crossed out the sentence, but then reinstated it with a set of dots in the margin. But when he came to copy the whole piece out as 68 he once again removed it. On that December day in Zürau, though, he then moved on to what would become 69: 'Theoretically there is the possibility of perfect happiness by believing in the indestructible element in oneself and not striving towards it.' No two 'aphorisms' could demonstrate better than 68 and 69 how diverse in style these pieces are and how different in their ability to affect the reader. 'Aphorism' 69 is clearly related to the thought: 'He who seeks does not find, he who does not seek will be found', which, as I've said, did not make it into the little anthology, though 'the indestructible element in oneself' still smacks of the books of 'positive theology' he has been reading, and as for perfect happiness, who, least of all

Kafka, ever expected it? However happiness comes, as it does when his writing suddenly takes off, he is clear that it is never because of an effort of will or because he has applied himself, but is rather a gift from heaven. Kafka always felt there was a gulf between himself and jobbing writers, even those like Brod and Werfel who were both highly successful and driven by a belief in their own genius. His torment lay in the fact that the god was fickle – the gift came suddenly and went just as suddenly. And when it did so, despair would set in and the chin would sink onto the chest.

Having unburdened himself of the thought Kafka finished writing for the day. The next entry consists of two sentences. First the laconic 'Telegram to F.', then the thought: 'Adam's first domestic pet after the expulsion from Paradise was the serpent.' This compresses into one memorable sentence many of his earlier musings about the Fall and how thought and even language itself, whereby one hopes to escape the clutches of Evil, are somehow complicit with it. Yet it never made it into the little anthology. Indeed, 69 was the last he wrote in Zürau that year. On 22 December, a Saturday, we find him in Prague. That day he noted: 'Lumbago, mental arithmetic in the night'. The next day: 'Fortunate and to some extent dull, listless [*matt*]. Heard much.' Was that in the train? On the 24th: 'Slept badly, strenuous day.' Clearly he was having a miserable time in Prague.

A brief entry, oddly dated 25, 26, 27, summarises those awful days. 'F. leaves. Weeping. Everything difficult, wrong and yet right after all (*unrecht und doch richtig*).' A letter to Ottla, who had remained in Zürau, fills that out: 'My days with F. were dreadful (apart from the first day, when we had not yet tackled the main thing), and the last morning I cried more than I had in all the years since my childhood. Naturally it would have been even more dreadful or even impossible if I had had the slightest remainder of I don't know what doubt

about the justice of my actions. There was none of that, only unfortunately the justice of an act does not contradict the fact that that act is in itself an injustice and an injustice aggravated by the calm and especially the goodness with which she responded to it.' Brod, in his biography of his friend, provides us with a third-party perspective on the drama: 'Franz came to see me at the office... He had just accompanied F. to the station. His face was pale, hard and cold. But suddenly he began to cry... murmuring between his sobs, "Isn't it terrible that it should have come to this?" The tears streamed down his cheeks; it's the only time I've ever seen him collapse, having totally lost control.'

Stach quotes Brod's diary, which gives a clearer sense of the horror of those days, with Kafka dragging along a desperate Felice to outings with his friends: 'In the afternoon, Schipkapass [a pub on the outskirts of Prague] with Baum, Weltsch, the 3 women. – Kafka unhappy. He is not sparing himself the pain of inflicting pain on her... He said to me, "What I have to do I can only do alone. Become clear about the ultimate things. The Western Jew is not clear about them and has no right to marry. There are no marriages for them."' As with much of Brod's testimony and that of Gustaf Janouch after Kafka's death, we must be wary. Kafka's words – pronouncements might be a better term – as they relay them too often seem to fit in with an idealised image of him as a wise and solitary figure, a martyr to his own higher calling. But there is clearly a kernel of truth in what Brod has him say here – we have after all seen him at work in the notebook trying to 'become clear about the ultimate things'. Also, seeing the problems his friends, especially Brod, were having with their marriages, he may well have tried to relieve them of some of their guilt at the way they were behaving by generalising about 'the Western Jew' and marriage – and a part of him may even have believed it.

All this painfully conveys what both Kafka and especially Felice went through in those days. Forced to mingle with his friends in local cafés and pubs while trying to come to terms with the fact that the man she had grown to love made it clear to her that there was no future in their relationship, she must have longed to get away from it all and back to Berlin. They never saw each other again.

Kafka wrote to Brod at the end of the month, while still in Prague, though not to talk about Felice but to send him manuscript copies of recent stories ('The Bucket Rider' and 'An Old Manuscript') and ask him to have copies made at his expense for him to forward to a Berlin-based literary journal, *Das junge Deutschland*: 'I am not enclosing novels', he says. 'Why stir up the old struggles? Only because I haven't burned them yet?… What is the point of saving such "even" artistically misbegotten works? Because one hopes that these fragments will somehow combine to form a whole, some court of appeal upon whose breast I shall be able to throw myself when I am in need? I know it is not possible, that no help comes from there. So what should I do with these things? Since they cannot help me, am I to let them harm me, as they must, in view of this knowledge?' Then, after some brief remarks about Brod's strained relations with his wife, he adds: 'One more request: Would you send me the military regulation forms which I believe have to be filled out in January?'

Clearly as far as Kafka was concerned, Felice belonged to the past. For now he needed to get his recent stories published and above all to 'become clear about the ultimate things' and about how his burning need to write fitted into that. Did it help him or harm him? That was the question, and the octavo notebook was the place to try and work it out. On the 24 December he noted: 'The indestructible is one; it is each individual person and at the same time it is common

to all, hence the unparalleled strength of the bonds that unite mankind' – not a very illuminating thought, though he felt it was significant enough to copy out later as 70 (and 71, he misnumbered the pages again). In the notebook he jotted down a further thought about the interconnectedness of Paradise and evil: 'In Paradise, as always: that which causes the sin and that which recognises it for what it is are one. The clear conscience is Evil, which is so entirely victorious that it does not any longer consider necessary that leap from left to right.' There is no escaping the serpent/evil, it is so much a part of us that even efforts to escape its clutches, such as this, are in fact complicit with it. The worse thing is a clear conscience, for that means that one has lost forever the possibility of escape from evil – but does this not condemn one for ever to useless self-examination and self-condemnation, also the sphere of evil?

That will not stop him turning the problem over and over. He goes on with a thought that does not usually surface in his work, on the difference between the privileged and the oppressed, and then notes that 'there are different subjects in one and the same man', an attempt perhaps to move away from the idea that evil directs all our activities. This last he copied out later as 72 and then crossed out. After that nothing except the note about Felice, followed by what would become 73: 'He devours the scraps [*Er frisst den Abfall*] falling from his own table; although this means that he is better fed for a while than the others, he forgets how to eat at the table and this means that there are then no more scraps.' *Fressen* is what animals, not humans do, and *Abfall* is more pejorative than scraps, garbage really. And this, like the earlier thought about the different views of the apple of the child and the 'master of the house', takes a commonplace scene as the setting for a little drama (just as Herbert, to the opposite effect, uses the notion of a communal meal to

dramatise his relations with God). But what kind of a drama? Is he talking about his life? His writing? Any 'translation' or paraphrase may give us the impression that we have got a handle on it, but this risks numbing that initial impression of a scene of mad desolation.

On 30 December, after the enigmatic 'Not essentially disappointed', he writes down the last 'aphorism' (74) he would produce that year, another attempt to decipher Genesis 1–3: 'If what is said to have been destroyed in Paradise was destructible then it was not decisive; but if it was indestructible then we are living in a false belief.'

Before he left Prague he saw his doctor, who, while reassuring him, told him he certainly had a case for taking early retirement and approved his decision not to marry. As far as his parents were concerned the reason for his rupture with Felice was this and this alone.

He also, as he tells Ottla in a letter dated 30 December, had a confrontation with their father, in which he, for once, came out on top. Ever since Kafka had arrived in Prague, his father had been ranting on about Ottla's folly in shutting herself away in the country, pretending to be a farmer; she needed to get back to civilisation and find a suitable husband (her liaison with Josef David was still a secret). Franz, the father went on, was complicit in all this nonsense and even to blame for it. Kafka stood his ground. He was not going to allow his father to call him ungrateful any more or to have his actions described as crazy and abnormal. He writes to Ottla that he is quite pleased with his answer, which disconcerted him, 'by saying that the abnormal was not the worst, since the normal is for example the world war'. The decisive end of the long-drawn-out affair with Felice and his work in the octavo notebook had clearly resulted, if not in a brand-new Kafka, at least in a newly resolute Kafka. He had turned a corner.

A Sermon and a Funeral

In the first days of the new year the blind Oskar Baum came to stay. Kafka explained in a postcard to Brod that he was only acting as Baum's secretary, writing to say that he, Baum, would be back in Prague on the Sunday and would thereafter be free to come with Weltsch to hear Brod read from his new novel. In his own person Kafka added: 'We're having a nice time with Oskar.' But in a letter later in the month, when Baum had gone back to Prague, he was more open about the visit. He had grown so used to being alone, he confessed, that it had been a trial having anyone to stay. Baum had shown him his new work and he was as unsparing in his criticism of it as he always was about both his own and his friends' work: 'Up to now I have felt there was too much superficiality in Oskar's new technique. That is not so. Rather, there is truth there, but it beats against the far-flung and yet too-narrow limits and the result is weariness, error, weakness, rhetoric.' This did not stop him, as ever, feeling warm towards his friend: 'I would be very glad if Zürau had helped him a little, although I doubt it – glad both for his sake and mine.'

To Baum he wrote thanking him for the raspberry syrup he had sent him and Ottla on his return to Prague: 'I drink it in the spirit of freedom and because it is there and because it reminds me of your goodness towards me.' Nothing has changed here in Zürau, he goes on, except that you are no longer there. 'But,' he adds, 'you were a lucky fellow, for you were spared the mice. Three days after you left – I no longer take the cat into my room – noise woke me up in the night. My first thought was that it must be the cat after all, until it became clear that it was a mouse, who, impudent as a young

child was playing with the trap – that is, carefully plucked away at the bacon while the trap's door clattered up and down without opening wide enough for the mouse to fall through. The trap, recommended by Max in such good faith, is more alarm clock than trap. By the way, the next night the bacon was stolen out of another trap also. I hope you aren't thinking that I, half-asleep, go creeping under the sideboard to take the bacon myself. Besides, all this has quieted down in the last few days.'

Outwardly there is no change from the first part of the winter. He informs Weltsch at the end of the month that it is very cold, 'six to eight degrees below freezing, sleeping with open windows… breaking the layer of ice in the pitcher, ice which will form again in the washbowl, standing quite naked of course, and after a week still not a trace of a cold, after having become accustomed to the stove going day and night, you must have a try at this… it is really wonderful.' That does not stop him taking his walks to the nearby village and observing the life around him. 'There is an order here,' he tells Weltsch, 'a daily order and a seasonal one, and if one can adjust to that, all is well. The church too has some importance. I was recently there for a sermon. It had a businesslike simplicity. The text was Luke 2: 41–52, and three lessons were drawn. 1. Parents should not permit their children to play outside in the snow but should bring them into the church (see, all the empty seats!). 2. Parents should be as tenderly concerned for their children as the Holy Family was for their son… 3. Children should speak as piously to their parents as Jesus did to his. That was all, for it was very cold, but there was a kind of ultimate power in the whole thing.' We might think that the deadpan description of a village sermon consisting of nothing but pious platitudes would be a cause for laughter in a letter from one sophisticated city intellectual to another in the midst of discussions of Kierkegaard and Troelsch,

Brentano and Buber – but the opposite is the case, and if we understand why we come close to understanding Kafka. As the little piece about the staircase reminds us, he was always moved by the unthinkingly traditional, from which, for him, there emanated a kind of power which was unquestionable and beyond words.

He goes on in this letter to Weltsch: 'And yesterday, for instance, there was a funeral of a poor man from a nearby village which is even poorer than Zürau but it was very solemn and could hardly have been otherwise, with the village square covered with snow. Because of a trench cutting halfway across the square the hearse could not go straight to the church but had to make a big circle around the goose pond. The mourners – the whole population of the neighbouring village – were all standing at the church door while the hearse still continued slowly making its circle at peaceful plough-horse pace, in the van a small band of frozen musicians entwined by a tuba and in the rear the fire company, our steward among them. And I lay in my reclining chair at the window and watched it all to my edification, simply as a neighbour of the church.'

The window gives him an excellent view of the whole thing, yet at the same time of course it cuts him off decisively from the participants, an uncanny replay of the painting he had been so struck by in his youth of the joyful group of young people partying on a river bank and from which, as he meditated on it, he had felt so excluded. And yet with pride he informs Brod that 'in Zürau no one is worried about me. People (anonymous authors) have made up rhymes about almost everyone in Zürau. Mine, except for the shaky metre, is most comforting:

> The doctor is a goodly man
> God will forgive him all He can.'

Kierkegaard

Kierkegaard was much on his mind. Already in a letter to Baum from late October or early November he had confessed that 'Kierkegaard is a star, although he shines over territory that is almost inaccessible to me.' At that time he said he knew only *Fear and Trembling*, but in the early months of 1918 he seems to have undertaken a crash course in the Danish thinker – not, however, with any better results. 'Partly as a consequence of [Baum's] visit,' he writes to Brod in the middle of January, 'I started reading *Either/Or*, with a special craving for help the evening after Oskar's departure, and am now reading Buber's recent books, sent by Oskar. Hateful, repellent books all of them. To put it correctly and precisely, they are written – *Either/Or* especially – with the sharpest of pens... but they drive you to despair.' By mid-March he is more temperate: 'Perhaps I have really lost my way in Kierkegaard', he writes to Brod. 'I realise this with astonishment when I read your lines about him.' What fascinates the two friends is the similarity between Kierkegaard's renunciation of his fiancée Regine Olsen out of a sense that he had to devote himself to God, and his constant calling into question of that momentous decision, and Kafka's equally ambivalent feelings about Felice. Should Kierkegaard have renounced Regine? Would God not rather have preferred him to marry her? Would he not have been a better thinker and theologian had he done so? And how is one ever to know? As you say, Kafka tells Brod, 'the problem of arriving at a true marriage is his principal concern, the concern that is forever rising into his consciousness. I see that in *Either/ Or*, in *Fear and Trembling* and in *Repetition*. (I have read the latter in the last two weeks and have ordered *Stages* [*on Life's Way*]. But though Kierkegaard is always in my mind these days I have truly forgotten this point, so much am I roaming in other fields, even though I never completely lose touch

with it. The "physical" similarity with him that I imagined I had after reading that little book, *Kierkegaard's Relationship to "Her"*... has now entirely evaporated. It's as if a next-door neighbour had turned into a distant star, in respect both to my admiration and to a certain cooling of my sympathy.'

A week or two later, at the end of March, he returns to Kierkegaard, telling Brod that 'he is no longer much on my mind' since 'in this lovely weather I have been working in the garden'. He goes on, though, to deliver a passionate critique of the interconnection of the man and his writings which, as we have seen, was so central to his own thoughts about living well and the place of writing in such a life. 'I do not see how his having published books ran counter to his basic aim (I do not know *Stages* [he still had not received the copy he had ordered], but in this sense all his books are compromising after all)... Besides, his compromising books are pseudonymous, and what is more, their pseudonymous quality is almost of the essence. Taken as a whole, in spite of the wealth of confession in them they might well pass for perplexing letters by the Tempter himself, written behind clouds. And even if all of this were not so, under the softening influence of time they must have made his fiancée breathe a sigh of relief at having escaped the torture machine whose engine was now merely idling, or at any rate was merely occupied with her shadow. At that price she may have patiently endured the "tastelessness" of his almost annual publications. And as the best proof of the validity of Kierkegaard's method (to scream in order not to be heard and to scream falsely just in case you are heard), she remained after all virtually as innocent as a lamb.'

Surely much of the vehemence of this comes from Kafka's suspicion that his own treatment of Felice in the five years of their relationship had not been dissimilar to Kierkegaard's treatment of Regine. But that does not prevent what he says from being true (and bitterly funny). Even Auden's clerihew:

'Soren Kierkegaard / Tried very hard / To take the leap / But fell in a heap' does not rise to the level of humour and critical insight of Kafka's 'to scream in order not to be heard and to scream falsely in case you are heard'.

He does not stop there. He goes on to criticise both Brod's apparent idolisation of Kierkegaard and his interpretation of him. Rightly he recognises that what Kierkegaard in effect does in his theological works is to remove all intermediaries between himself and God, not only the Church, but Jesus too, so that in the end he is left with nothing but a Last Judgement. This is of course the kind of problem that has been troubling Kafka in those Zürau months, and he summarises it in a very Kafkaesque way: 'According to Kierkegaard,' he says, 'striving man must oppose the world in order to save the divine element within himself. Or, what comes to the same thing, the divine sets him against the world in order to save itself.'

And with that he leaves Kierkegaard, at least for the time being. The Danish thinker, however, cannot be brushed off quite so easily. Abraham, the protagonist of *Fear and Trembling*, now joins Kafka's pantheon of semi-mythical figures – Odysseus, Alexander, Don Quixote – whose exploits will go on giving him material for reflection to the very end of his short life. I feel that if he had had access to some of Kierkegaard's other writings, especially the *Journals*, but also *The Concluding Unscientific Postscript*, he would have seen profounder affinities between them than a conflicted view of marriage. In a series of journal entries from 1837, for example, Kierkegaard meditates on the difference between what he calls 'the mode of existence' and 'the mode of possibility', or what happens in life and what happens in our imagination. Cleverly, he relates this to the grammatical modes of indicative and subjunctive: 'The indicative thinks something as actual... The subjunctive thinks something as thinkable.' The writer sensitive to the difference between living and thinking will

reflect this distinction by choosing the subjunctive, the mode of possibility, not the indicative, the mode of actuality: 'One should be able to write a whole novel in which the present tense subjunctive was the invisible soul, as light is for painting.' This is coming close to Kafka's central insight in those months of something peculiar happening when the creature in despair writes down 'I am in despair'. And Kierkegaard is still struggling with this issue in 1850, after he has, he believes, written his most polemical books and is ready to devote himself to pious theology: 'To conceive something,' he writes in his *Journal*, 'is to dissolve actuality into possibility – but then it is impossible to conceive it, because conceiving something is transforming it into possibility and so not holding on to actuality.' In Kafka's formulation, in those Zürau musings, this becomes the idea that as soon as you start to think, to formulate ideas, you are doing the Devil's work.

But most important of all: does not his description of Kierkegaard's method in his pseudonymous works as 'To scream in order to be heard and to scream falsely just in case you are heard' sound uncannily like Kafka's own method of writing fiction, though in his case there is no screaming, only the quiet murmur of bureaucratic prose?

Friend and Author

When he was not writing to Brod about Kierkegaard, Kafka was (with much hesitation) advising him and Baum about the crises in their marriages. Brod's marriage was on the rocks and he was writing novels and plays about it, while Baum, during his stay in Zürau, had confessed to Kafka that he hated his wife – and was writing a novel about it! Kafka listened patiently and offered what advice he could.

He was still asking his Prague friends to send him books and journals as well as seeking their advice about which

translations and editions to acquire. Surprisingly, in view of his previous letter to Josef Körner, he wrote to him at the end of January to say that 'I would never have thought *Donauland* could have given me such pleasure', and thanking him for sending his Arnim piece, which he proceeded to discuss at some length, ending with advice about the pros and cons of seeking to get it published by Kurt Wolff Verlag, perhaps as the introduction to a selection of Arnim's letters, as Körner had suggested. 'One has to shout if one wants to be heard by such a publisher, who is besieged by authors', he concludes. 'I would be very glad if this succeeded.'

He was speaking from the heart. Wolff had sent him the proofs of *A Country Doctor,* but, though Kafka had stipulated the order of the stories, had placed the title story first. Kafka was furious, though polite as ever: 'May I ask that you arrange the stories in the order I indicated', he writes; that is, he reiterates, with 'A New Advocate' first and 'A Country Doctor' second. He also asks Wolff to add a dedication page inscribed 'To My Father', and adds that he would like to purchase the correspondence of the playwright Jacob Lenz, Goethe's friend and the subject of an extraordinary story by Büchner, which Wolff had just published. A few days later he writes to thank Wolff for 'the handsome gift of Lenz's letters'. 'This,' he goes on, 'is a book I wished for long before I knew of your intention to publish it. Your giving it makes it doubly precious.' However, by the end of March he is complaining to Brod that Wolff is no longer answering his letters and he wonders whether he should look for another publisher. 'Ever since I decided to dedicate the book to my father,' he writes, 'I am deeply concerned to have it appear soon. Not that I could appease my father this way,' he goes on, 'the roots of our antagonism are too deep, but I would at least have something.' *A Country Doctor* was not in fact to appear in print – with Wolff – till 1920.

What this correspondence shows is that once he had made up his mind that something of his was worth publishing,

Kafka was as keen as any author to see it in print. What he was not willing to do was put out into the world material he felt he had failed to bring to proper fruition. Thus to Johannes Urzidil, the editor of the journal *Der Mensch*, he wrote, as he had so often before to other editors: 'Dear Herr Urzidil, many thanks for your kind invitation and the copy of your magazine, but I must ask you not to expect any contribution from me at least for the present, since I have nothing I could publish.'

What is striking about Kafka's correspondence from Zürau in 1918 is what few traces it bears of the torment and anxieties of the last months of 1917. There are hardly any references to his illness or to Felice. The tone, rather, is firm, thoughtful, argumentative and at times very funny, as in this from a letter to Brod, which would not be out of place in an exchange between Eliot and John Hayward: 'By way of thanks for this, may I quote you a sentence from an appeal for the Frankenstein Sanatorium, since I have no one else to share my delight. A Herr von Werther, a captain of industry, delivered a major speech at the first meeting of the board of directors at Frankenstein... "Labouring long years in the vineyards of practical life, my philosophy, untrammelled by visionary theories, sounds its ultimate note in the perception: Being healthy, working efficiently and successfully, honourably acquiring a modest fortune for ourselves and our families, leads humanity to contentment on earth."'

The Notebook

In the middle of February Kafka paid a flying visit to Prague to discuss his future with the Institute and deal with his call-up. What a relief to be back in Zürau, he tells Brod on his return, though the letter is mainly about his inability even to write letters. Putting anything into words seems to be beyond

him, he says, 'in contrast to the happily-unhappily transported Kierkegaard who so wonderfully steers the undirigible airship'.

But his inability to write letters perhaps only meant that he was now focused entirely on the little octavo notebook and did not want to have to make the effort of putting on a performance for his friends. On 2 January, back in Zürau, he jotted down: 'True undoubting on the teacher's part, continual undoubting on the part of the pupil.' Baum's visit distracted him after that and there is only one entry for the week: 'Test yourself against mankind. It makes the doubter doubt, the believer believe.' Later he copied it out on sheet 75 and then, continually doubting, scratched it out. On 12 January he noted with relief: 'Tomorrow Baum goes away', and followed it with one of the simplest and most moving of the little meditations: 'This feeling, "I am not dropping anchor here", and instantly feeling the billowing, uplifting swell around me [*die wogende tragende Flut um sich fühlen*].' Nothing here is difficult to understand, neither the words nor the sentiment, and yet Kafka manages to set so many contradictory and complex feelings into play that it would take a whole essay to unpack, and the danger would then be that we had lost the essence. First, the way he starts, 'this feeling [*Dieses Gefühl*]', plunging us at once, like so many of the openings to the most successful 'aphorisms', into a little drama. And then does '*hier ankere ich nicht*' mean 'I will not anchor here' (because I don't want to), as Pasley takes it in his translation, or 'I wish I could but it seems I can't'? Michael Hofmann and Shelley Frisch, with their 'I am/I'm not dropping anchor here' preserve at least some of the ambiguity of the German. And then the way the language itself lifts us up, carries us onwards – but is it to a blissful future or to a death at sea, or perhaps both? Certainly it catches Kafka's frequent lament that there is no solid ground under his feet and so he is compelled to wander for ever, a *Luftmensch* or air-person, a Yiddish term applied to those who have no income and must rely on the community for support but often used by Zionists to

refer to the Jewish masses and by antisemites to refer to Jews as a whole. Yet there are none of these negative connotations here; we seem closer to Rimbaud's ecstatic vision in *Le Bateau ivre* than to the world of Sholem Aleichem, but all done so briefly, so quietly. A little miracle.

He follows this in the notebook with the uninteresting: 'Dealing with people engenders self-scrutiny', which he nevertheless thought well enough of to copy out later onto sheet 77, followed at once by 78: 'The spirit becomes free only when it ceases to be a source of support', and the day's entry ends with a short paragraph in the form of another 'aphorism', which feels effortful and confused, and he does not transcribe it. On 13 January he notes that Baum left with Ottla (she was going to accompany their blind friend back to Prague) and that he took a walk to Eischwitz, and ends with a remark about sensual love blinding us to heavenly love, though he gives it a Kafka twist by suggesting that it can only do so because it has an element of heavenly love within it.

The next day he notes: 'Dim, weak, impatient', and then the banal comment: 'There are only two things: truth and lies.' This leads, though, to one of his most acute insights: 'Truth is indivisible and so it cannot recognise itself; whoever claims to recognise it must be a lie.' Earlier he had written: 'Evil can speak to man but cannot become man.' Is this not absolutely central to his search, in those Zürau months, for answers to the deepest questions of life and the role of writing in that quest? For if he is right, then what he says opens up a role for art which elsewhere he finds it difficult to acknowledge: conceptual thought seeks to recognise 'the truth', and in so doing entangles itself in lies, but narrative and drama can show us the truth precisely by bringing 'the lie' out into the open. But is that not what all of Kafka's stories, from 'The Judgement' in 1912 to 'The Burrow' in 1924 actually do? Strangely, after copying this onto sheet 80 Kafka crossed it out.

The next day, 15 January, he began by noting: 'Impatient. Improvement. Walk at night to Oberklee.' (One wonders how many of his walks to nearby villages that winter were undertaken at night.) This is followed by one of his most laboured 'aphorisms': 'No one can desire what ultimately harms him. If in the case of a particular person it appears to be so after all – and perhaps it always does – this is explained by the fact that someone within that individual desires something that is of use to that someone but inflicts grievous harm on a second someone, who is brought in partly to judge the case. If the individual had sided with the second someone from the outset rather than waiting until the judgement, the first someone would have been defunct, and with him the desire.' I quote it in full only to show how clunking Kafka could be when he tried to write 'philosophy'. The puzzle is that he didn't see this and thought well enough of it to copy it out onto sheet 81. But then of course he never gave the anthology a title or sought to get it published. It may be that he realised that it had no unity either of feeling or expression but was simply a ragbag of confused thoughts, images, mini-dramas and fantasies. Today, thanks largely to Brod, they are venerated as the distillation of a wise man's thoughts about life. I have tried to counter this view here by suggesting that they were rather the anxious jottings of a man under sentence of death.

On 16 January he changed tack completely. Without any warning he produced one of the richest of his meditations on ancient myths and legends which, like the 'aphorisms', merge seamlessly into many of the 'stories' that make up *A Country Doctor*. We have already seen him write about Odysseus and the Sirens while in Zürau. Here too the voice is impersonal, timeless, authoritative. Kafka begins with a general remark that presents itself as clarificatory but at once plunges us into paradox: 'Legend tries to explain the inexplicable. Since it arises out of a foundation of truth it must end in the realm

of the inexplicable.' The voice goes on: 'There are four legends about Prometheus. According to the first, because he betrayed the gods to men he was chained to a rock in the Caucasus and the gods sent eagles that devoured his liver, which always grew again. According to the second, Prometheus in his agony, as the beaks hacked into him, pressed deeper and deeper into the rock until he became one with it. According to the third, in the course of thousands of years his treachery was forgotten, the gods forgot, the eagles forgot, he himself forgot. According to the fourth, everyone grew weary of what had become meaningless. The gods grew weary, the eagles grew weary, the wound closed wearily. What remained was the inexplicable range of mountains.'

This is familiar Kafka territory, but there is nothing second-hand about it. The writer who was drawn to depict the horrors of 'In the Penal Colony' and described almost with relish the ugly death of Josef K. in *The Trial* would naturally be drawn to the travails of Prometheus, and the unfolding of the narrative, drawing us towards an understanding of the nature of forgetting, aligns it with all those stories about messengers urgently setting out but losing their way and forgetting why they ever set out, as well as with the earlier 'aphorism' about kings and messengers. Yet in its brief span it is also a comment about truth and about tradition, as well as about the nature of legends themselves. Yet the most striking thing about it, I think, is the way Prometheus's torments are gradually folded into the larger geological history of the earth in a way that seems neither ironic nor cynical but, because perfectly natural, almost comforting. Kafka, however, chose not to include it in his little anthology and it remained locked in the rock of Octavo Notebook G until Max Brod rescued it and brought it into the public domain.

In the notebook it is followed by a little meditation on the misfortunes of one who finds himself in the middle of a

quadrille with no partner – one which moves, like 'Prufrock', effortlessly from the comic to the cosmic and back again. Though we know instinctively what the term Kafkaesque implies, it is worth remembering how many different registers Kafka could work in, his abundant imagination allowing him to switch from one to the other at the drop of a hat.

The following day, two brief comments: 'Walk to Oberklee. Limitation'. And: 'Respecting the Devil even in the Devil [*Im Teufel noch den Teufel achten*]'. What was the limitation (*Einschränkung*)? And as for the Devil, he was never far away in those months in Zürau. Then from 18 to 22 January Kafka is more expansive. First: 'The complaint: if I shall exist eternally, how shall I exist tomorrow?' – a nice rejoinder to Dostoevsky's 'Do you believe in eternal life? – Yes, in the here and now.' Then several paragraphs grappling with notions of Paradise, the Fall and the Tree of Life. Four of these he later copied into the little anthology as 83–6, the last a meditation so lengthy he had to use the reverse of 86 as well. Just before it he notes: 'Attempt to walk to Michelob. Mud'. And reading these entries we actually feel as if we are walking through mud. Though it's easy enough to find links with many of the preoccupations of those months, they strike me as both opaque and lacking in imaginative vitality, as though while Kafka clearly felt that he was, through his unique circumstances, peculiarly qualified to comment on the Fall, the opening chapters of Genesis didn't fire his imagination as Homer and Cervantes did. By contrast, the paragraph that follows bursts into life: 'In amazement we beheld the great horse. It broke through the roof of our room. The cloudy sky was drifting faintly along in mighty outline and its mane flew in the wind.' The *Diaries* are full of such extraordinary beginnings or fragments of stories, which are never developed yet even in such fragmentary form feel completely realised, but the little octavo notebook had until then been singularly free of them. Odysseus and the Sirens,

yes, Don Quixote and Sancho Panza, yes, thought-provoking remarks about leopards in temples and forlorn modern staircases, yes. But these grotesque and violent fragments, appearing out of nowhere and disappearing before we have even begun to take them in – no. Yet they now start to appear more and more frequently in the octavo notebooks, as the intensity of Kafka's quest to 'become clear about the ultimate things' begins to abate and his old urge to give free rein to his imagination returns.

For the present, though, he is still grappling with the issues that had been in his mind since the outset of his Zürau sojourn. 'Art flies around the truth, but with the decided intention of not getting burnt. Its capacity lies in finding in the dark void a place where the beam of light can be intensely caught without this having been perceptible before.' This follows on from 80, about truth being indivisible, and 63, about art only being able to show the mask of horror recoiling from the light of truth. All three bring out the subterfuges art has to resort to in order to go on doing its work in our dark times.

Then comes one of those compacted sentences that flash out every now and again from the notebook, mysterious, unparaphrasable, yet instantly understandable: 'A belief like a guillotine, as heavy, as light.' Part of its mysteriousness rests in the grammar. Kafka wrote: '*Ein Glaube, wie ein Fallbeil so schwer, so licht.*' When he copied it out into the new little anthology (87), he wrote: '*Ein Glaube wie ein Fallbeil, so schwer, so licht.*' What a difference a comma can make! The first version stresses the belief: 'A belief like a guillotine, so heavy, so light.' The second the guillotine: 'A belief, like a guillotine, just as heavy, just as light.' Both formulations leave it in the air whether this is a belief I hold, one I would like to hold, or one I can just about imagine holding. But no paraphrase can convey the shock, both of horror and of recognition, of comparing belief to the Revolution's deadly instrument of justice. It is,

I think, the violence combined with gentleness – the victim hardly feels a thing as his head is cut off – that makes the quiet sentence so memorable.

It is followed in the notebook by a far more laboured and less resonant remark: 'Death is before us, rather like a picture of the Battle of Alexander on the classroom wall. It is imperative for us to use our actions to obscure or even obliterate this picture in our lifetime.' Stach suggests that this was a reproduction of the so-called Alexander Mosaic found in Pompeii and dated second century B.C., which was on display at the secondary school in Prague that Kafka attended. Pasley directs us rather to the sixteenth-century German painter Albrecht Altdorfer's painting of the same subject. It doesn't matter who is right. Alexander's triumph in the battle against the Persians at Issus was a decisive moment in his life, in that of the army he commanded, and perhaps in European history. Kafka had long been fascinated by the legendary quality of Alexander's life. The story he was so insistent should come first in his recent collection, 'The New Advocate', reimagined Alexander's battle horse as a modern functionary, spending his days immersed in old documents while a vestige of his former glory still seems to cling to him in the eyes of all who see him. Here he appears to suggest that we must make every effort to obliterate the image of the heroic, triumphant Alexander. Why? Because to carry it about in our minds keeps us from accepting that we no longer live in that heroic world? Because it makes of death a single decisive, heroic moment? But if it is not that then what is it? Kafka had come to Zürau to confront his own mortality, but, as he quickly understood, even to put things in such terms is to confer a heroic quality on death, which keeps us from understanding it. Rather, we should spend our lives trying to remove this image from our minds.

The next entry, on 25 January, presses on with these thoughts: 'The suicide is the prisoner who sees a gallows

being erected in the prison yard, mistakenly thinks it is the one intended for him, breaks out of his cell in the night and goes down and hangs himself.' We are back, by a roundabout route, to the theme of patience and impatience he started these short pieces with: suicide is a form of impatience, a mistaken desire to be a second Alexander, triumphing over death this time, rather than the Persians. And he follows it with a long paragraph which, in the form of a Hasidic or Buddhist parable, tells us that before the Holy of Holies we must shed not only our possessions and our clothing but even our nakedness 'and everything that is under the nakedness and everything that hides beneath that… and then the residue and then even the glimmer of the undying fire.' And he adds, in a sentence that could stand by itself: 'Not the shaking off of the self but the consuming of the self. [*Nicht Selbstabschüttelung sondern Selbstaufzehrung*.]' Instead of nurturing the merest glimmer of 'the undying fire' we must somehow allow ourselves to be consumed by it, in a fulfilment rather than a denial, but a fulfilment which would lack all sense of heroism or decisiveness. Remember the burning bush? We are in Rilke territory here and though I'm sure Kafka means every word of it, that is not really where his instincts tend to take him.

The last date in Octavo Notebook G is 28 January. Kafka starts the entry as he so often does with a brief comment on his state of mind: 'Vanity, self-forgetfulnesss, some days'. Then: 'Two possibilities: to make oneself infinitely small, or to be so. The first is perfection, that is, inaction, the second is beginning, that is, action.' The first part is clear enough. Kafka always longed to disappear. Not just merge into the crowd and not be the tall awkward man he was, immediately noticeable, but to vanish entirely in order to avoid the objectifying gaze of others. ('There is no finer fate for a story than to disappear', he says to Milena, and the title he envisaged for his first novel was *Der Verschollene, The Man Who Disappeared.* This was not

a unique aspiration. 'I should have been a pair of ragged claws, / Scuttling across the floors of silent seas', says Prufrock/Eliot, and Stevens often wishes to be the opposite of the equestrian statue of the triumphant horseman, to be no thing, a snow man, or 'the listener, who listens in the snow, / And nothing himself, beholds / nothing that is not there and the nothing that is'. What they are all searching for in their art – and in their lives, actually – is a kind of perfect anonymity, something that is the opposite of the image of the entrepreneur, the figure of Progress, linked to capitalism in society and, in art, to fictions with beginnings, middles and a nice resolution at the end. The puzzle with Kafka's formulation is that in the second part he has clearly mixed the two positions up, in that inaction has to be connected with *being* infinitely small rather than trying to make oneself that. After copying it into the little anthology (90), he anyway crossed it out.

And then this: 'For the avoidance of a verbal confusion: Whatever is to be actively destroyed must first be held quite firmly in the hand and the eye: what crumbles crumbles but cannot be destroyed.' As that early letter to Oskar Pollack from Liboch attests, Kafka was fascinated by the physicality of the earth that it was possible to pick up and run through one's fingers when out in the countryside, something which is singularly absent from the modern city. It is the image of renewability, the life and death cycle of nature as opposed to the concrete and iron of the city. When he came to copy the sentence out on sheet 91 he removed the phrase 'in the hand and the eye', which he must have felt was redundant. But he kept the wonderful double 'crumbles', which is unnecessary as far as meaning goes but enacts what the sentence is saying. And again as in all the best of these, we are pulled in two directions at once: total destruction may be desirable, the idea of holding something 'quite firmly in the hand' may be enticing, but is it not perhaps a lure and a temptation? And why

'verbal confusion?' Why not just 'confusion'? Yet *Wort-Irrtums* is what Kafka wrote and later recopied. The Wittgenstein-like phrase, though, sits oddly with the rest of the little pieces in his notebooks.

Two more paragraphs bring that notebook to an end. The first appears to belong more to the genre of pulp fiction but becomes more understandable if we see it as an allegory of the internal forces tearing him: A., we are told, could neither live congenially with G nor get a divorce, and so shoots himself. The second is another meditation on good and evil, death and eternal life. It ends: 'Expulsion from Paradise was not an act but a happening', harking back to the thought about the Battle of Alexander. Kafka is still trying to find the correct way of saying what he felt was happening to him.

Octavo Notebook H

Some time between 28 and 31 January Kafka must have reached the end of one little octavo notebook and started another. He begins the new one with a long meditation on idol worship, some of which he copied out later as 'aphorism' 92. The thought is neither original nor particularly illuminating and the writing flat. He picks up the underlying theme, though, the nature of personal responsibility, in the following paragraph, which he did not copy out: 'If all responsibility is imposed on you then you may want to exploit the moment and want to be overwhelmed by responsibility; yet if you try you will notice that nothing was imposed on you but that you are yourself this responsibility.' This is typical of Kafka in the way it highlights the fact that when we are dealing with the inner life then both everything and nothing may be at stake at the same time. And very Kafka too is the twist: 'you are yourself the responsibility', which seems at moments

profoundly meaningful and at others quite devoid of meaning. Then comes a little parable about Atlas, going on with this theme: 'Atlas was permitted the opinion that he was at liberty to drop the earth and creep away; but this opinion was all that he was permitted.' And this in turn leads to a different, almost untranslatable formulation: 'The apparent silence in which the days, seasons, generations and centuries follow upon each other signifying a pricking up of the ears [*bedeutet Aufhorchen*]: so do horses trot before the cart.' As so often in these pieces, the elements out of which they are made seem to offer meaning and then withdraw it. Do the alert ears pick up the passage of time which takes place only in 'apparent silence'? But then how does the final phrase modify this? Do the alert ears of the horse pick up where the driver wishes to go? But how does that translate into the human awareness of the passing of time?

Now comes the first date in the new notebook, 31 January. 'Gardening,' he notes, 'hopelessness'. And then, reflecting this mood, another little vignette about hand-to-hand combat: 'A fight in which there is no way, at any stage, of getting protection for one's back. And in spite of knowing this one keeps on forgetting it. And even when one does not forget it one seeks protection all the same, solely in order to rest while seeking it, and in spite of the fact that one knows one will pay for doing so.'

However, by the time of the next entry, 1 February, his mood seems to have lifted. He notes the receipt of Lenz's *Letters*, which Wolff had just published and sent him, and then, in very Wittgensteinian mode: '*Zum letztenmal Psychologie!*', which can be translated, as Frisch does, 'Psychology, for the last time!', or, more freely, with Hofmann, catching the sense and giving due weight to Kafka's use of the exclamation mark here: 'No psychology ever again!' Kafka later copied it into the little anthology (93), the shortest piece there, but then crossed

it out. It summarises succinctly what he had often said in his diaries and in his letters to Brod, that simply studying the self will never get at what makes the self tick, and therefore is less than useless in trying to change course if one feels one has been going in the wrong direction all one's life. In the musings of the Zürau months he had also, as we've seen, frequently used Genesis 2–3 to make the same point: psychology is not a neutral instrument, it is the instrument of the serpent. He will return to it as he comes to the end of the 'aphorisms', on 25 February, when, in an extended series of meditations, he comes as close as he ever does to summing up his thoughts on the subject.

On the next day he notes the receipt of a letter from Wolff, probably the one in which he wrote that he would of course respect Kafka's wishes regarding the order of the stories in *A Country Doctor*, and follows this with a brief meditation on the subject of evil, later copied as 95, then crossed out. On 3 February he reports a visit from his cousin Irma, followed by a tortured little meditation on 'this life' and a 'higher life', which became 96.

On 4 February he begins by noting: 'Lying for a long time, sleeplessness, becoming conscious of the struggle [*Bewusstwerden des Kampfes*].' That struggle finds expression in a brief thought on truth and lies, and then one on suffering which with a few changes became 97. The first entry for the next day shows how volatile were Kafka's moods at the time: 'A good morning, impossible to remember everything.' He then proceeds, though, to note down, in two longish paragraphs, what he presumably remembers from the previous night, which once again goes over the paradoxes of evil, Eden and the two Trees of Life and of Knowledge. The following day he notes that he has been to Flohau, and this is followed by thoughts on the infinite expanse of the cosmos, which became 98 and was then crossed out.

The entry for the following day starts with the enigmatic: 'Soldier with stones. Island of Rügen', a reminder that we are in the middle of a war, not all that far from the front, and that Kafka is as ready as ever to see what is going on in the village and to talk to those who are passing through. Then come several pages in which a note rarely found in the writings of those months is struck: pleasure, perhaps even joy. He begins, as so often, with weariness: 'Weariness does not necessarily signify weakness of faith – or does it? In any case weariness signifies insufficiency. I feel too tightly constricted in everything that signifies myself; even the eternity that I am is too tight for me [*selbst die Ewigkeit, die ich bin, ist mir zu eng*].' But then the tone starts to shift: 'But if, for instance, I read a good book, say an account of travels, it rouses me, satisfies me, suffices me… From a certain stage of knowledge on, weariness, insufficiency, constriction, self-contempt, must all vanish: namely at the point where I have the strength to recognise as my own nature what previously was something alien to myself that refreshed me, satisfied, liberated and exalted [*erfrischte, befriedigte, befreite, erhob*] me.'

At the start of his stay in Zürau, we remember, he had wondered whether the very ability to write down the words 'I am in despair' was not 'a merciful surplus of powers at a moment when the pain has actually visibly used up all my powers to the bottom of my being'. The joy he had experienced on finishing 'The Judgement' on that September night in 1912 had seemed far away, all but forgotten. He had felt a burst of joy on first arriving in Zürau, but then, as he began the long process of attempting to understand what his illness meant for him, such feelings had dropped away. Now, though, he acknowledges that reading a book that is to his taste drains the weariness from his limbs and spirit, that there is a moment when what had previously been alien to him has the ability to refresh, even to liberate and – yes – exalt him. It's a remarkable turn.

He of course goes on to question this and gets into a long argument with himself, clearly influenced by Kierkegaard, about 'commandments' and how we respond to them, ending with the enigmatic 'Christ, moment', in a separate paragraph. The next day carries only the laconic remark: 'Got up early, chance to work'. Work clearly has nothing to do with his notebook, but refers to work for Ottla in the fields. This is followed, the next day, by what seems to be an account of happenings in the village: 'The windless calm on some days, the noise made by those arriving, the way our people come running out of the houses to welcome them…'. But we gradually realise that this is the start of a story set by the sea, for 'the boats, instantly gripped by a hundred arms, push up onto the beach, the foreign men gaze round them and climb up into the broad daylight of the square'. The need to write fiction is beginning to re-assert itself.

Yet it is not so easy to distinguish the personal from the fictional where Kafka is concerned. In what follows it is impossible to say whether he is writing a note to himself about a story he is at work on, a note to himself about a thought generated by the story, or is still within the story: 'Why is what is easy so difficult? Of seductions I have had – let there be no enumerations. What is easy is difficult. It is so easy and so difficult. Like a game of tag where the only "home" is a tree on the far side of the ocean. But why did they ever set forth from that place? – It is on the coast that the billows crash most freely, so narrow a room do they have here, and so unconquerable… Ever and again the straits will oppress me.'

Then we are back to sin and faith in two tortuous paragraphs. Here is a fragment of the second: 'How much more oppressive than the most uncompromising conviction of our current state of sin is even the weakest conviction of the erstwhile justification for our temporality. Only the fortitude to endure this second conviction, which, in its purity, entirely

encompasses the first, is the measure of faith.' In its convoluted syntax and abstract vocabulary this is reminiscent of much of the humdrum theological writing of the time, and shows how Kafka's self-imposed exile and leisure in Zürau could lead to some of his worst as well as his best writing. He obviously felt it spoke to his concerns, though, for he copied it into the little anthology (99) and in 1920 even added another, slightly more resonant 'aphorism' to it.

On 10 February he noted: 'Sunday. Peace Ukraine'. In the chaos of the Bolshevik revolution Ukraine had made a separate peace with Germany and Austro-Hungary, and of course all things to do with the war were of immediate concern to the citizens of the Austro-Hungarian Empire, and especially to those, like Kafka, who still felt the threat of an imminent call-up. Yet what follows in the new notebook is something we have rarely seen before in the Zürau jottings but which will become more and more prevalent as the weeks go by: he starts to use the notebook to try out stories as well as to go on trying to make sense of what is happening to him. On 11 February he notes: 'Peace Russia' and follows it with: 'Ever ready, his house is portable, he lives always in his native country.' A story? A dream? He who never felt at home anywhere to live always 'in his native country'? And is the fulfilment of such a dream simply a matter of re-orienting the self? At times Kafka tried to believe it was.

He follows this with a long, convoluted iteration of many of the ideas that had been preoccupying him that winter: transience, the nature of hope and faith, our fight against the world. 'Look into it' he admonishes himself, and then, to an imaginary 'you': 'All you offer me is proof that I had to ask the question.' But there is no answer. 'And so that means: you either will not or cannot answer me.'

In the middle of February he went briefly to Prague, noting on the 19 February: 'Back from Prague. Ottla in

Zarch.' Then comes a fragment of fiction, tiny, but as so often with Kafka, profoundly resonant: 'The moonlight dazzled us. Birds shrieked from tree to tree. There was a buzzing in the fields.' And then, a new paragraph: 'We crawled through the dust, a pair of snakes.' It is unclear, though, if the last sentence belongs with the first three and the 'us' is the pair of snakes, or is the start of a separate story.

More abstract philosophising follows, and then two 'aphorisms' (100 and 101): 'There can be knowledge of the diabolical but not a belief in it, for more of the diabolical than is actually present does not exist.' And: 'Sin always comes openly and can be grasped instantly with the senses. Transparent, as something self-created. It comes from the outside and, if asked, names its provenance.' Both show the degree of Kafka's immersion in Protestant theology at this time and both seem far too vague and abstract to convey his thoughts. Yet he copied them into his little anthology, changing the second significantly as he did so: 'Sin always comes openly and can be grasped instantly with the senses. It walks on its roots and needn't be torn out.' Like the early piece (4) about the river of death which rears up in disgust and has to be stroked to be appeased, this one suddenly comes alive when sin is made to 'walk on its roots'. It is rare that we can be present as Kafka makes a correction that will improve his work, and this shows how, at his best, he transforms abstract ideas into the animated and dramatic.

Two more turgid and abstract paragraphs follow, the second of which he chose to incorporate into the anthology (102), though when he did so he removed a sentence which read: 'Christ suffered for mankind but mankind must suffer for Christ' – proof, if one were needed, that he was reading a lot of Christian theology. The next day he added a further thought on suffering and then one about free will, both later transcribed into the anthology (103 and 104). This last is

one of the longest and most theological/philosophical of the lot, though it has a characteristic twist in the tail, for, having started 'Man has free will of three kinds', it ends: 'Those are the three facets of free will, but it is also… one single facet and is fundamentally so utterly one single facet that it has no place for a will, whether free or unfree.'

On 23 February he notes, 'Unwritten letter', followed by a thought on marriage as 'the representative of life with which you are meant to come to terms', which shows that, despite the break with Felice and his insistence that no one with TB should even think of getting married, the idea of marriage was still much on his mind. But he goes on with a confused set of remarks that couches his current concerns in language that seems to come straight out of the misogynist playbook of early twentieth-century Europe: 'The seductiveness of this world and the token guaranteeing that this world is only a transition are one and the same. Rightly so, for that is the only way the world can seduce us, and it is in keeping with the truth. But the bad thing is that once a seduction has been successful we forget the warranty, and so Good lured us into Evil, the woman's gaze into her bed.'

The next day, after jotting down the single enigmatic letter 'H', he wrestles with thoughts about humility and prayer which he later copies out into the anthology as 106. A meandering paragraph about modern inventions follows and then he returns to thoughts about the elasticity of time: 'Evidence of a real pre-existence: I have seen you before, the marvels of primeval times and at the end of time.'

He begins 25 February the way he often does, with a note about the day and how he is feeling: 'Morning clearness'. There follows perhaps the fullest and most lucid account of himself and his place in the world that we have, and which for that reason is worth examining in detail. 'It is not inertia, ill will, awkwardness – even if there is something of all this

in it… that causes me to fail, or not even to get near failing: family life, friendship, marriage, profession, literature', he begins. 'It is not that but the lack of ground underfoot, of air, of direction [*der Mangel des Bodens, der Luft, des Gebotes*].' We have seen how prone Kafka is to blame himself for everything, how, as Max Brod noted (and Kafka's violent reaction to this suggests that it hit the mark), he sometimes seems to take a perverse pleasure in doing so. Here we feel he is really getting somewhere because for once he dismisses this (though of course, being Kafka, he half-acknowledges it in the same breath – 'even if there is something of all this in it'). He goes on: 'It is my task to create these, not in order that I may then, as it were, catch up with what I have missed, but in order that I shall have missed nothing, for the task is as good as any other.' This is vague and difficult to understand because at this point Kafka himself is groping. 'What is my task?' he asks, pulling himself up. And how does one 'create' 'ground underfoot' and 'air'? He tries for an image: '… just as one may, on climbing to heights, where the air is thin, suddenly step into the far-distant sun.' 'Of course,' he acknowledges, 'this is no exceptional task either; it is sure to have been set often before. True, I don't know whether it has ever been set to such a degree.' And then: 'I have brought nothing with it of what life requires, as far as I know, but only the universal human weakness. With this – in this respect it is a gigantic strength – I have vigorously absorbed the negative elements of the age in which I live, an age that is of course very close to me, which I have no right ever to fight against, but as it were to represent… I have not been guided by the hand of Christianity – admittedly now slack and failing – as Kierkegaard was, and have not caught the hem of the Jewish prayer shawl – now flying away from us – as the Zionists have. I am an end and a beginning.'

When he had first moved to Zürau he had written in his diary: 'You have as far as this chance exists at all, the chance

to make a beginning. You won't be able to avoid the filth that wells up out of you if you want to penetrate. But don't wallow in it.' After months of perhaps undue wallowing he seems, on this morning of clarity in February 1918, to have recognised that perhaps the hardest thing is not unduly blaming himself. In any other writer these remarks might have sounded arrogant, even egomaniacal. 'I am an end and a beginning' is as Nietzschean as you can get. Yet in Kafka, after these months of soul-searching, it sounds like simple self-understanding. With no ground beneath his feet, no guiding set of beliefs, Christian, Jewish or Zionist, the only task is to represent the age by being yourself. Suddenly his very weakness, his very lack of outer props, instead of being the impediment he had always tended to see it as, becomes a source of gigantic strength.

He carries on writing in his notebook on that February day in Zürau, turning now to the nature of death, his own imminent one and how it is viewed in the modern world: 'After a person's death for a short span of time, even on earth, a special beneficial silence sets in with regard to the dead person; a terrestrial fever has ceased, a dying is no longer seen to be continuing, an error seems to have been remedied, even for the living there is an opportunity to breathe freely, for which reason, too, the windows are opened in the room where death took place – and then everything turns out to have been, after all, only a semblance, and the sorrow and the lamentations begin.' Life is a long dying, but it is also a false dying, a playing at death; with the real thing clarity is, perhaps only for a moment, present.

The mood of clarity in relation to the self and the world persists the following day: 'Sunny morning', he notes, then gets down to further thinking about death. 'Our salvation is death,' he writes enigmatically, 'but not this one.' 'Everyone is very kind to A,' he writes, 'rather in the way that one tries to protect an excellent billiard-table even from good players,

until such a time as a great player arrives, carefully examines the surface, will tolerate no premature blemish, but then, when he begins to play himself, runs riot in the most restless manner [*sich auf die rücksichtsloseste Weise auswütet*].' Only Kafka, who could inhabit the feelings of a beetle, a jackal, a bridge, a staircase, could imagine himself as a billiard-table. But then who is the great player? Felice? Art? It is Kafka at his enigmatic best, in that we sort of understand even as we are baffled – perhaps it is the sudden controlled violence with which this single long slow sentence ends that does it, the explosion, after the careful examination of the table, of the restlessness of the great player suddenly breaking out into a frenzy of activity.

Later this became 107 in the little anthology; now, however, he takes a new direction. Surprisingly, it begins with a quotation: '"But then he returned to work as though nothing had happened." We are familiar with this remark from any number of old tales, though it may not be found in any of them.'

This type of remark is familiar to us from the work of another Austrian writer, Peter Handke, but it is extremely rare in Kafka. A quotation from a letter he wrote to Felice on 17–18 January 1913 should help, though, to set it in context: 'I have now, dearest,' he writes, 'for the first time in a long time spent a lovely hour reading again. You would never guess what I have read and what has caused me such pleasure. It was an old issue of the *Gartenlaube* from the year 1863. I didn't read anything in particular but leafed slowly through 200 pages, examined the (at that time, due to the costly reproduction, rare) images, and only here and there read something of particular interest. Time and again I am drawn to older eras in this fashion, and the pleasure of experiencing human relations and ways of thinking in a complete yet still wholly understandable version (my God, 1863, that was only fifty years ago), in spite of this no longer being able to experience them in detail from

below, emotionally, and hence being confronted with the need to play with them according to my mood and fancy – this contradictory pleasure, for me, is tremendous. Time and again, I like to read newspapers and journals. And this old, heart-wrenching, expectant Germany from the middle of the previous century! The modest circumstances, the closeness that each person feels to others, the publisher to the subscriber, the writer to the reader, the reader to the great writers of the period (Uhland, Jean-Paul, Seume, Rückert...).'

We have met this 'old, heart-rending, expectant Germany from the middle of the previous century' before in the Zürau jottings, in the form of the well-worn stairs, but here it is drained of all pathos. 'He' here is not a simple substitute for 'I', as it is in most novels, but an assertion of the authority of the storyteller: this is how it was. In its refusal of psychology, of any search for motivation, it is wonderfully calm and restful, in stark contrast to all the breathless fiction of our time. A sliver of an older order amidst the torment and anxiety that permeates the octavo notebooks.

After this masterpiece of effortless compression come a few random phrases about knights and Abraham, no doubt sparked off by his reading of Kierkegaard's *Fear and Trembling* and the depiction there of Abraham as a 'knight of faith', followed by a convoluted paragraph about the meaning of life, and then what became the last 'aphorism', 109, which takes the form of a dialogue: '"It cannot be said that we lack belief. The very fact that we live at all is an inexhaustible wellspring of belief." "That would indicate a wellspring of belief? Surely one cannot not live." "The incredible power of belief lies squarely in that 'surely one cannot'; it takes on its form in this negation."' To this rather clumsy and unmemorable piece he later (1920) added the very Kafkaesque: 'It is not necessary for you to leave the house. Stay at your table and listen. Don't even listen, just wait; be utterly still and alone. The world will offer itself to you

to be unmasked; it cannot do otherwise; it will writhe before you in ecstasy.' And with this the little anthology comes to an end. Kafka added nothing more to it and, as I have said, never sought to publish it.

The Last Pages of Notebook H

27 February is the last date in Octavo Notebook H, so it is impossible to know when in the next two months the fragments that follow were written. In many of them Kafka seems to be engaged in sorting out his thoughts about Kierkegaard and especially his depiction of Abraham in *Fear and Trembling*. But as he thinks and writes about this he appears to grow tired of Kierkegaard, as he told Brod. Here he simply notes: 'He has too much mind and by means of that mind he travels across the earth as upon a magic chariot, going even where there are no roads. And he cannot find out from himself that there are no roads there. In this way his humble plea to be followed turns into tyranny and his honest belief that he is "on the road" into arrogance.'

But now comes a strange intrusion into Notebook H. Kafka was used to drawing up reports for the Institute, but here we have a blueprint for, as the title has it, *The Brotherhood of Poor Workers,* in numbered paragraphs. The obligations for those joining are 'to possess no money... the most simple dress (to be defined in detail), whatever is necessary for work, food for one's consumption. Everything else belongs to the poor.' Here you earn your living by working for it, and 'either to choose the work oneself or, if this is not possible, to fall in with the arrangements made by the Labour Council, which is responsible to the Government'. One will work for no wages 'other than is necessary to support life... for two days' and 'eat only what is absolutely necessary to support life'. The

relationship of employee to employer is 'to be treated as a relation of mutual trust'. In return one has certain rights, such as a maximum working time of six hours, less for manual work, to be looked after by the state when sick or old. Strangely, '[p]rovisionally at least, expulsion of independent persons, married persons, and women… Five hundred men upper limit. One trial year.'

Had someone requested such a document? Was it a socialist or Zionist dream of Kafka's? There it is, with no comment and we know of no such Brotherhood planned or proposed, though there were many similar plans drawn up by Zionists at the time for a communal life in Palestine, and we know Kafka was interested in these, was learning Hebrew and even dreamed of one day settling in Palestine – one of many unrealised dreams. Seeing it there in the notebook reminds us that while trying to make sense of the illness that had so unexpectedly manifested itself in his body he was also living the life and dreaming the dreams of many middle-class intellectuals in central Europe in those years of war and change.

There is a space in the notebook and then a story fragment about the building of a great temple, followed in turn by what could be another fragment, notes for a story or a number of stories, or an account of village life: 'Upstream towards the wandering water. Clumps of birches. The teacher's voice suddenly raised. Murmuring of the children. Sun fading red, abandoning itself, overawed. Stove door slamming. Coffee is being made. We sit. Leaning on the table, waiting. Thin little saplings on one side of the road. Month of March. What more do you want? We rise out of the graves and want to go roaming through this world too, but we have no definite plan.' Then come other fragments, including one of Kafka's reworkings of classical legend: 'Poseidon grew tired of his seas. The trident fell from his grasp. Silent, there he sat on a rocky

coast, and a gull, stupefied by his presence, flashed in wavering circles round his head.' Then one of those strange suggestive sentences catching things in motion in four brief words: 'The wildly bowling carriage.'

This is in turn followed by lines written out as verse, striking for being much less immediate and evocative than the preceding prose fragments. It begins '*Ach was wird uns hier bereitet*', and peters out after twenty or so lines:

> Ah, what has been readied for us here
> Bed and couch under the trees
> Green darkness, dry leafage,
> Little sun, damp scent of flowers
> Ah, what has been set before us here…

Is it an evocation of Eden? A memory of that youthful sojourn in Liboch? Whatever it is, it fails to spark. Kafka's peculiar vision after his early experiments in fantasy has its basis in an unadorned realism which is immediately disturbed ('As Gregor Samsa woke up from uneasy dreams he found himself transformed into a gigantic insect'), yet remains ever-present, the ground upon which the story is played out. The formal qualities of verse would seem to go against that, and this little venture into it lacks conviction and is never repeated.

He now starts a story about a count sitting down to lunch, and keeps it going for well over a page, more than he has given the other fragments in the notebooks. It too stops abruptly though, and he begins another story, or perhaps tries another version of the same one: 'We were drinking, the sofa was becoming too small for us, the hands of the clock on the wall never ceased to whirl round and round. The servant looked in, we beckoned to him with raised hands. But he was held spellbound by an apparition on the sofa at the window. There an old man in a thick, black, shining robe was slowly rising

to his feet, his fingers still toying with the arms of the sofa. "Father," the son exclaimed, and "Emil" responded the old man.'

The next paragraph consists of one sentence: 'The distance to my fellow man is for me a very long one.' And the last entry is headed simply: 'Prague.' Under it: 'Religions get lost as people do.' And with that Octavo Notebook H comes to an end. More important, 'Prague' signals that we are in the last days of April and that the whole Zürau experiment is over.

Kafka returned to Prague on 30 April 1918. Ottla had visited the capital in February to try for one last time to get the Institute to offer her brother early retirement, but the firm was adamant. They needed Kafka and there was no medical reason why he should not return to his old job; the most they were prepared to offer was to extend his leave till the end of April. That, then, was the reason for his return, and on 1 May he was back in the office. He was to remain there and work for the Institute as assiduously as he had always done till his TB eventually made it impossible for him to continue. As he wrote with rare insight to Ottla in 1921: 'The Company is for me a feather bed, it weighs on me as much as it keeps me warm. If I were ever to manage to escape from it I would at once be in danger of catching cold, for the world is not heated.'

And though the break with Felice was indeed final this time, and his ostensible reason that a man with TB should not think of marrying was given to all as the reason for the break and was accepted by most, it did not stop Kafka's quest for a life companion, nor seemingly make him any less attractive to women. There were to be three more in his life between 1918 and his premature death in 1924. The first of these, Julie Wohryzek, he met early 1919. Her father was the sexton (*shames*) of a synagogue in Prague and she was twenty-eight when they met. Her fiancé had been killed in the war and Kafka, as though the long travails of his relationship with Felice had taught him nothing, was soon asking her to marry him, much to his father's horror. The arrival of Milena on the scene put an end to that.

Milena Jesenská was born in Prague in 1896 and after briefly studying medicine had married a Czech Jewish intellectual, Oskar Pollack, and moved with him to Vienna,

where she started translating to supplement his income and came across 'The Stoker'. She wrote to the author to ask if he would allow her to translate it into Czech and a passionate correspondence ensued, punctuated by two brief meetings. Here was someone, quite unlike Felice or Julie, who was his intellectual equal, someone with whom he could exchange views on artistic and political and not just emotional matters. The letters he wrote to her are the most honest, passionate and painful he ever wrote. She, however, had her own problems, which included an egotistical over-possessive father and an addiction to cocaine, and was besides in thrall to an abusive husband. It gradually became clear to Kafka that she would never leave Pollack and by November 1920, heartbroken, he ended their relationship. Yet they continued to correspond sporadically throughout 1921 and 1922 and it was to her that he entrusted his diaries. She was later to join the underground resistance to the Nazi occupation of Czechoslovakia and, among other exploits, help numerous Jews escape. She was eventually caught and died in Ravensbrück in May 1945. A memoir by a fellow inmate, Margaret Buber-Neumann, was published after her death and she is remembered in Yad Vashem as one of the 'righteous gentiles'.

Kafka's final love was Dora Diamant, a much younger Jewish woman with whom he seemed at last to find some semblance of peace. Although he was already a very sick man when they met she managed to do what no one else had done, get him to move away from Prague and his family and settle in Berlin. To Baum he wrote on 26 September 1922: 'Within the limits of my condition that is a foolhardiness whose parallel you can only find by leafing back through the pages of history, say to Napoleon's march to Russia' – showing that the image of Napoleon never ceased to haunt him. But the Berlin they settled in in the winter of 1922 was in the throes of rampant inflation and the lack of heating and food were fatal to

someone with Kafka's fragile constitution, so that their time together turned into a life of successive nursing homes, and it was in one of these, in Kierling, not far from Vienna, that he died of tuberculosis of the larynx in the middle of correcting the proofs of his final book of stories, in June 1924.

Thus though Kafka was to write to Milena in 1920 that those eight months in the village were 'perhaps the best time of my life', he seemed to settle back into his old life and habits in Prague as though nothing had happened. But of course spiritually and artistically a great deal had. For one thing he had hit upon a new literary form, call it aphorism or maxim or *pensée* or adage, it doesn't matter. It's not quite any of those things, for they all imply authority, an author summing up and passing on a thought, a reflection, a piece of instruction or advice. Auden described the aphorism as an aristocratic mode, meaning that it is very much advice or admonition handed down from above. Kafka's short pieces, by contrast, those he thought well enough of to cream off from his notebooks and inscribe into his little anthology as well as the many others scattered throughout the two octavo notebooks, are, apart from rare exceptions, characterised by their exploratory, groping quality, by their refusal of closure. That this form appealed to him is clear not only from the fact of his starting the little anthology and including in it over a hundred items, but also that even as late as 1920 he was still revising and adding to them, and that in January of that year he began a new collection, usually known as 'He', since the subject of these is always in the third person. At the same time the fact that both collections were abandoned suggests that in the end he was not satisfied with the form. They lay there with the rest of his unpublished papers, saved by Brod from the fire to which Kafka had instructed him to consign them. And, as I hope has become evident in the course of the foregoing discussion, a close reading of the notebooks in which, along

with much else, he first jotted them down, along with much else, makes it difficult to see what led him to select one little item rather than another, and impossible to treat it as a unified whole, a 'testament' or 'theology'.

No, the discovery of the short form was not the main lesson of those months. Kafka had gone to Zürau with the explicit intention, as he wrote in his diary at the start of his stay, of using his time there to dig down and try to understand what his life was about. For the whole of his early writing life he had been complaining to his diary and his friends that without freedom from the drudgery of office work he would never be able to write what he felt he had it in him to write. And it is clear from his letters to Felice over the five years of their tortuous relationship that he also felt that sharing his life with her would be the death of his art. At the same time, as we have seen, he felt that the life of a bachelor cut him off from normality and that without marriage and children not only would his father be fully justified in seeing him as a dismal failure but, more important, his writing would have no foundation. Now the blood had given him the opportunity to break free of the office, his family and Felice. He needed to grasp it with both hands.

And the diagnosis of TB was not something like learning that his leg was broken and he would have to take time off till it healed. It was, in effect, a death sentence, precisely what, even in the most unthinking person, would act as a spur to reflection on the meaning and purpose of life and of one's place in it.

Kafka thus began his stay in the country with an overriding sense that this was his chance to ask himself the most fundamental questions: Why had this happened to him? What was the meaning of his life, of his overwhelming compulsion to write and the strange product of that urge? And why did it, instead of bringing him closer to the world, as he felt it should, seem only to further distance him from

it? These questions, which we might broadly term religious, were what tormented him in the aftermath of the blood. And so Brod was in a sense right in the first title he chose for his publication of those short pieces, 'Thoughts on Sin, Suffering, Hope and the True Way', except that this gives a totally wrong impression of what follows. It might have been right for Kierkegaard, but Kierkegaard was in the end a theologian, though a strange one. Kafka was not, not even the most negative of theologians. To repeat what he said in his most lucid moment: 'I have vigorously absorbed the negative elements of the age in which I live, an age that is of course very close to me, which I have no right ever to fight against, but as it were to represent… I have not been guided into life by the hand of Christianity – admittedly now slack and failing – as Kierkegaard was, and have not caught the hem of the Jewish prayershawl – now flying away from us – as the Zionists have. I am an end and a beginning.'

That does not stop him, at various moments in his struggle for meaning in those Zürau months, from employing the vocabulary of both Christian and Jewish religious thought and turning to both the Hebrew Scriptures and the New Testament. Yet when he does so the writing too often starts to feel flat and second-hand. At other times he creates brief stories or dramas, such as the river of death writhing in anger and leopards breaking into a temple, which are both enigmatic and highly resonant, just as his best stories are; or little parables, such as those of Ulysses and the Sirens or Don Quixote and Sancho Panza, which are no different from the parables he wrote throughout his life. And the gradual giving way of intense concentration on questions of the ultimate meaning of life as the winter of 1917–18 began to turn into spring suggests that the search for answers had begun to lose its grip.

The reason for this, and the real lesson of Zürau, I want to suggest, is his gradual recognition of the fact that there are

no answers and that the search itself is at once a very human need *and* one that can never be satisfied. In fact this is what so many of the brief pieces are saying: 'Like a path in autumn: scarcely has it been swept clear than it is once more covered with dry leaves.' 'Truth is indivisible; hence it cannot recognise itself. Whoever wants to recognise it must be a lie.' And the many, often quite turgid, explorations of the Garden of Eden story merely repeat that the serpent is thought itself and that imagining we can get at the truth by thought and introspection is to be already in thrall to it. One of the brief items in the 'He' collection puts the same thing a little differently: 'He has the feeling that merely by being alive he is blocking his own way. From this obstruction, again, he derives the proof that he is alive.' This is a hard lesson for a man under sentence of death to learn, and in a sense it is not a lesson one can ever fully learn. But slowly, in those months, it came to be accepted by Kafka. By the time he was ready to return to Prague he understood it in his inmost heart, just as by December he had understood that everything was over between him and Felice.

In those months Kafka came to understand that you cannot articulate or grasp final truths, only dramatise the burning need to do so and the impossibility of so doing: Sancho Panza exorcises his demon by inventing Don Quixote and Cervantes his by inventing them both. But the question Kafka posed about writing at the very start of his Zürau sojourn stays with him all his life: 'And it is not at all a lie and does not still the pain, is simply a merciful surplus of powers at the moment when the pain has actually visibly used up all my powers to the bottom of my being, which it scrapes. But then what sort of a surplus is it?' It is not a lie, but, as he says over and over again to Max Brod, and as he keeps telling himself in his notebooks, is it not a form of vanity? Does it not spring at least in part out of the desire to impress both oneself and others, to show off? 'So what should I do with these things?' he asks Brod about his writings.

'Since they cannot help me am I to let them harm me, as they must?' This already troubled him when, in 1911, he recalled in his diary that traumatic episode in his childhood when he sat ostentatiously writing at the kitchen table after lunch at his grandparents' house and it is still troubling him in 1922 when he pours out his heart on the subject in a long letter to Brod: 'Writing sustains me, but is it not more accurate to say that it sustains this kind of life? By this I don't mean, of course, that my life is better when I don't write. Rather, it is much worse then and wholly unbearable and has to end in madness. But that, granted, only follows from the postulate that I am a writer, which is actually true even when I am not writing, and a non-writing writer is a monster inviting madness.' 'But,' he goes on, 'what about being a writer itself? Writing is a sweet and wonderful reward, but for what? In the night it became clear to me, as clear as a child's lesson book, that it is the reward for serving the devil. This descent to the dark powers, this unshackling of spirits bound by nature, these dubious embraces and whatever else may take place in the nether parts, which the higher parts no longer know when one writes stories in the sunshine. Perhaps there are other forms of writing, but I know only this kind; at night, when fear keeps me from sleeping, I know only this kind. And the diabolic element in it seems very clear to me. It is vanity and sensuality which continually buzz about one's own or even another's form – and feast on him. The movement multiplies itself – it is a regular solar system of vanity.' And, in a thought which he had not articulated so clearly before, he pins this vanity not just to the desire to show off, to be praised, but to the wish to evade his own death. For writing gives you the feeling of being immortal, even writing about your death, and that, he feels, at this moment, is the ultimate denial of reality.

All these thoughts come to a head in the terrifying story he wrote at about this time and which he was in the process of proofreading when the TB which had been diagnosed seven

years previously finally took away his life. That story, 'The Fasting Showman' or 'The Hunger Artist' as it is sometimes called, tells of a fairground showman whose particular 'turn' involves simply fasting in public. But the attraction of this unusual act begins to fade and the crowds drop away. As his fasting leads inexorably to his death the management decide they have had enough, and as soon as he is dead remove the corpse and install in his stead a vibrant, lively panther whose presence quickly brings back the spectators. But before he dies, the fasting showman confesses to his overseer that, had he found food to his liking, he would never have fasted – so his act is less willed than forced upon him. The story expresses Kafka's own sense that he would much rather have written like Werfel or Brod and enjoyed worldly success, but he simply could not do it. It is as if his commitment to truth in writing was too great, and this was not just an ethical imperative but a physical one: his body rejected falsehood, could not process it. This in turn meant not just a tiny readership but the growing sense that anything he wrote was tainted. At the same time he couldn't not write, as he explained to Brod. The contradiction was killing him.

Of course he went on writing and was even occasionally happy enough with what he wrote to seek to have some of it published. For, as he had once said to Felice, 'I have no literary interests, I am made of literature.' And as such he was ready to make use, for his purposes, of all that life threw in his way: the horror and pathos of his relations with his father; the drudgery of his job in the insurance company; the pain that racked his body; the sense that his feet had never rested and never would rest on solid ground, that his ship had weighed anchor in his earliest childhood and he had to make do with choppy seas beneath his feet.

And so we come to the final lesson of the winter in Zürau. Or rather, of the final fruit of that long winter. I am thinking

not of profound thoughts or great insights but of the Night of the Mice. For without his unsettling encounter with that 'frightful mute and mighty race', that 'oppressed proletarian race to which the night belongs', Kafka could never have written, six years later, his last and one of his greatest stories, 'Josephine the Singer, or the Mouse Folk'. Here he explored for one last time the paradoxical place of art in our lives, at once of fundamental importance and utterly without importance, and was able, in the last sentence, which follows with remorseless logic from the first, thirty pages earlier, to articulate his deepest wish: 'So perhaps,' says the narrator of Josephine's death, 'we shall not miss her so very much after all, while Josephine, redeemed from the earthly sorrows which to her thinking lay in wait for all chosen spirits, will happily lose herself in the numberless throng of the heroes of our people, and soon, since we are no historians, will rise to the heights of redemption and be forgotten like all her brothers.' Truly, life bestows its gifts in unexpected ways.

NOTE

I have felt it important to tell the story as much as possible in Kafka's own words, in extracts from his diaries, from the octavo notebooks he wrote in at the time, and from his letters, mainly to his friends in Prague. This in turn has meant relying on translations from the German. I have used the standard translation of the *Diaries*, by Joseph Kresh, Martin Greenberg and Hannah Arendt, with occasional help from the new translation by Ross Benjamin; the standard translation of the letters by Richard and Clara Winston; and the only existing translation of the octavo notebooks, by Ernst Kaiser and Eithne Wilkins in *Wedding Preparations in the Country and Other Posthumous Prose Writings*. In all cases, but especially the last, I have silently emended where the English did not seem to reflect the German. On the other hand many translations of the aphorisms exist and I have consulted most of them and again emended where I saw fit, though in most cases I discuss what is at stake as the need arises.

Volume Three of Rainer Stach's great biography of Kafka, *The Years of Insight*, translated, like the other two volumes, by Shelley Frisch, has been a constant companion.

Many thanks to Michael, Andrew and Maren at Carcanet, and to Tamar and Steve, for making this book the beautiful object it is.